I've Been Killing Slimes for 300 Years and Maxed Out My Level

Kiseku Morita

Illustration by Benio

9

GW01495376

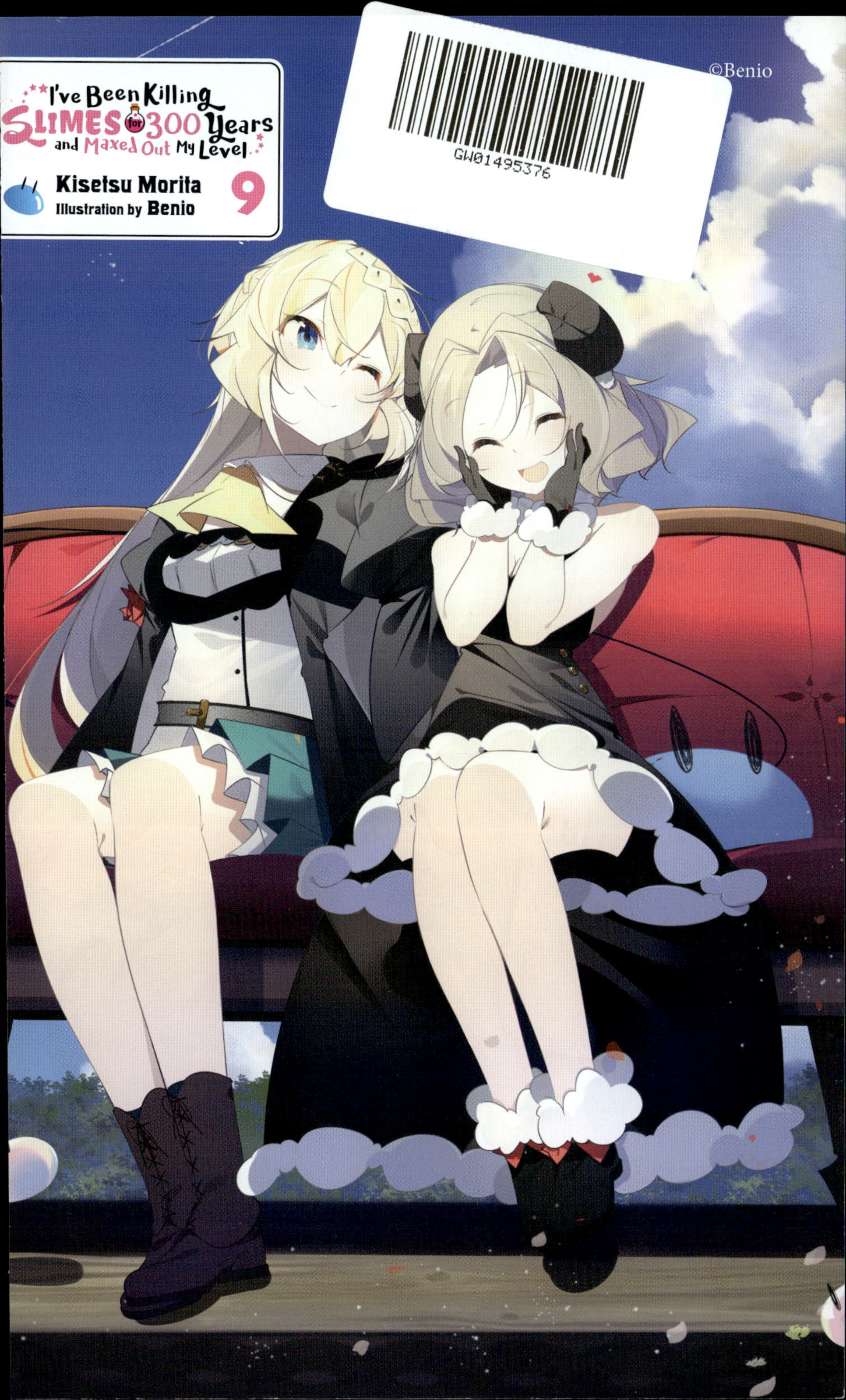
©Benio

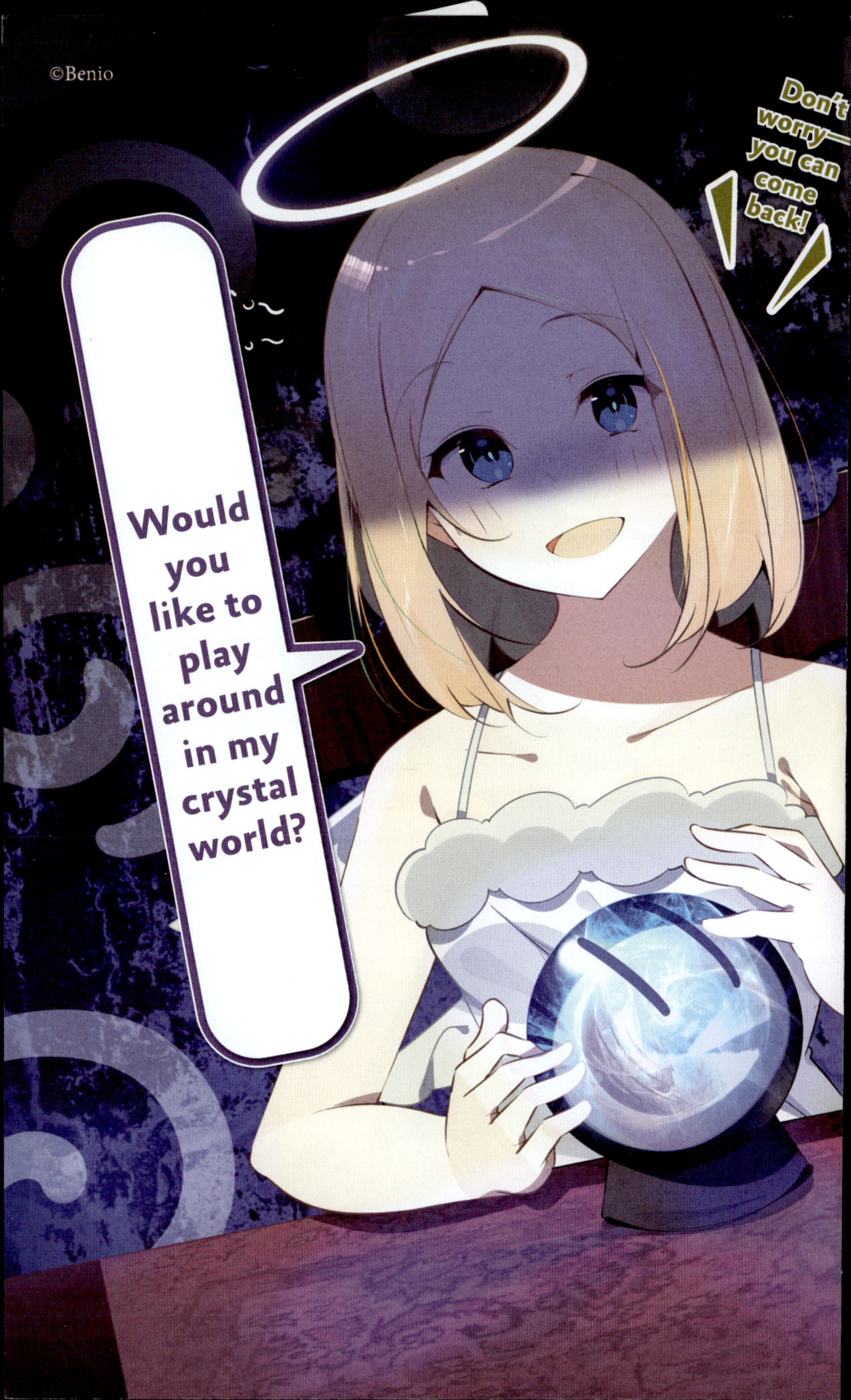
©Benio
Don't worry—you can come back!
Would you like to play around in my crystal world?

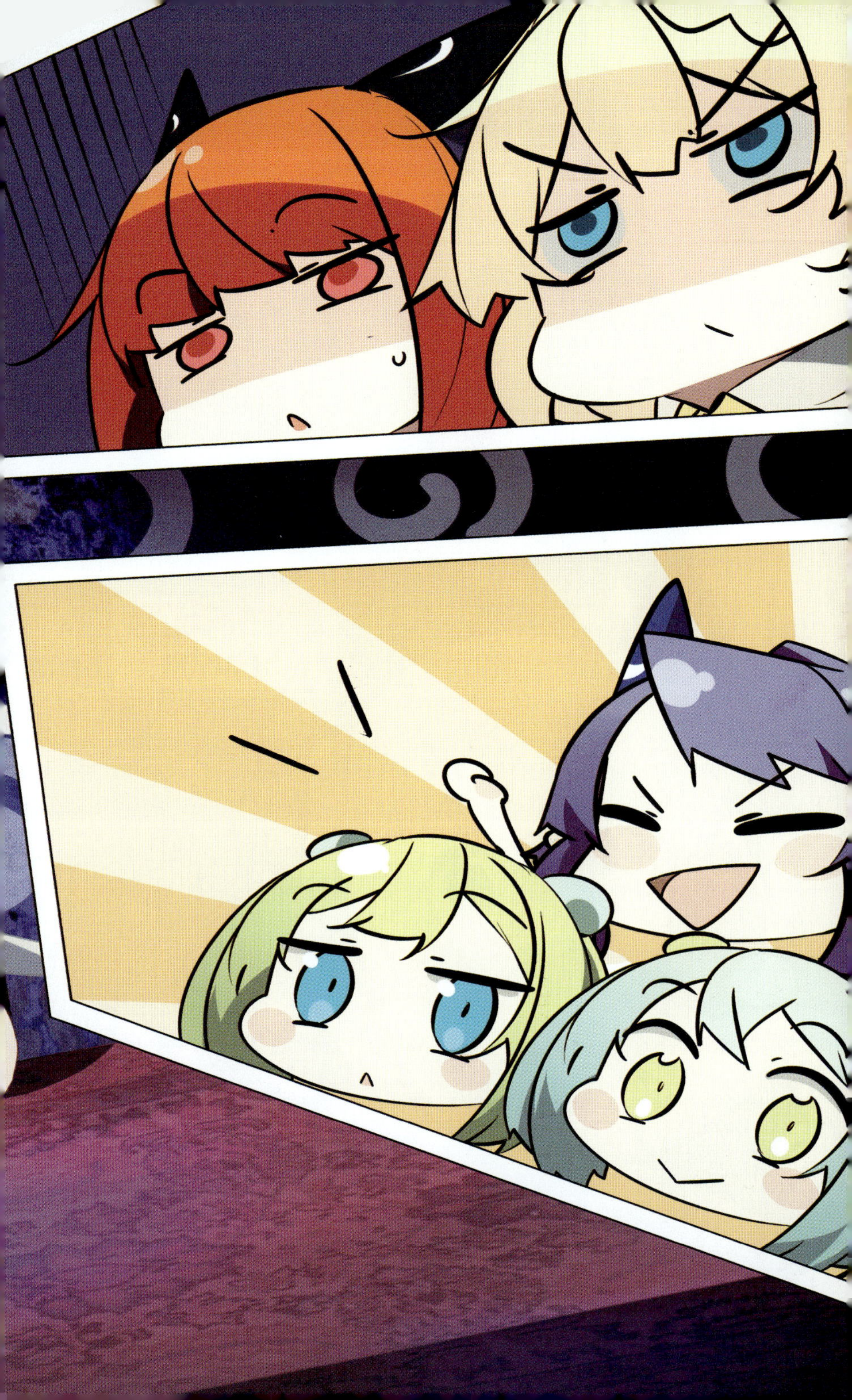

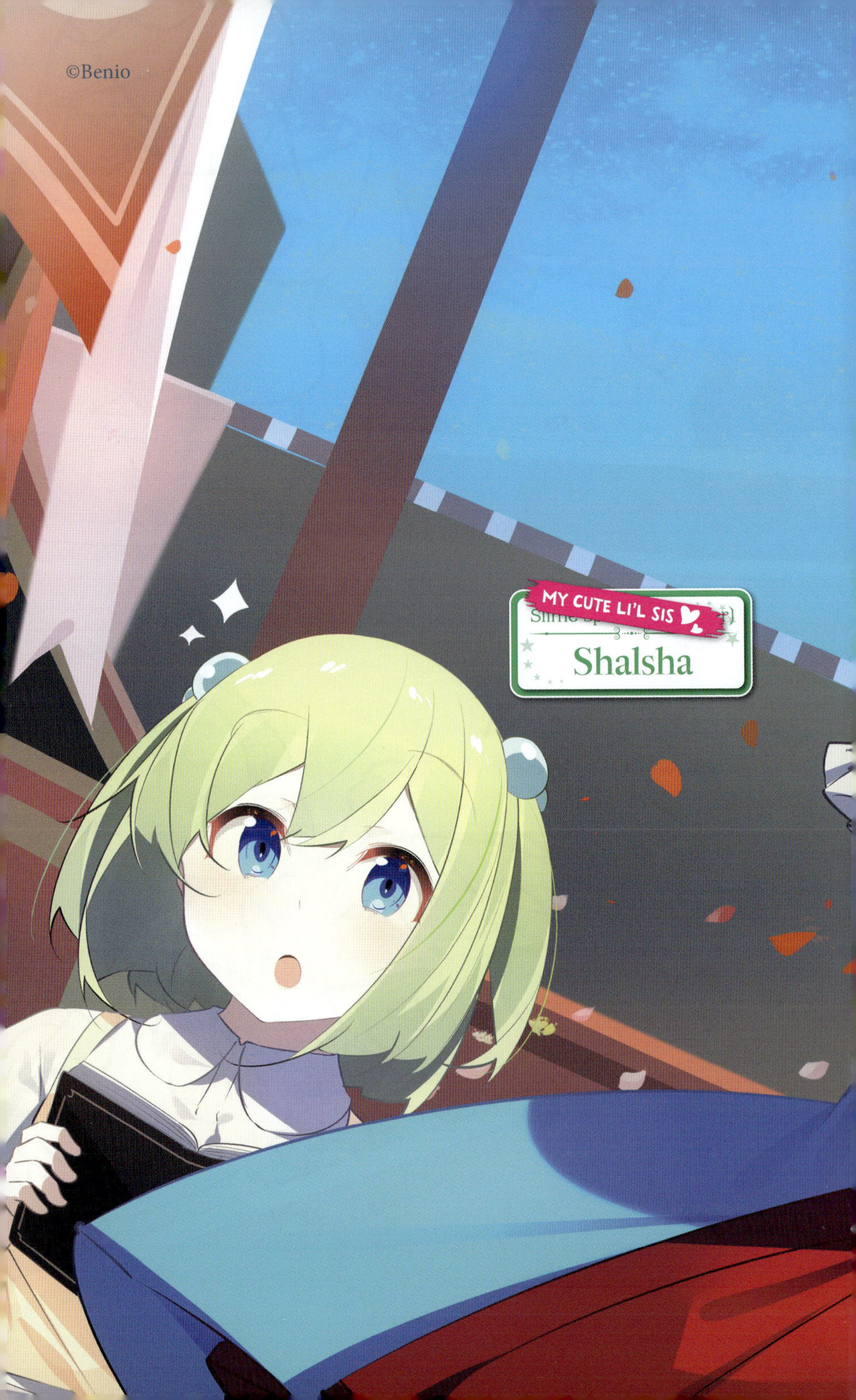
©Benio
MY CUTE LI'L SIS
Shalsha

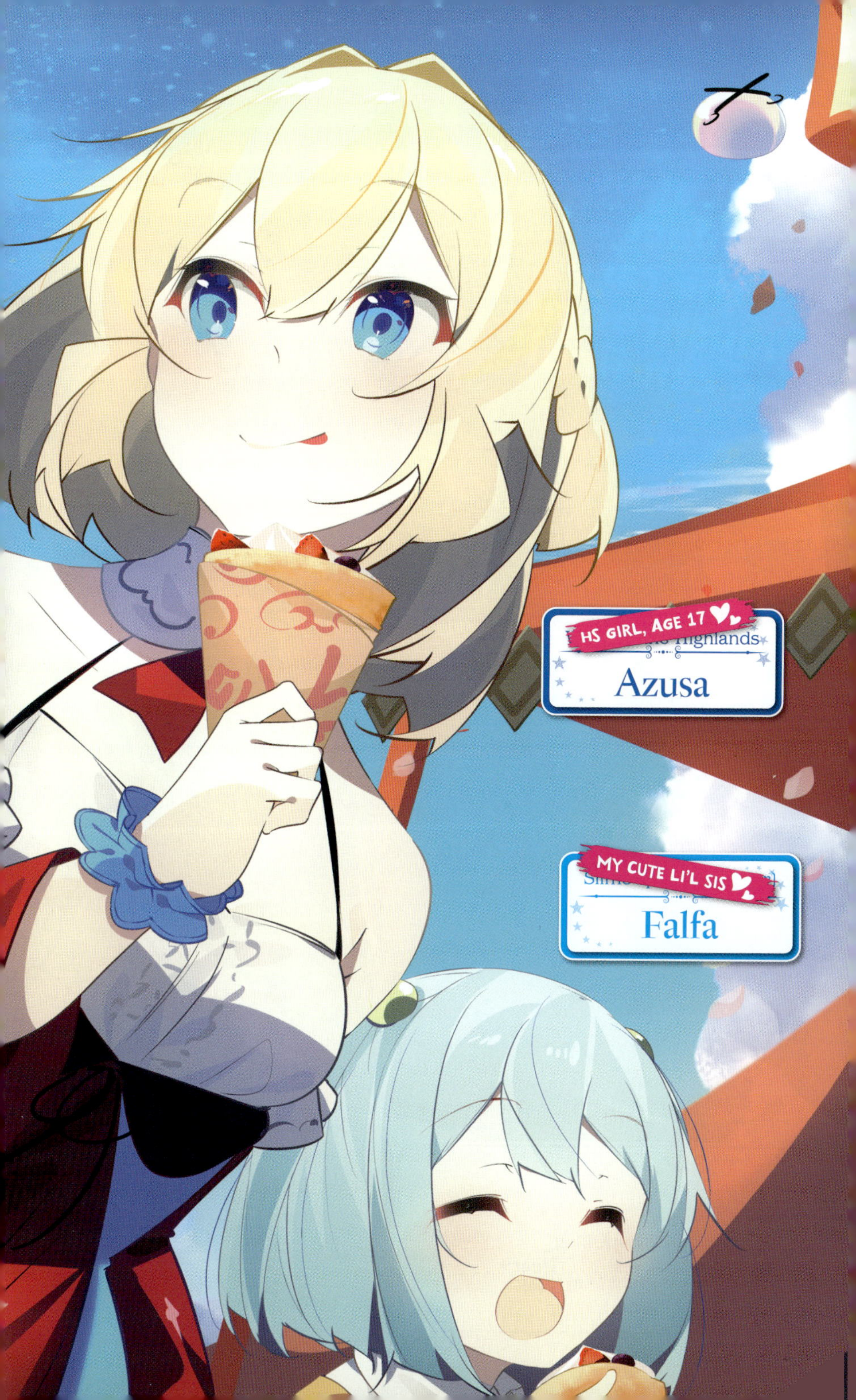
HS GIRL, AGE 17
Azusa
MY CUTE LI'L SIS
Falfa

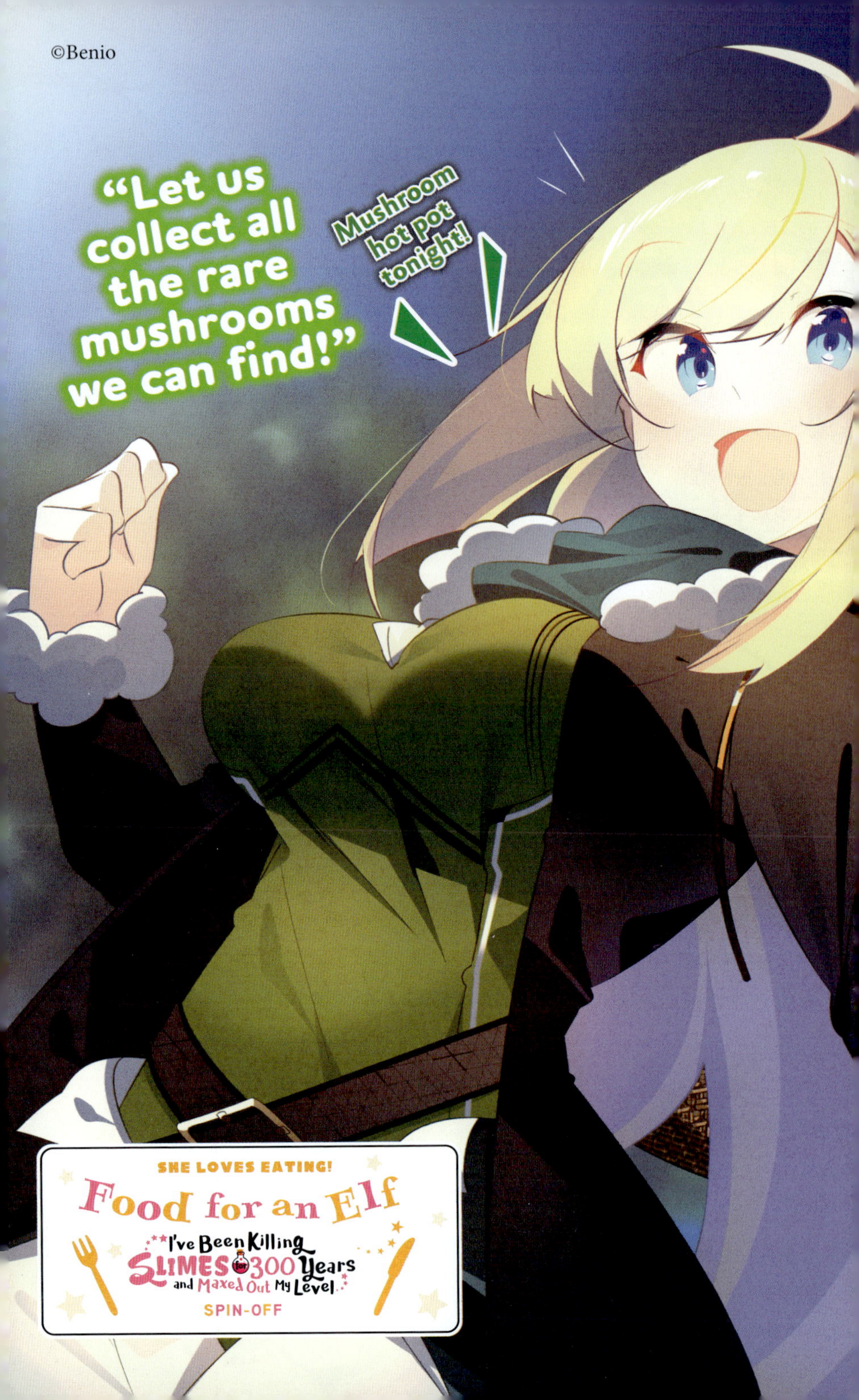
©Benio
"Let us collect all the rare mushrooms we can find!"
Mushroom hot pot tonight!
SHE LOVES EATING!
Food for an Elf
I've Been Killing Slimes for 300 Years and Maxed Out My Level
SPIN-OFF

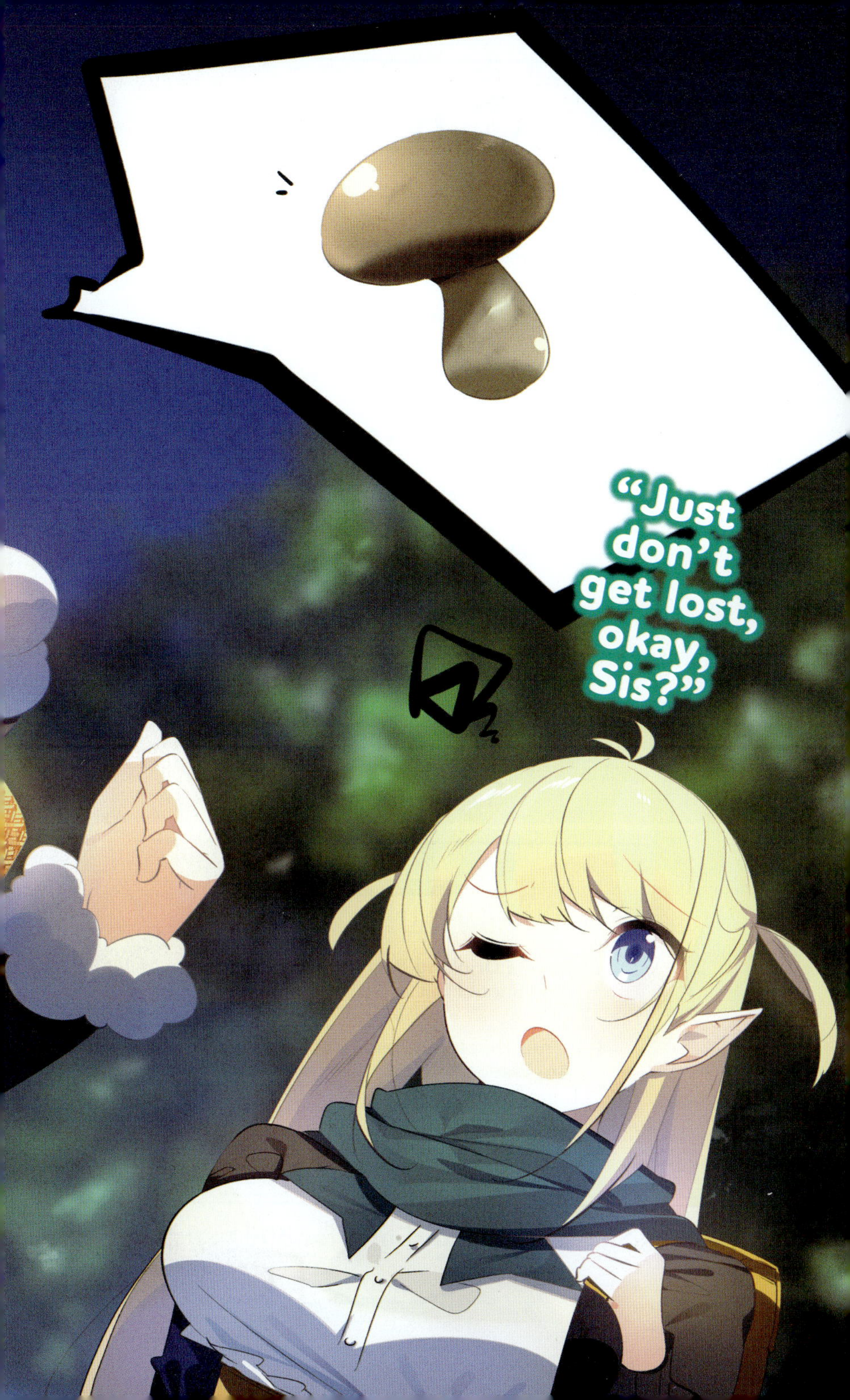
"Just don't get lost, okay, Sis?"

Contents

A Deity's Strange Request
1

We Drained the Pond
21

We Went to Another World
45

I Cut My Hair Too Short
63

I Used Hair Growth Magic
87

We Went to a Meat Festival
103

We Watched Bullfighting
119

We Visited the Great Slime
137

I Got a New Daughter
149

Sandra Sprouted a Hat
167

SPIN-OFF
Food for an Elf

I'll Be at a Drinking Party Until I Go Home, So I Should Eat to Sober Up, Right?
193

Is It True That Ingredients You Get Yourself Are Tastier Than Ingredients You Buy?
211

Story by Kisetsu Morita   Illustration by Benio

She slaughtered slimes for 300 years...

©Benio

I've Been Killing SLIMES for 300 Years and Maxed Out My Level 9

Kisetsu Morita
Illustration by Benio

YEN ON
NEW YORK

I've Been Killing SLIMES 300 Years and Maxed Out My Level 9

KISETSU MORITA
Translation by Jasmine Bernhardt
Cover art by Benio

This book is a work of fiction. Names, characters, places, and incidents are the product of the author's imagination or are used fictitiously. Any resemblance to actual events, locales, or persons, living or dead, is coincidental.

SLIME TAOSHITE SANBYAKUNEN, SHIRANAIUCHINI
LEVEL MAX NI NATTEMASHITA vol. 9
Copyright © 2019 Kisetsu Morita
Illustrations copyright © 2019 Benio
All rights reserved.
Original Japanese edition published in 2019 by SB Creative Corp.

This English edition is published by arrangement with SB Creative Corp., Tokyo in care of Tuttle-Mori Agency, Inc., Tokyo.

English translation © 2021 by Yen Press, LLC

Yen Press, LLC supports the right to free expression and the value of copyright. The purpose of copyright is to encourage writers and artists to produce the creative works that enrich our culture.

The scanning, uploading, and distribution of this book without permission is a theft of the author's intellectual property. If you would like permission to use material from the book (other than for review purposes), please contact the publisher. Thank you for your support of the author's rights.

Yen On
150 West 30th Street, 19th Floor
New York, NY 10001

Visit us at yenpress.com
facebook.com/yenpress
twitter.com/yenpress
yenpress.tumblr.com
instagram.com/yenpress

First Yen On Edition: January 2021

Yen On is an imprint of Yen Press, LLC.
The Yen On name and logo are trademarks of Yen Press, LLC.

The publisher is not responsible for websites (or their content) that are not owned by the publisher.

Library of Congress Cataloging-in-Publication Data
Names: Morita, Kisetsu, author. | Benio, illustrator. | Engel, Taylor, translator. | Bernhardt, Jasmine, translator
Title: I've been killing slimes for 300 years and maxed out my level / Kisetsu Morita ; illustration by Benio.
Other titles: Slime taoshite sanbyakunen, shiranaiuchini level max ni nattemashita. English |
I have been killing slimes for 300 years
Description: First Yen On edition. | New York : Yen On, 2018– | v. 1–2, 6: translation by Taylor Engel. |
v. 3–9: translation by Jasmine Bernhardt
Identifiers: LCCN 2017059843 | ISBN 9780316448277 (v. 1 : pbk.) | ISBN 9780316448291 (v. 2 : pbk.) |
ISBN 9781975329310 (v. 3 : pbk.) | ISBN 9781975382636 (v. 4 : pbk.) | ISBN 9781975382650 (v. 5 : pbk.) |
ISBN 9781975382674 (v. 6 : pbk.) | ISBN 9781975312916 (v. 7 : pbk.) | ISBN 9781975314811 (v. 8 : pbk.) |
ISBN 9781975318338 (v. 9 : pbk.)
Subjects: CYAC: Reincarnation—Fiction. | Witches—Fiction.
Classification: LCC PZ7.1.M6725 Iv 2018 | DDC [Fic]—dc23
LC record available at https://lccn.loc.gov/2017059843

ISBNs: 978-1-9753-1833-8 (paperback)
978-1-9753-1834-5 (ebook)

1 3 5 7 9 10 8 6 4 2

LSC-C

Printed in the United States of America

I've Been Killing SLIMES for 300 Years and Maxed Out My Level 9

AZUSA AIZAWA

> PERSE-VERANCE EQUALS POWER. I ONLY DO THINGS I CAN STICK WITH!

The protagonist. Commonly known as the Witch of the Highlands. A girl (?) who was reincarnated as an immortal witch with the appearance of a seventeen-year-old. Before she knew what was happening, she'd become the strongest being in the world. Although she's had some rough times, it has ultimately given her a family, and she's delighted about it.

HALKARA

A young elf woman and Azusa's apprentice. She is an upstanding CEO who runs a company using her knowledge of mushrooms, but in the house in the highlands, she's known for her knack for screwing up. She is the main character of the bonus story, "Food for an Elf," that's included in this book.

> WELL, WHAT SHOULD I HAVE TODAY? ♪

FALFA AND SHALSHA

Spirit sisters born from a conglomeration of slime souls. Falfa, the older sister, is a carefree girl who's honest about her own feelings. Shalsha, the younger sister, is considerate and attentive to others. They both love their mother, Azusa.

LAIKA AND FLATORTE

Red and blue dragon–girls who live in the house in the highlands. Laika is Azusa's apprentice and a good, hardworking girl. Flatorte is a cheerful, energetic girl who obeys what Azusa says. They tend to compete with each other as fellow dragons.

BEELZEBUB

A high-ranking demon known as the Lord of the Flies and the demons' minister of agriculture. She frequently shuttles between the demon realm and the house in the highlands. She's Azusa's reliable "big sister" surrogate and the protagonist of the spin-off in this book, "I Was a Bottom-Tier Bureaucrat for 1,500 Years, and the Demon King Made Me a Minister."

ROSALIE

A ghost girl and resident of the house in the highlands. She's devoted to Azusa, who didn't shy away from her as a ghost and instead reached out to her. She can go through walls but can't touch people. She can also possess others.

SANDRA

A mandragora girl. After growing for three hundred years, she gained sentience and the ability to move around. She is a literal plant and lives in the vegetable garden in the house in the highlands. She's often stubborn and puts up a front, but she also craves the company of others.

GOODLY GODLY GODNESS

The very being who reincarnated Azusa into this world. An upbeat and affable but careless goddess who fits perfectly in this world. She has a soft spot for women and tends to make lenient decisions.

PECORA
(PROVATO PECORA ARIÉS)

The demon king. A girl with a devilish temperament who loves to use her power and influence to bewilder her subordinates and Azusa. She actually has a masochistic desire to be subordinate to someone stronger than she is, and she adores Azusa.

FATLA AND VANIA

Leviathan sisters who work as Beelzebub's secretaries. They can transform into giant dragons, and they transport Azusa and company to the demon lands as well as look after them. The elder sister, Fatla, is a stable and capable woman. The younger sister, Vania, is ditzy but a good cook.

THE GODDESS NINTAN

A goddess long worshipped in this world. She is a troublesome one, always looking down on others and turning people she doesn't like into frogs, but after losing a fight to a human (Azusa, who broke the level cap), she softened a bit.

A DEITY'S **STRANGE REQUEST**

Suddenly, I was in an odd space with magic circles floating all around me. I recognized this sight.

Azusa, We are speaking directly into your mind.

Nintan stood right before me.

She was an eminent goddess in this world, one I had ended up fighting in the past. Last time, she said I didn't have to address her formally, so I planned to take her up on the offer. But I still end up being deferential when I talk to her. She is way, way, way more important than I am…

"Uh, there's, like, subtitles here…"

Indeed, the words *Azusa, We are speaking directly into your mind* sat in front of Nintan. She could just speak normally to me.

This is inside your mind. You have not come to Our world, so you cannot heed Our voice directly. The voice of a god is not a sound to be heard so easily.

"I'm not sure I'm following all this, but something is going on, right?"

Maybe it was a problem unique to deities.

Yes. And to make this easy for you to comprehend, We are utilizing a script from your previous life. We can use all languages.

Oh yeah, they were like Japanese subtitles in a movie. Literally in Japanese, and not in any language of this world. I could read it either way, so I didn't even notice at first.

We can even use other accents, yeah, mate.

Where the heck was that supposed to be from?

So We have a request to ask of you, and thus, We are calling to you like this.

Eep… This is going nowhere good…
"I'm sorry, I don't know if I can listen to the request of a god. Don't you think it's a bit much to ask?"

All your dreams starting tomorrow will be about you turning into a frog.

For a god, her methods were awfully insidious.

To be honest, We are losing the ability to control Our power, and it has become a cause for worry.

Now *that* was a god problem. *I can't control my power!* was such an edgelord thing to say. Well, to express via subtitle, if you want to get technical.

* * *

Our temple is surrounded by a manmade pond. You have come to Our temple, so you know this. This pond is meant to venerate Us.

Well, that was a sudden topic change. What do ponds have to do with power?

Strangely enough, the pond has become infested with power... Even Our believers are starting to get frightened...

How does power infest a pond? Is that like how magic naturally gathers in divine spaces or something?

Among Our believers are those who think this is Our wrath. We have sent oracles saying they have misunderstood, yet they do not accept them... But even believers with deep faith are staying away from the temple. One day, people will no longer come, all because of power... How dreadful power can be...

Power is dreadful...? Maybe she's talking in subtitles because this is too embarrassing to say aloud.

You are likely thinking We should erase everything, power and all. However, though We are a god— No, *because* We are a god, erasing a part of creation isn't something to be done lightly.

Is power something you "create"? I guess it has to be brought into existence sometime, so in that sense, it is created. This conversation was too abstract, so I was starting to get confused.

                            * * *

And so, Azusa, We have a request of you, a human. Will you wrestle the menace of this power under control? With your fame as the Witch of the Highlands, you may also be able to contain it. Essentially, We want you to fight against the power in Our place.

F-fight the power?!

Sure, I'd fought with gods in this world, so I didn't think I'd be contending with anything even more absurd than that. To think I'd be asked to literally fight against the concept of power. It's a word with all kinds of meanings.

I guess the power creep's gotten so bad, I have to fight against the concept itself... We're really starting to enter philosophical territory here...

You are human. It is acceptable for you to control and kill power. We shall trust you to choose an acceptable method.

Kill power...? Now that was another edgelord thing to say...

I guess once you reached max level, you could even defeat power. In a surprising twist, I'd reached even greater heights. Somehow.

But I wished I didn't have to involve myself in all these troublesome affairs and could just live my relaxing life.

"By the way, do I have the right to say no?"

Tree frog, bullfrog, a rare golden frog—take your pick.

She sure was ready and willing to turn me into a frog if I said no.

"Let me just ask one more time, but how dangerous is this going to be? My opponent is so abstract, it's hard for me to tell."

I was going to mitigate my risks as much as possible. I couldn't just take on this job and hope everything would be okay.

* * *

There is not even a one-in-a-million chance that you would lose. We cannot guarantee you will be itch-free, however.

Why would I get itchy…? Does power give people rashes…? Does it act like poison ivy…?
Well, whatever. Saying no wouldn't be an option.
I was apparently the strongest being on this planet, after all.
I was probably the only one who could fight against something so extraordinary as power itself.
"Understood. I'll take on your request, Nintan."
Nintan's expression softened.

Aye. We believed you would say that.

But still, she essentially just threatened me…

Also, this is a little off-topic, but We rather enjoy those magic livestreams the demons are conducting. We thought it might be a nice way to speak to Our believers, too.

"Oh no, you really shouldn't force yourself to incorporate new essentials! They'll just think it's fishy! It'll cheapen your image!"
I really wanted gods to stay solemn beings. Even the spirits started participating in the magic streams—please, god, not you, too!

And recently, We have heard of treats made with tea in the south. We see them occasionally in Our offerings.

Now this conversation is turning into a weird teatime chitchat. I'm fighting against power, hello?! Don't just bring up sweets while I'm here!

* * *

Azusa, prove victorious against power and grasp glory for yourself.

The next moment, I realized I was in my bed in my house.

"It was just a dream...or not, I guess."

If it wasn't just a dream, then I'd be turned into a frog if I ignored it...

◇

I hopped on Laika in her dragon form, and we headed to the grand temple that worshipped the goddess Nintan.

"This has truly become quite extraordinary, Lady Azusa," Laika said to me. Even a dragon would be surprised to hear I would be battling against an abstract concept.

"That's one word for it. How am I supposed to fight it? Does power even exist in the temple pond in the first place? Is this a riddle?"

What's the scariest thing a pond can have?

I dunno. I have no answer for that.

"But you really are special, Lady Azusa, for a god to ask a favor of you! As your apprentice, I am truly proud!"

"No, please don't flatter me like that! It's just how things turned out!"

Laika would always immediately try to praise me, and I wished she would stop. It was so embarrassing.

"Battles with such powerful enemies are typically given to heroes and the like. That means you are this world's greatest hero, Lady Azusa."

"I mean, I probably *could* defeat any party of heroes that came my way..."

Did heroes even exist in this world? If so, then I'd be a target for vanquishing, considering I'm friends with the demon king...

* * *

We arrived at the outskirts of the capital city, then made our way to the town of Nintania, where the Grand Nintan Temple was.

But there was clearly something strange about this place.

Most of the people passing by had covered their entire bodies with skintight, stocking-like clothing, and some even covered their faces. It was like the whole city was filled with people wanted by the police.

"What's with this dystopian vibe...?"

It was like a world where the air was too toxic to breathe without a mask.

"Lady Azusa, I am frightened of this place..." Laika's fear was perfectly normal, despite her power. Her values were quite ladylike, after all. This was like something out of a nightmare—worse than a nightmare.

"I'm scared, too. I really have my work cut out for me this time. Thanks, Nintan..."

Not only that, but as we walked down the main avenue, we suddenly heard a scream.

"Eegyaaaaaaah! Eegyaaaaah! It hurts, it huuuurts!"

A man with his face covered writhed in agony.

What is going on...? This is terrifying!

"Laika, were there any prophecies that the world was going to be destroyed this year?"

"Hmm... There are always a number of cults announcing the end of the world in any era..."

Now that she mentioned it, I realized she was right. I guess there weren't any doctrines that said we didn't need faith anymore in modern times.

Everyone who passed by walked too quickly for us to clearly hear what they were saying, but we still caught snatches of conversations.

"This must be the wrath of the goddess Nintan—it has to be."

"What other explanation is there? Some of her priests are saying it isn't, though."

"We need to find a way to soothe her anger quickly; otherwise, this town is done for..."

"Hey, speed up, or they'll get you!"

A Deity's Strange Request

I guess that would be the obvious line of thinking when you lived right at the foot of her temple.

Not only that, but since Nintan herself actually had nothing to do with this, she would surely be bothered by it.

"Laika, I know it's uncomfortable, but let's go to the temple. We'll probably find out what's causing this, at least."

"Indeed… I must brace myself…"

We made our way toward the temple and its sparse crowd of visitors.

Then, when we arrived at Nintan's temple, we were greeted by a shocking sight.

The pond was swarming with a seemingly infinite number of tiny black things. There were even swirls and vortices in the cloud.

We could also hear an unpleasant whining: *eeeeee, eeeeee.*

"Laika, is this…?"

"An insect that rarely makes its home in the cool highlands—mosquitoes," Laika said, smacking her arm. Even as she did so, more came to land on her.

There had been a terrible misunderstanding.

× **Kill power (力)**
✓ **Kill mosquitoes (力, or when written in kanji: 蚊)**

"She wants me to do something about the *mosquitoes*! The Japanese subtitles made me think she wanted me to deal with her *power*!"

Was that my fault or hers…?

But *power* (力) and *mosquito* (力) really look awfully similar in Japanese… They're practically indistinguishable… It's like trying to tell apart *earth* (土) and *gentleman* (士), or *pending* (未) and *ending* (末) when someone has terrible handwriting.

"The area around the temple is surrounded by a pond, so they must have come in because there was a massive outbreak there."

Mosquitoes did pop up wherever there was standing water.

"There's so many. How are we supposed to get rid of them?"

Then a priest approached us, his body completely covered. "You are Azusa, the great Witch of the Highlands, yes?"

To be honest, he just looked like a cultist straight out of a horror movie. Laika even darted behind me in shock.

"An oracle told of your arrival. Please do something about these dreadful mosquitoes. Use whatever means necessary."

For a moment, I thought, *Don't ask me to do this!* Getting rid of the little bugs might be harder than you'd expect. This might be more of a challenge than a boss fight.

"Very well… I'll do what I can…," I said. Quietly, so that no mosquitoes would fly into my mouth.

"You will get bitten if you stand still, so please be careful. I believe you both have been bitten fifteen times already by now."

""What?!"" Laika and I yelped in unison.

And the second he pointed it out, I immediately realized how itchy I was.

"Ack, everything itches!"

"Oh goodness, me too! They got my back! They got a spot I cannot reach!"

To think two of the strongest beings on this planet—me and my red-dragon apprentice, Laika—would both be laid so low!

Such is the power of mosquitoes. Were they really the strongest creatures in this world?!

All of a sudden, I sensed bloodthirst.

Laika's eyes were glazed over. "Lady Azusa, let us exterminate these things. I am terribly cross at the moment."

Oh no, her dragon anger was coming out…but then again, so was mine.

"You're right. I'll fight them with all I've got. We'll burn them to a crisp."

I'd show them what I could really do, and then they'd be sorry!

Laika and I went right to eradicating them.

"For bugs, we should stick with fire, right, Laika?"

"Indeed. I shall burn them all!"

I cast my Scorching Heat spell, and Laika breathed flames from her mouth. She was still in her human form—her flames could reach a much wider scale if she returned to her dragon form, but it was much harder for her to control her power because of that. We couldn't afford to incinerate the temple; Nintan would be furious with us.

"Now burn, burn! Be gone!"

"*Fwoooo, fwoooooooooooooom!*"

"You take all my blood, and I'll turn into a mummy. All things in moderation, you little bloodsuckers!"

"*Fwoooo, fwoooooooooooooom!*"

*Laika was breathing fire from her mouth, so she couldn't talk.

When the flames made contact with the swarm of mosquitoes, there was a short sizzling sound as the legions died.

There was a saying that went *even a worm will turn*, but couldn't we catch a break? I'd killed a lot of slimes, too, huh…? This was also a divine request, so I doubted we would be punished for this.

For the first five minutes, the priests had gathered to cheer us on—"Wow, incredible!" "Yes, please get them!"—but then they started worrying they would get bitten if they stayed still for too long and cleared out.

No one could afford to stick around and cheer—you had to keep moving if you didn't want to suffer.

We burned and burned them for about thirty minutes, but—

"The mosquitoes are dispersing, which is making our attacks less effective…"

—they didn't want to be torched so ungracefully. The swarms were gone, and the new strategy involved keeping their distance from one another. Or hiding in the grass or behind the trees, it seemed.

"There is only so much we can do like this… We cannot burn down the trees on the temple ground…"

Laika sat on a bench next to the lake, likely tired from breathing so much fire. But we were up against an incredibly formidable opponent this time. They would not allow us to rest.

"Hey, Laika, your neck and arms are all red. Did they bite you?"

"Oh, now that you mention it… And, Lady Azusa, your legs look awful…"

I had a feeling we had a lot more mosquito bites than when we came.

"Argh! Now that I'm thinking about it, I'm all itchy again!"

"This is torture! I can bear pain through the power of concentration, but I cannot do the same with itchiness! The impossible is most certainly impossible!"

We were so stupid!

It wasn't like we were running around all over the place while we were spewing fire everywhere. We didn't stand totally stock-still, but we hadn't moved all that much.

That's when the mosquitoes got us! All they had to do was get behind us while we were making the flames, and we were totally unprepared for them. They devoured our necks and legs!

It was like in old action games—if you got in a boss's blind spot before it made an attack, you could deal all the damage you wanted.

Why were mosquitoes using boss strategies against us…? *Ugh, they are really pissing me off!*

"Laika, let's retreat for now. This strategy isn't working."

"Yes. And, Lady Azusa, we perhaps should not stand still to have a conversation… We will be bitten in the meantime!"

"Yeah, if we move randomly, we might be a bit safer…"

We took shelter in the temple, doing a strange dance as we made our way there.

Also, at the entrance of the temple, there were three screen doors, possibly as a measure against the mosquitoes. It was almost unbelievable that they had to go that far.

When I entered the temple, I felt a force guiding me.

This sense was coming from the statue of Nintan.

"Oh, I get it now."

"What is it, Lady Azusa?"

"Laika, hold my hand. If I treat you like my companion, then she'll probably see you, too."

"Your hand...? A-all right..." Laika gripped my hand. Shyly, for some reason. "I am somewhat embarrassed to be holding your hand, Lady Azusa. You are much greater than I am... But it is an honor..."

"Oh hey, the place where you're squeezing doesn't feel as itchy anymore."

"...I-indeed."

I had a feeling Laika was a bit fed up with me.

I picked up speed as I made my way straight toward the statue of Nintan.

"What?! Lady Azusa, we're going to run into it!"

"It's fine! Just trust me!"

The moment we leaped into the goddess statue—we were standing in Nintan's realm.

It was the same as when I came with Goodly Godly Godness.

Like before, Nintan was standing right in front of us. It was more like she was floating, though.

"It seems your flame method did not go well, Azusa."

"I mean, this is terrible. I had a feeling that strength alone wouldn't be enough for this..."

Even though I was the strongest in the world, there were still things I couldn't do.

"Lady Azusa, is the one floating there really the goddess Nintan?"

This would be Laika's first time meeting her.

"Yes. We are the goddess Nintan. To think you would be unable to fend off these mosquitoes..." Nintan looked embarrassed. "Feel free to use this space and the temple as you see fit in order to solve this problem. Once you have successfully and safely dispatched the mosquitoes—"

"Then?"

"—then We shall praise you as the Mosquito Slayer! We will recognize you as Our patron saint who slays mosquitoes!"

"Please don't!"

That would just make me a joke character.

What the heck would a witch who's strong against mosquitoes *be* anyway? Someone who's researched what plants to use in mosquito-repellent coils...?

Nintan's gaze darkened into something a bit sterner.

"And We will not condone any partial efforts. You cannot merely try; you must succeed. We will not allow you to return home until you do something about the mosquitoes."

Eep... That was some unethical treatment for a deity...

"Why not ask another god for help instead of me? There has to be some god community out there, right?"

"No one will solve the problem for Us. As We mentioned in your dream, casually killing off the mosquitoes will send the message that mosquitoes, despite being a divine creation, should not have been brought into this world in the first place. It is a manner of honor, so I cannot do that."

Though mosquitoes must be doing what they could to survive, they were causing harm to a lot of people, so this wasn't easy.

"Is there no mosquito god?" Laika asked. "There is a jellyfish spirit, so there might perhaps be one."

Good suggestion. If jellyfish have a spirit, why not mosquitoes?

"Unfortunately, no. If there were, We would have heard about it immediately."

Yeah, they would probably be treated like a joke by the other gods...

"Rather, We would have crushed that mosquito god. Remove them from existence!"

"No need to go *that* far!"

But the mosquito god was a good starting point.

"Hey, I have an idea!"

"Excellent. We have solved it."

"Wonderful, Lady Azusa! There is truly nothing you cannot do!"

No, wait, all I did was get an idea, so please don't praise me just yet...

"Even if there is no mosquito god, there must be a specialist for bugs. I think we should leave this to a professional. And luckily, I happen to know one."

"You know someone who is knowledgeable about mosquitoes, Lady Azusa?"

"I'm not sure if she knows about mosquitoes, but she might. I want to give her a call, so I'll just go to an empty room, okay?"

If I summoned her into Nintan's personal space, I was afraid something might bug out because of the difference in space-time. Accidentally erasing someone from existence is no laughing matter.

After leaving Nintan's realm, I tried using the summoning spell in an empty room. I drew the magic circle in the carpet. It would still be effective even if I didn't actually make permanent lines.

"*Vosanosanonnjishidow veiani enlira!*"

Nothing around me changed.

"Oh, I guess I was off again…"

After I finished casting, I searched around the temple and finally found Beelzebub.

As always, the summoning spell brought her somewhere nearby. At least she hadn't been placed right above the lake.

"Hey, Azusa, where is this?"

"The grand temple of the goddess Nintan."

"'Tis a deity the humans worship. Should a demon like me be in such a place?"

I had Nintan's permission, so it shouldn't be a problem. Also—

"There's a powerful foe that I must fight that crosses the boundaries between demons and humans!"

I brought Beelzebub into Nintan's space, and we talked. About the mosquitoes, of course.

"…Aye. I understand there are more mosquitoes now, and things have grown troublesome."

"Yes, exactly. We're so busy taking care of them that we literally can't stay still."

But the expression on Beelzebub's face told me she still wasn't satisfied with something.

"And so then why have you summoned me? Mosquitoes have naught to do with demons or monsters. They are insects, no?"

"See, they call you the Lord of the Flies, right? Mosquitoes are like their cousins, so I figured you might be able to do something. Operation: Ask a Fly About a Mosquito!"

"Oh-ho, I see, I see. I understand now. ♪"

For some reason, Beelzebub was grinning at me. It was creeping me out. Like the calm before the storm, the harbinger of anger to come…

"Are you a fool?! No, you *are* a fool! One can only be so foolish!!"

"I knew you'd get mad!"

I guess what I said brought her wrath on me…

I thought it was a pretty good idea, though…

"Huh? But mosquitoes fly, too. Aren't they similar? They're annoying and hover around people…"

"They bear some resemblance, but they are entirely different! I may be able to transform into a fly, but *this* is still my basic form! I am nothing like a simple fly! And I know nothing about mosquitoes!"

My plan was already crumbling.

"You could at least turn into a fly and then ask the mosquitoes to move somewhere else, right…?"

"No. I cannot converse with flies anyway."

"Oh, so you're just a fake fly…"

Beelzebub pinched my cheek and stretched it out! She was attacking me!

"Listen here, you! Real flies may be inferior creatures, but I am a

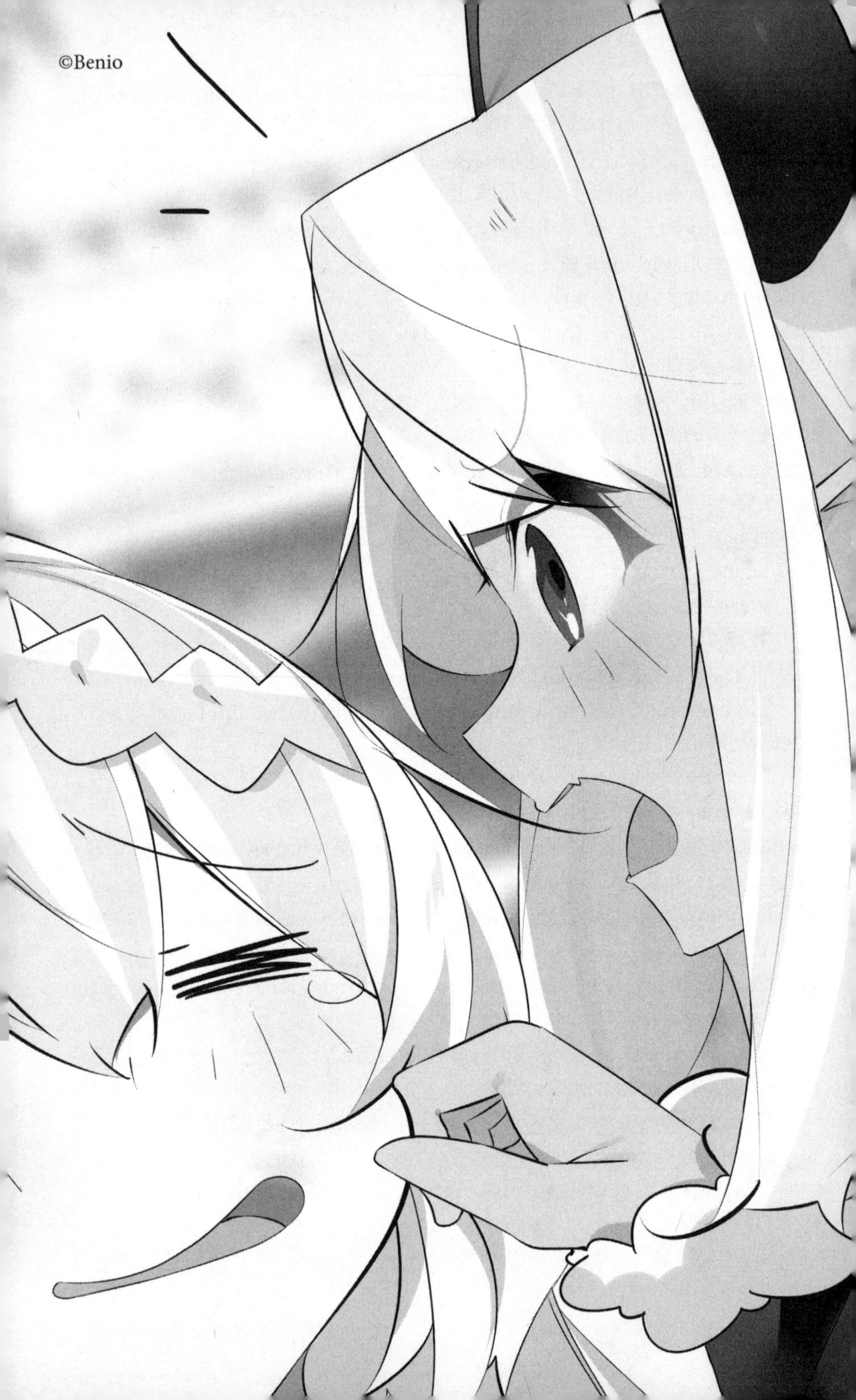
©Benio

proud member of demonkind! Do not look at me as the same as other flies out there!"

"Oh-hay! I geh ih, leh me go!"

I went to all the trouble of summoning Beelzebub, and my only accomplishment so far was getting her to stop pinching me.

"Listen. The outbreak of mosquitoes is indeed great, but they are still no more than mosquitoes. You are all larger than life. All three of you, even that human-faith goddess, are larger than life."

It didn't seem like the demons had any respect for human deities at all. Not everyone could say that in front of a god. Although a human might lose some reverence for a goddess after being dragged in for pest control.

"Hmph, Beelzebub, was it? Do you mock Us?"

Oh no... I can already imagine a fight breaking out...

"Then go into the garden! Learn how terrifying and dreadful mosquitoes can be!"

Or not...

"Very well, then I shall prove to you that mosquitoes count for nothing!" Beelzebub marched out of Nintan's space with purpose.

"Demons don't worship human gods, do they? Though I guess that's obvious," I asked.

"Demons believe the current demon king's ancestor is the deity who birthed them," explained Beelzebub. "That god also appears in human myth, but they consider other gods from human myths to be inconsequential."

If I asked Shalsha about that stuff, I bet she would tell me all about it. She would probably tell me *so* much that I might not be able to keep up, but I'd ask her next time.

Then, about thirty minutes after Beelzebub left for the garden with the pond...her whole body was covered in mosquito bites.

"I'm so itchy... Everything itches... Please give me itch cream..."

"Ha! This is your punishment for scorning the likes of mosquitoes," said Nintan. "Rushing headfirst into a swarm with so much exposed skin is suicide! Be mindful of the mosquitoes from now on."

Wait, so disrespecting the mosquitoes is a bigger offense than disrespecting a god...?

Maybe she had a point. As of right now, a god, a high-ranking demon, and the apparent strongest being in the world (me) had all lost to the mosquitoes, so—

Strong people < Mosquitoes

—that would put a sign of inequality between us... *I don't like that...*

"Mmm... I shall mend my ways... Next time, I will turn into a fly in areas with lots of mosquitoes to avoid getting bitten."

That might be effective, sure, but that only works for you, Beelzebub.

"But how I share your hatred for mosquitoes. I will make it so they can stay here no longer!"

Hey! Beelzebub joined our side in the end!

"Do you have a plan, great demon?" Nintan asked. The goddess was willing to rely even on a demon if the option was there for her.

"I do!" Beelzebub extended her right index finger. "What you have been doing thus far is symptomatic treatment. You simply killed some mosquitoes because there were more of them. There will be no end to them. You must attack at the source."

"And what is your plan?"

Beelzebub grinned.

"Drain the water in the garden pond!"

Wh-what?!

Laika, Nintan, and I were all shocked.

I see—doing that could probably work as a fundamental solution.

"Listen. The mosquitoes multiply because the stagnant pond water creates an optimal environment for them to lay their eggs. Without the water, they will lose their habitat!"

Back in medieval times, people thought mosquitoes and other small insects came from nothing, but it seemed it was common knowledge in this world that they sprang up from those tiny larvae.

"But there are all sorts of other creatures that live in the pond…"

I also understood Nintan's apprehensions. She was not in a position to sacrifice the other creatures in the temple.

"We simply need to move those other creatures to another spot temporarily. That will also allow us to remove the excess invasive fish and clutter in the ponds, thereby improving the water quality. I believe the mosquitoes have increased so much due to problems with the water."

Hey, so the demon did have a rational idea.

"We are not convinced that Our believers would throw garbage into Our waters, but We did suspect the pond was dirty. Perhaps it would be a good idea to drain the water in earnest at least once…"

Nintan sounded like she was on board. Problem solved?

"The pond in the garden takes up quite a bit of acreage, however. It seems to be quite deep as well. We may need a considerable workforce to do this." Laika seemed uneasy as she put her hand to her lips.

This wasn't just getting rid of a puddle.

"This great goddess may be able to do something about that, no? She *is* a great goddess, yes? Does she not have a considerable number of believers?"

Beelzebub was very obviously nudging Nintan.

"Of course We do! We shall send out an oracle to have all Our believers gather here from across the country right away! This is the goddess Nintan's all-out attack on the mosquitoes!"

Did she just call this an all-out attack on mosquitoes? At this rate, she was going to lose her goddess card…

"Either way, the engineering work will take at least a few days. I shall return to Vanzeld Castle." Beelzebub left immediately.

"Nintan, could we go back home, too?"

"Yes. We shall summon you again in a dream."

I kind of wanted her to show just a little more appreciation. We were working for free, but at least the goddess was actually listening to us. Some companies won't even give you that...

Except that wasn't really what was happening.

When we returned to the temple, the priests gave us all sorts of treasures as gifts.

But despite their generosity, it was still a little too much for Laika to take back on a single return trip. We had no choice but to leave the better half of it here.

"The goddess bade us give these to you. Please, take them."

"Huh...? We can't accept this..."

"We have been given all sorts of donations over the ages, so they will simply pile up if we do not pass them along to others. Please accept these gifts."

They were just getting rid of their knickknacks...

But I had a feeling there were a lot of shrines and temples in Japan that received treasures from important figures, so maybe religious institutions just tended to collect those kinds of things. And Laika seemed rather interested in the items, so I guess it was fine.

"This golden mask is quite an article. And this sword is of such fine make!"

They did say dragons collected gold, so maybe she was just broadly interested in these curios.

On the other hand, it didn't seem like Flatorte would be very interested in them, so maybe I was generalizing too much.

Guess we'll leave the treasures in an empty room.

I had a feeling the house in the highlands was going to have a lot more of these knickknacks before we were through.

WE DRAINED THE POND

Ten days later, Nintan appeared in my dream with subtitles that read *Come.*

I did, and Beelzebub apparently had arrived at the temple ahead of time to coordinate the work. That wasn't the whole story, though, because there were about twenty other demons there.

I recognized the sisters Fatla and Vania among them, but the rest were unfamiliar faces.

"Um… Why are there so many demons here…?" I asked Fatla.

"Under Lady Beelzebub's orders, the Ministry of Agriculture is conducting a survey on the water quality and ecosystem in this pond. If we research the ponds in human lands, we may be able to make use of the data for demons as well," Fatla explained in her typical clerical manner.

"Most of the people here are national civil-service personnel~ But more than half are researchers~"

Vania was acting as casual as she always did.

I see… Beelzebub really did put in some serious effort to tie this together…

Beelzebub flew over to us, her arms folded.

"Well? When it is time to work, I do everything I can. And we are carrying out legitimate research on the water quality in human lands while we are here."

"You're a testament to the work ethic of a minister. Um, by the way, why are you hovering around like that?"

Beelzebub was darting this way and that in the air as she was talking to us. Were her fly instincts taking over?

"The mosquitoes will bite me if I do not keep moving…"

It didn't seem like they'd taken any measures against the mosquitoes themselves. Maybe in the future, I should learn a spell that's effective only against mosquitoes. It sounds stupid, I know, but I think it's just plain important.

"I'm not going to make the same mistakes twice, though! I brought help!" I said.

Coming up behind me, pulling a cart, was the Witch of the Grotto, Eno. "Hello, everyone~! When the mosquitoes get you, use this cream, Itch-B-Gone! The most bothersome itches vanish in an instant! There are no harmful ingredients in the cream, so you can safely use this on even a child's sensitive skin! Bug bites? Itch-B-Gone! One tube is eight hundred gold!"

I had Eno make medicine for us.

But still, I was surprised to see her selling medicine that was effective against bugs. She had her fingers in all sorts of pies.

"I want itch cream, but I do not wish to be bitten in the first place…"

I know how you feel, Beelzebub, but you could stand to cover up a little more. Coming here in what she usually wore was suicide.

"It's all right. I've prepared something for people just like you." This time, Eno produced a bottle filled with liquid. "Insec-Away works on even the most persistent bugs. I've very carefully collected the liquid from plants with natural, bug-repelling components! After all, there are plenty of plants that have ways to protect their leaves from insects!"

Eno's voice loudly rang through the area.

There were a surprising number of creatures that had evolved to fight against insects in the natural world. Plants especially, since they couldn't photosynthesize if their leaves got eaten up.

"Rub some on yourself, and the bugs will stay away! Children can also have some peace of mind when they play outside! A bottle of Insec-Away is fifteen hundred gold!"

That wasn't cheap. But sometimes, sacrifices must be made.

"I'll have one, Eno."

"Oh, thank you very much as always, Miss Azusa!"

I could keep the mosquitoes away with this, so I guess it was time to start draining the pond.

And so we carried out our plan to remove all the water in the temple garden. I did wonder where it would go, but a little water channel had been dug down to a nearby river.

That was a lot of construction to take care of, but Nintan's believers had already built it for us. She sure had a lot of followers at her disposal. I guess that's what happens when you're worshipped for a long time.

There were also a few screens attached in the space between the garden and the water channel.

It was built to catch everything—both trash and critters.

Some believers were keeping their distance because of all the demons, but it didn't seem like there would be any trouble; maybe Nintan had already told them in an oracle that demons would be coming.

"By the way, who's taking charge here?"

A project this big needed a leader. It wasn't like Nintan could show up in a corporeal form or anything.

"You do it." Beelzebub pointed at me at point-blank range.

Urgh... I guess whoever brings it up has to do it...

"But, like, the demon's Ministry of Agriculture has really come out in force for this. Shouldn't the minister be directing this?"

"I am little more than the ministry's leader. You were asked to take on this project by the goddess herself, no? You do it. If something happens, you take responsibility."

I had a feeling that last sentence was her real point. Well, everything did technically start when Nintan asked me to do this.

I lightly slapped my thighs. "Okay. I'll do it. I'll be the leader."

I floated straight up into the air so I, the project representative, could see everyone.

"Hello! I'm Azusa, Witch of the Highlands. The goddess Nintan gave me a revelation, so I am now working to do something about these mosquitoes. This time, I received an oracle, so I'm cooperating together with the demons. I know we have a mix here of demons and humans, but let's make sure to get along."

From both the humans and demons, I heard comments like "Hey, that's the Witch of the Highlands!" "Incredible, the goddess herself commanded her to deal with the mosquitoes!" "That's amazing!"

I was getting even more famous when I wasn't looking...

Everyone was actually listening to me—so I was going to leave it at that.

I'd just get Nintan or Beelzebub to yell at whoever wasn't cooperating.

"I don't want to talk forever, so we should get started. The mosquitoes will bite us if we stay still for too long... All right, let's begin draining the water!"

The demons pulled a thick wooden board that had been built between the lake and the channel up and away.

Now with the path open, all the pond's water flooded into the water channel with a thunderous noise.

Fwooooosh!

"Ooh, this is the best part."

Still floating in the air, I watched everything going on below.

The simple waterway was transforming into a river. It was interesting observing it from the sky.

"Quite a sight to see, no?" Beelzebub came up to float beside me.

"I'd say it's more of a sight to river, if you get what I mean."

"...Was that supposed to be a joke? Either way, I only have to look at this water to tell how old it is. 'Twas difficult to notice beneath all the green algae, but the water itself is quite cloudy. 'Tis not a surprise that there was such a great outbreak of mosquitoes."

Right, I guess the environment itself wasn't in total working order...

"Then it wasn't so much the mosquitoes' fault, but the fault of whoever failed to manage the pond. In a way, this was a man-made disaster."

As the water level in the pond went down, the scenery quickly changed.

Meanwhile, fish and bugs got caught in the different-sized nets in the waterway. In the lake bed, there were still a lot left flopping around in the mud.

"All right, Azusa, give the order to everyone to finish checking the types of fish and bugs and transfer the appropriate ones to the readied water tanks. Any species that seem invasive should be placed in their own specific tank."

"Shouldn't you be saying that?" I felt like a puppet sovereign being controlled by my adviser.

"Some humans may be too prideful to follow my instructions. I, too, find it strange for me to be ordering humans around. I do not worship the goddess here, you know."

"We're on the same project, so it's fine, right? But maybe I'm not as mindful of this as I should be…"

It was my job to give commands and take responsibility, and so I would.

I gave the order to start sorting out the different species of plants and animals.

Strictly speaking, checking them wasn't directly related to dealing with the mosquitoes, but if we were going through with this anyway, we may as well do it thoroughly. For the demons, that was the point of this job. And it was probably easy for mosquitoes to breed somewhere in the pond.

People who looked like demon researchers started leaping into the drained pond. I was impressed with their decisiveness.

But then most of them got stuck in the mud and started to panic.

"Oh no, it's way deeper than I thought!"

"His face is stuck!"

"My legs are so heavy, I can barely move!"

I was not expecting a bunch of amateurs!

"They are the lab workers, you see. Some of them do not have much physical strength. Those who specialize in fieldwork are putting up quite a good fight, however."

"I guess some demons are more athletic than others, huh?"

There were humans who were also jumping in and facing a similar predicament. The mud, which had accumulated over the years, was rather deep, so it was hard enough just to pull your leg free. Most of the people involved had sunk into the mud.

But getting all muddy did seem kind of fun.

I was joining in, too. Time to let my hair down a little.

"Laika, come here."

Back at the temple, Laika and I changed into old, shabby clothes.

"Um, Lady Azusa, what are we going to do dressed in these work clothes?"

Apparently, Laika hadn't figured it out yet.

"We're getting our hands dirty, Laika!"

"Dirty…?"

Laika had been watching hesitantly, probably because she was such a prim and proper young lady—which made me really want to take her into the muddy pond. It was time to throw off the standards of ladylike behavior.

"Yeah. See, I think getting all messy is a good way to relieve stress. You can at least relieve the irritation from all those mosquito bites last time."

Laika didn't seem all that interested, but—

"Understood. If you insist, Lady Azusa…"

Well, I ended up having to force her to join me—she definitely wouldn't come on her own. It was a master's job to broaden her apprentice's horizons.

I took Laika's hand, and we leaped into the mud together.

"Whoa, I'm stuck in so deep…"

"I cannot even lift my leg…"

A weird, chilly sensation wrapped around my calves.

It was insanely hard to move around in the mud. Just taking a few steps splashed it all over my clothes.

I had no intention of flailing or struggling, so where was it all coming from?

"Oh, Lady Azusa, I've lost my balance!" Laika cried and slowly, slowly, slooowly fell backward.

It was like watching a slow-motion movie as she plopped into the sludge.

"Oh no, what have I done…?"

"You don't do so well in unfamiliar environments like this, do you? Adapting isn't really your forte."

It was typical of Goody Two-shoes types like her. They can execute a form perfectly, but they can't work at full potential when you throw them into an unexpected situation.

"I don't intend to be this way, but… I'm sure I'll find myself in a miry battle one day, and being unused to the environment will be no excuse."

She was so stiff. *Miry*? She could just say *muddy*.

But it seemed like Laika understood now. Keeping yourself even relatively clean in a situation like this would only lead to despair. I guess I could call that her real starting point.

The moment you decide you don't mind getting dirty, you can't lose anymore. You're invincible.

"All right, Laika, then let's get to work. Amateurs like us can't tell fish apart, so why don't we look for garbage?"

The demon researchers would be classifying the fish, so it would probably be more effective if we specialized in picking up the garbage. There was nothing for us to worry about with that.

"Garbage, yes, but this is a sanctuary, so I doubt—" Laika stopped, pulling up the remains of a ladder.

"You'll be surprised at how much we'll find. That's humans for you."

"I suppose so…"

Even if no one meant to litter in the lake, sometimes things just fell

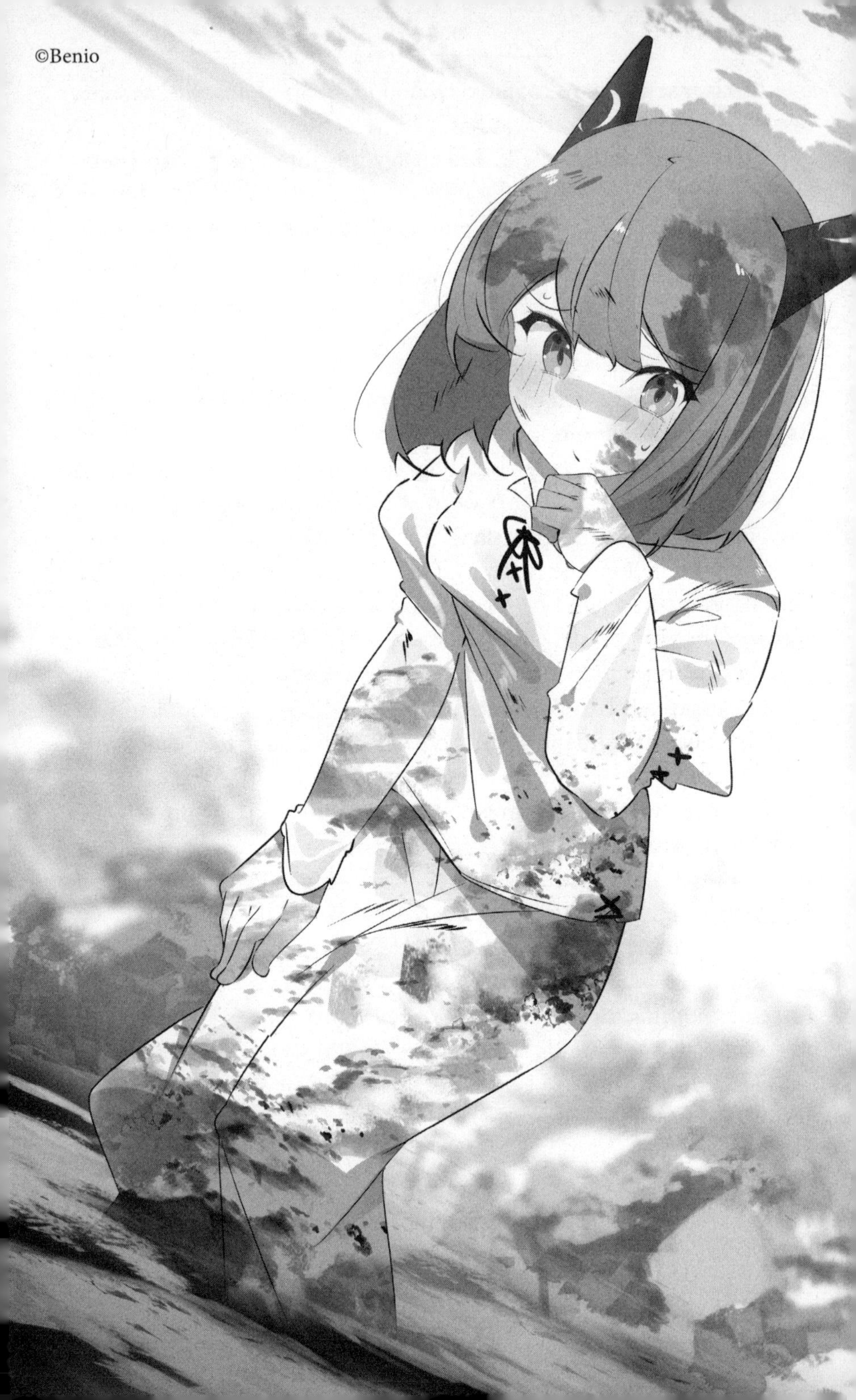
©Benio

into the water, and people let them be. The mud was so deep, it was super hard to pull anything out anyway.

The garbage had sunk to the bottom of the mud. It must have obstructed the water flow, which caused that huge outbreak of mosquitoes.

I searched around my feet.

"Oh. I got something again. Whatever this is, it's not alive." I pulled out something that looked like a doll with a missing head. "Oh god, this is terrifying! Why would you throw this away here?!"

"Perhaps the owner was not sure how to dispose of it and chose the temple pond. I wonder if they believed the goddess's power would prevent it from becoming a cursed object."

"I can see that line of thought. But I'd think they'd be more afraid of her wrath before throwing it away…so don't toss it here."

I doubted Nintan had so much time on her hands that she'd punish people for the tiniest wrongdoings.

We found all sorts of trash after that, and a lot of it had us wondering how they even got in here in the first place. Collecting garbage was a truly fascinating activity.

"A carriage! There's a carriage in here!"

Who put this here, and when? Someone would have definitely found out and raised a fuss, surely.

Some of the other participants started laughing at the sight.

"Lady Azusa, I found a treasure chest!" Laika was cradling a rusted box.

"Seriously?! Is there treasure inside?!"

Laika immediately pried it open. "It's empty, unfortunately."

"I guess we're not that lucky, huh…?"

Before I realized it, the population density within the pond—well, the mud where the pond had once been—had increased.

The people who were hesitant at first must have decided to join the fun.

Their decision was correct. Because it *was* fun.

And there was one more very important thing.

The mosquitoes were keeping their distance thanks to the mud coating our skin. Plus, Eno had started burning the plants that mosquitoes hated. With all our efforts combined, the mosquitoes didn't even try to interrupt us and make it hard to work.

Beelzebub did not come into the mud and instead flew around in the sky. Not surprising that a minister wouldn't want to get all dirty.

"Azusa, how is this supposed to work when the supervisor is in the mud, too…?" she asked.

"Lighten up. I don't need to give out orders that are *that* detailed, right? The more people, the better."

"Very well. So be it. I shall direct the Ministry of Agriculture employees, then."

Yep, that was where she belonged, and she'd take care of that end how she saw fit.

"By the way, how's the fish sorting going?"

"Take a look at the tanks there." There were two massive glass tanks sitting side by side. "The left one is for invasive species, and the right one is for the fish that were here originally."

The invasive-species tank was full of fish.

"So many outsiders!"

"There are quite a number of species that do not belong in this region. Similarly, turtles that do not live in this land have propagated. The ecosystem is a mess."

It was like the rivers in Japan with the growing number of black bass, bluegill, snakeheads, pond sliders, and other critters…

"The mosquito problem aside, it was good that we drained the water. The pond was in chaos. A pilgrim would have gotten bitten by a turtle sooner or later."

"Yeah, a turtle bite would hurt a lot more than a mosquito…"

—Then I saw something big moving around in the mud. And it was getting closer and closer to me.

"What's that? A big turtle? Sorry, fella, but you can't live here anymore."

"No, turtles that big do not exist. It must be something else."

The massive creature came before me and slowly rose from the muck. The first thing I noticed was the long mouth, then the tough skin. It'd probably make for good armor material.

"Wait, is this…a crocodile?"

"Ooh! A crocodile! They are valuable creatures that only live in the south! How lucky I am to have seen one!"

"Hey, wait! Don't act like you're excited to see it in a zoo! It's right in front of me!"

The crocodile opened its mouth wide and came right at me. I guess that was its way of saying it was going to eat me.

"Aaargh! Go away!"

I dealt it a punch, and the crocodile drew a beautiful arc in the air and out of the pond.

And right into the invasive species tank. It floated motionlessly, so it must have lost consciousness.

"Whoa! There was a crocodile, too?! Incredible!"

Vania was getting excited over the crocodile. Kind of a childish reaction—but if I heard there were crocodiles in the local pond, I would probably get worked up, too, so I couldn't talk.

"I've always wanted to prepare a dish of crocodile~ Such a rare ingredient."

She was going to eat that…? I wonder what crocodile tasted like. I'd heard that snakes and frogs taste like chicken, so maybe it was similar?

"But if there's one around, then that probably means there's more—"

A crocodile popped up right in front of Laika this time!

"What is this creature?! Its face looks somewhat dragon-like…"

Oh right, by itself, the face was kind of similar…

Laika would never lose to a crocodile, and she quickly squared it away, but they soon started popping up in other spots, bringing trouble.

"This thing just appeared!"

"Somebody, do something!"

"There's another big turtle over there, too!"

The mud was full of dangers…

Wait, who threw away the crocodiles in the first place?! They probably got rid of them because they couldn't keep them anymore!

"Lady Azusa, I found this..." What Laika had picked up was a ruined wooden sign.

"'These crocodiles are named Crocomax, Crocodina, Crocolate, and Crocodilla. Free to a good home.'"

Don't throw 'em out like abandoned kittens! And don't abandon kittens, either!

◇

After a day of draining the water in the pond, cleaning out all the mud and garbage that had built up, and sorting out the plants and critters—

—the pond was so much cleaner, it looked like a completely different place.

Well, the absence of the water helped with that, too, but...

By sundown, all the manpower we had on our side managed to get most of the mud and garbage squared away, and we got to a point where if we put the water and fish back in, we'd get a revitalized, holy-temple pond.

But our goal this time around wasn't to clean the pond.

It was to do something about the mosquitoes.

We'd managed to lessen the number of mosquitoes for now, but I wanted to have a plan in place to prevent more of them in the future.

I guess it was time to talk.

In the evening, we gathered in the temple meeting hall to discuss the pond work.

Laika and I were still covered in mud, but we participated anyway. You think about it, you lose. So I wasn't going to think about it!

"Um... Our representative is covered in mud, but please do not mind her."

"Beelzebub, maybe they weren't going to until you mentioned it! If you don't need to say it, don't!"

I felt like I'd been betrayed by an ally. Not a full backstab, though, just a little poke.

I sat at the head of the long table, as if it were my birthday. I was formally the leader here, after all.

"Um, ahem… I am Azusa, Witch of the Highlands. I would like to hear what you all have learned from draining the water here. If you have anything to share, please raise your hand."

One of the demon researchers quickly did so.

"We discovered roughly fifteen spots where the mud contributed to unwanted growth. By removing the mud, I believe we have greatly reduced the chance of another mosquito outbreak."

I had no idea when they put it together, but someone was handing out some documents.

They really had it together here. Good thing we had all these researchers.

"Thank you. Anybody else with similar information?"

Well, wouldn't this solve the problem for the most part?

It was practically confirmed that the mosquitoes appeared because of the pond anyway.

This time, a temple priest raised his hand.

"We have not done any work to clear the water in quite some time now. I believe we should strive to continue improving the water quality by regularly replacing it in the future. I was also thinking we could prepare a channel that connects to the pond to create a consistent flow."

"Yes. I think keeping the pond clean is very important."

Everyone was saying the most obvious things, but the tricks to solving this problem kind of were the obvious things. There was no shortcut to improving the water quality. We had to take the smallest actions one step at a time.

Just when I didn't think there were any other suggestions, Fatla raised her hand.

"Yes, Fatla. What is it?"

"We must find whoever abandoned the crocodiles and make them pay a fine."

Did we?! Well, I guess they were way bigger than a stray fish!

"Those crocodiles were big, and they are not native to this area. Which means not many people could have been keeping them as pets here. I can only imagine it must be someone like a noble or a rich merchant. By investigating them, we should happen upon the culprit in due course."

I guess ordinary people wouldn't try to keep them as pets, huh?

One of the priests chimed in. "Now that you mention it, I feel like I saw someone walking a crocodile…"

"Then the next time you see them, please fine them. The same goes for the turtles—if you find the owner, I believe a monetary penalty should suffice."

Right, and that should be it for suggestions.

But there was still another raised hand. Beelzebub.

"Yes, go ahead, demon minister of agriculture. Talk as much as you like."

"I found this item among the garbage that came from the pond." Beelzebub was holding a bright-red stone that was about the size of two fists.

I didn't know what it was, but Laika looked astonished.

"Oh! If it isn't a flame-spirit shard!"

That sounded quite special.

"Aye. Exactly. As you all know, a flame-spirit shard generates its own heat, and it is generally said they can exude this heat for two hundred and fifty years postexcavation."

It wasn't like *I* knew that. I had no idea.

"The royalty and nobility have long valued these. By wrapping one up in a towel and placing it on your back, it can warm you up quite nicely, especially in wintertime."

It was just a pocket hand warmer!

"'Tis hot, so I am putting it down now."

Beelzebub placed the hand-warmer rock on the table. *Yeah, I'm just going to call it that.*

"And we discovered this stone within the pond."

Fatla stood up this time. She wasn't even going to raise her hand anymore. My role was gone now. *I'm still the chair here, by the way.*

"It seems that since someone disposed of this flame-spirit shard in the lake, the water temperature rose much higher than before, which kept it the same in winter as it was in summer. And so the environment morphed into something more hospitable for mosquitoes."

"Wh-what?!" I exclaimed.

Sure, if the water temperature went down in the winter, then mosquitoes couldn't breed.

And yet the recent and dramatic increase of mosquitoes meant there had been a climate-level change in the pond.

"The hand-warmer rock is the culprit here, then! That's the reason why there were so many mosquitoes!"

"Hand-warmer rock? Do you mean the flame-spirit shard?"

Whoops. I got swept up in the conversation and forgot to use the real name. "But I guess this settles this whole thing, then. The culprit is the flame-spirit shard."

"No, Miss Azusa, that is a rash conclusion," Fatla immediately countered. "Since we are talking about a culprit here, it must be a person. Whoever discarded the flame-spirit shard in the pond is the culprit."

Now she was just nitpicking.

"You're probably right, but how are we going to find whoever threw the rock in?"

Things would be different if there were security cameras around, but nothing like that existed.

"Flame-spirit shards are extremely valuable. I doubt anyone would throw one away except in extreme circumstances, and only those of considerable standing own them. That naturally narrows down who it might be."

Fatla slowly started walking along the long meeting table. Essentially, she was playing detective.

"Not only that, but there had been creatures living in the pond that would not have been able to otherwise without this stone."

"Like what? A fish that lives in warm water?"

"No, Miss Azusa, an animal that tried to attack you."

"Oh, the crocodiles…"

The dots were starting to connect for all of us.

"A precious stone had been tossed into the pond at the same time the crocodiles had been abandoned. It is much too well put together to be a coincidence. In essence…the culprit threw the flame-spirit shard into the pond so that the crocodiles they abandoned could live there!" Fatla's voice rose a little at the very end of her sentence.

We were all surprised and getting a little excited.

"Incredible, Fatla… I'm impressed you figured this out… You're just like a detective…"

"I am not a detective. I am merely a leviathan assistant to a minister."

But it was still amazing.

And though her expression still seemed impassive, I bet she felt good about this, too.

"This may be redundant, but if we reason a little further, we know that whoever came to abandon such large animals as a crocodile would indeed draw attention. It would be rather difficult to stay out of sight, unless one is rather knowledgeable of the temple. For example, a guard on night du—"

"Enough!" One of the priests stood. "Yes, it was me! I could no longer care for the crocodiles at home, so I abandoned them in the pond!"

Fatla was dead-on!

The culprit-priest slammed both hands on the table. "But I still love my crocs… I believed Crocomax, Crocodina, Crocolate, and Crocodilla could live a happy life in the big pond…"

If you really loved them, would you have given them those names?

"I will pay for my sins… I believe many people have suffered because of the mosquitoes… I will buy five hundred units of Itch-B-Gone from the Witch of the Grotto."

Are you paying for your sins or paying for itch cream?!

"Five hundred units of Itch-B-Gone! Thank you very much for your purchase!"

Eno was super happy. Five hundred was a pretty big order.

The other priests took the culprit away, probably to make him confess to the statue of Nintan.

On the other hand, Fatla stood there and sighed. "And so love sometimes brings unhappiness. Things never turn out the way we want them to, do they?"

This felt exactly like the ending to a crime drama.

"Though I believe I could own all the crocodiles I want if I kept them on my leviathan form."

Yes, but not all of us have a leviathan form. *You* haven't even been using your leviathan form during all this.

That aside, it seemed like the massive mosquito outbreak was over. I guess my position meant it was time for me to wrap things up.

"Well done, everyone! Now the temple won't have to worry about mosquitoes anymore, and we should be receiving visitors again! You are all dismi—"

"Please hold on a second!" This time, it was Fatla's little sister, Vania, who stood up.

Was there a mystery that was yet unsolved? Were the sisters a detective duo?

No, Vania couldn't pull it off. Nope, she definitely couldn't. She didn't seem suited for it at all.

"Miss Azusa, you look as though you're thinking rude thoughts..."

Oh no, Vania found me out. But Fatla was unusually brilliant, so anyone would panic at the idea of being compared. Wouldn't you?

"We still have one big problem remaining. We cannot be dismissed yet."

"What problem?"

"I will cook something up to show you!"

And that's exactly what she did.

Rows of spoons and knives were laid out in the temple meeting hall, and plates of food were placed before us.

The first dish we got was a thick sauce over fried fish. *Starting off with a bang, huh?*

"Here we go! These are special, Vania-made invasive-fish dishes! We cannot allow them to be set free into the river, so we will enjoy them right here!"

Vania the chef was showing off her true ability.

"The extra animals sure are a big problem, aren't they?"

I didn't think it was just because that's where the crocodiles were kept, but at some point, fish, turtles, and other critters that didn't originally live in the temple pond had settled there. If they escaped to another pond or river, they would certainly cause ecological damage.

In Japan, I'm pretty sure it wasn't okay for anyone to catch and take an invasive fish home alive, but if you wanted to kill it there then cook it later, you were safe. You could release it, too.

There were no laws on invasive fish in this world, but it was probably still better to eat them here.

All right, let's get this party started! We completed a job well done, and now it's time to celebrate!

"I prefer red meat over fish, but this is rather tasty. ♪" Laika was enjoying her meal with perfect table manners. She was clearly devouring it much quicker than anyone around her without losing any of her prim and perfect charm.

"Yeah, the fish doesn't taste like mud at all, even after being in that pond."

"She has seasoned it with herbs, 'tis why. She has hidden the flavor well," Beelzebub explained as one familiar with Vania's cooking.

"I see. I guess cooks know how to make things taste good."

I did wonder if we should really be eating the critters from the temple pond, but they *were* technically trespassing. The priests looked like they were eating without much objection, too.

"We have so much food, you see. It would be best to finish it all while we have plenty of people to dine with."

"You look like you're having fun, Vania."

Her expression was so animated.

"It's because I'm using so many ingredients I don't often get to use!

The next dish I am bringing out is fried fish mince. It has such an excellent texture!"

I imagined a fish cake patty of some sort, and the servers brought in something that more or less matched the description. And they were thick, too—easily in the five-hundred-grams range.

"It's good, but there's a lot of food in each dish…"

"This is the perfect serving size for me."

"'Tis also a regular size for me."

Dragons and demons sure ate a lot…

This was only the second dish, but it seemed the human priests were already having a hard time eating.

Please save any leftovers for dinner.

But the main course hadn't even arrived yet. I knew it was going to be massive.

After somehow fitting the entire fish cake into my stomach, they brought out several huge pots.

"Here we go! Turtle hot pot! Eat it and feel the power!" head chef Vania called out enthusiastically.

"Hot pot after all this…? I can't eat any more…"

"Shall I have yours, then, Lady Azusa?"

I was so glad Laika was with me. "Yeah, go ahead. I'll just have a little bit of turtle…"

I took a piece and put it on a small plate.

I thought it might stink of mud, but it didn't at all. It was probably similar to firm duck meat. It was tough, but biting it set free all the nice flavors.

"Still, I made the right decision calling you, Beelzebub."

I had been grasping at straws, wondering if she could do something about the mosquitoes because she was a fly, but then she suggested draining the water. Fatla even found the culprit who had accidentally invited the huge outbreak of mosquitoes.

"What I mean is, calling on you means I didn't make a mistake!"

"Do not twist logic to be more favorable to you!" Beelzebub complained to me.

She could stand to be a little more honest with herself, considering she had still helped me all she could.

"Honestly, building that survey-project team wore me out. I must have the girls massage my shoulders after this." Beelzebub dramatically rolled her shoulders.

I think Falfa and Shalsha would massage her shoulders at any time, though.

"Why don't I do it for them?"

"You are much too powerful! And I would really rather Falfa, Shalsha, or Sandra instead!"

"At least you're being honest now…"

I took a spoonful of the collagen-loaded (probably) turtle hot pot and put it in another, smaller bowl, then sipped it directly from there. For a Japanese person, this really did feel like hot-pot time.

After the feast was finished, Laika, Beelzebub, and I went to Nintan.

We had to report officially to the client, after all.

"We solved it splendidly! I felt like the demons did most of the work, though…"

"Yes, We saw everything. We never suspected the culprit would be here in Our temple…"

Nintan seemed embarrassed. But of course she would—there was a scandal right in her own organization.

"Indeed, why did a goddess not know of what your own priest had done? It seems a major flaw in your divine power, no?" Beelzebub made a rather sharp indictment. I thought the same.

"Silence! One goddess cannot know everything! If a goddess were able to manage all her priests, then no priest on earth would ever sin. Would that not be too eerie for you?"

Now that she mentioned it, she was right. It would be weird to live in a world where everything the priests said was absolutely correct.

"I am glad we solved this without incident," said Laika. "Mosquitoes have caused plagues in the past, and I believe everyone is glad that we took countermeasures quickly." She put a nice bow on it all.

"Indeed. Though it was the demons who reached a breakthrough, it was Azusa who made a request to the demons, and it was Us who sent an oracle to Azusa. Thus, Our strategy was correct! A worthy god We are!"

"You are twisting logic even more than Azusa did!"

Nintan's train of thought sure was a lot like mine...

The goddess then looked away hesitantly. "We must show Our appreciation to the demons for their contributions in solving the mosquito problem... We will let Our priests know there are indeed some outstanding demons..."

I hoped this could provide the first spark for reconciliation between demons and humans. I had a feeling that reconciliation was already happening little by little, though.

"Yes, thank us demons more. Wah-ha-ha-ha-ha!"

"But how you do irk Us... We shall turn you into a frog."

"Do not take vengeance on someone who has helped you! What do you take me for?!"

I stepped between the two. "Okaaay. That's enough now. Let's be nice with each other."

Despite the pout on her face, Beelzebub extended her hand to Nintan. "This might be a chance for some of the demons to worship you."

"Perhaps We will accept the demons, if it means more believers for Us..." Nintan grasped Beelzebub's hand in turn.

Good, there was now a bridge between god and demon. What a relief.

"Um, there has been something on my mind." Laika seemed to have made a realization. "What should we do with the crocodiles? We could take them back to the south. They were not served as a meal."

You can't just eat someone's old pet... But keeping them in the pond would bring the water temperature back up.

And that would defeat the purpose of everything if that led to more mosquitoes again.

"Oh, We have already dealt with that."

On our way home, we saw a small hut had been built in the corner of the garden.

"Acolytes? She definitely made that up!"

But I didn't think it was a terrible idea for a crocodile to also be a goddess's servant.

CROCODILE CORNER

These crocodiles used to belong to a priest, but as fate would have it, they are now acolytes of the goddess Nintan. Please close the door when coming and going to keep in the heat.

DO NOT PUT YOUR HANDS
IN THE CAGE.
THEY WILL BITE.

WE WENT TO **ANOTHER WORLD**

—Azusa, can you hear me? I'm speaking directly into your mind.

As I was making lunch in the kitchen, a voice rang in my head.
This was probably Goodly Godly Godness using her god powers. That's all fine and well, but...
"You have the volume on way too high! Wait, does telepathy have volume...? Anyway, you're making my head rattle!"

Oh, I'm sorry! It is rather difficult speaking to you. How about thi—? EEEEEEEEEEEEEEEEEEE, WOOOOOOOOOM!

"Was that feedback?!"
Why were her powers acting like cheap communication equipment...? Was this good enough for a god?

Gosh, gosh, speaking to someone, speaking to someone, in the same world, in the same world, comes with its own difficulties, comes with its own difficulties.

"Now you're echoing! I hear everything twice!"

Only some people could probably understand what I mean by this, but listening to her was making me sick. In my past life, making phone calls on messaging apps with a bad connection sometimes sounded like this.

"Is something wrong, Mistress?"

I was yelling my comebacks out loud, so Flatorte was now eyeing me strangely. *I agree, this is strange.*

"It's nothing, Flatorte… Don't worry about it."

Hmm, hmm, these settings are— Khhhch… Beeeeep, beeeeep, beeeeep—

"The line cut!"

Her lack of dignity in this was getting impressive now.

"What line cut, Mistress? Are you angry with something? If you are, then I, Flatorte, will go and pummel it for you anytime."

"No, nothing violent. It's not that big of a problem."

After a little while, the connection came back.

—Khhhccchhhhh, um, Azusa? Can you hea—? Cchhhhhhhh—

"The static is really bad, but I can pick up some sound? Isn't there a spell that can make telepathy a little easier…?"

I am still—kkkhhhhhccccchhh—a god, so I should use— Kkkkkkccchhhhhh—

Oh, sounds like I could just communicate with her in my mind without speaking. I just tend to retort out loud when things don't make sense.

I was trying out something new to pass the time, so I was wondering if you would humor me? Beep beep, beep beep. Oh, another god is calling me.

※ ※ ※

"This telepathy function needs some work!"

Why did it have ringtones? Actually, I'd say it was more of a shock that she wanted me to humor her just because she needed to kill the time.

That said, I still owed her because it was Godly Godness who reincarnated me into this world.

Very well. If that's okay with her, I'll participate.

Thank you! I'll be right there!

What? She's coming here?

Thirty minutes later, Goodly Godly Godness arrived at the house in the highlands.

"Hello~ It's me, Goodly Godly Godness! I hope we're living virtuous lives by collecting virtue stamps! Let's all try to do one good deed a day!"

I didn't really want her coming over, but she had before when Nintan was angry with her. Because of that, the family treated her like a friend.

Laika gave her polite thanks. "Thank you very much for all your help."

Shalsha talked to her from a scholarly angle. "I want to hear about the divine psychological world. I believe it will have a major impact on theological studies."

I think it would probably change theological studies forever, actually, so please don't.

Everyone else accepted her easily.

To be honest, I did think we were a little too accommodating. Someone here had to have common sense; otherwise, our values would get skewed, and we might make some major mistake.

"Thanks to your help, the virtue-stamp-card system has reached far and wide. There are more people giving up their seats on carriages and more dungeon-diving adventurers leaving signs that say, *All treasure chests beyond this point have been opened, so there's no point in going farther.* I believe the world is truly becoming a better place."

I wasn't completely convinced that was true, but I guess it didn't matter right now so long as things weren't getting worse.

"Well? What was that new thing you were trying out?"

"Here we go. Ta-daaa!" Godly Godness pulled out a perfectly round crystal ball.

"Are you going to start fortune-telling? I think it's a bit mean-spirited for a god to tell fortunes."

"Oh, Azusa, equating crystal balls with fortune-telling is so uninspired."

She just insulted me. Ouch.

"This is, in a word—a world!"

I couldn't believe it! "Huh? What do you mean by 'a world'…? Uh, what…?"

My comprehension hadn't caught up yet.

"See, it may be possible for higher beings to create worlds, and those beings must necessarily be gods, yes?"

With the way she worded that, it was hard to tell if they created them or not.

"For me, I can only create simple worlds. See, you all can construct a pond in your garden, let fish swim free in it, and make a new mini ecosystem. This is similar, but to a greater degree. I suppose you could even call it a pocket world created within this world~"

She was talking casually about it, but there was no doubt this was an extraordinary topic. Case in point, Shalsha fainted dead away on the spot.

"Oh no, Mommy! Shalsha is frozen with her mouth open!" Falfa was shocked by her little sister's reaction, too. "I'll hug her. I'm sure she'll go back to normal soon!"

I lifted Shalsha up to cradle her, and she immediately recovered.

"Shalsha has a question... What is the world? What is space? What is truth...? The missing link..."

"Calm down, Shalsha! You'll freeze up again if you think too hard!"

I guess when a god shows up out of the blue, all the rules go out the window.

"Oh, I'm so sorry. I suppose it was too much stress for little Shalsha."

And as always, Goodly Godly Godness was the relaxed one here.

I was starting to sweat, imagining this crystal-ball world falling on the floor.

"Oh dear, my hand slipped! I almost dropped it."

"This is scaring me! Please just put it on the table!"

I would be unbelievably traumatized if I saw a world destroyed in front of me, so please just keep it together!

We laid down a purple cloth on the table, and Godly Godness put the crystal ball on top of it. I didn't think it would roll around now, but the cloth made the place look even more like a fortune-telling house.

"This crystal world has a very simple makeup. Creating worlds is generally too much for me to do on my own, but I did this in my spare time as a fun little project."

"No need to be so humble. I'll start feeling bad for the people in that world..."

"Oh, no, no. There aren't any intelligent life-forms in there~ There is still only one type of creature."

That does sound simple.

I wonder what the ecosystem looked like. I was actually having a harder time imagining a world with only one kind of life-form.

"And if I may get straight to business..." Godly Godness used her free hand to point to the crystal world.

"Please play in this world as one of the life-forms!"

* * *

There she went, saying these wild things like they were nothing…

"I will explain it in a way that will make it easy for you to understand, Azusa. It's like VR."

Yes, it was easy for me to understand. Me and literally no one else.

In short, I guess that meant that from the perspective of this world, where Godly Godness was, the crystal world she made was just a simulation.

"Even if you enter the world I made, it will not have any effect whatsoever on your physical bodies. It is not like entering another world by some mistake and finding yourself suddenly unable to get back. You will definitely, definitely be able to return."

"Please don't say that twice. It's just making me more nervous."

This is what you call jinxing yourself…

"I am interested, though I would be lying if I said I was not uncertain…" Laika was looking dubiously at the crystal ball. As she should be.

"This sounds fun. I, the great Flatorte, will be among the first to explore your world!"

"I suppose if everyone else is going, I will, too," Halkara added.

"Will it work for a ghost like me?"

And so we threw together the party of Flatorte, Halkara, and Rosalie!

"Hey, are you sure you can just casually say *yes* to entering another world like that? You do realize how unbelievable this is, right? It's okay to stay on the safe side every once in a while. You do know that?"

"Both you and Laika worry too much. I, Flatorte, don't mind at all!"

Yeah, Flatorte wasn't the type to think too deeply about anything…

"Madam Teacher, she said it was all right, so it is most definitely all right."

Whenever Halkara said something was *most definitely all right*, that immediately added to the danger. To her, *most definitely* meant she was about 60 percent sure.

"I'm dead anyway, so if we do run into trouble, I'll just cross that bridge when I get to it. I'm already sticking around on borrowed time."

Rosalie thought like a ghost, but that was hard for the rest of us to sympathize with!

"Shalsha is not so much interested in experiencing the world, but in how the world itself was put together."

"Falfa wants to see the world for scientific reasons!"

My two girls were very enthusiastic scholars.

"I see~ I could explain it to you now, but the knowledge could be beyond your comprehension and drive you to madness~"

"Please do *not* explain it to anybody, then!"

That was *really* dangerous.

"Can I photosynthesize in this world?" Sandra asked a very plant-like question.

"This world has no concept of plants, so I doubt that will be a problem at all~"

I'd be lying if I said I wasn't unsure about this, but if it was that dangerous, then she wouldn't have come all the way to the house in the highlands to make us try it out. Goodly Godly Godness wasn't spiteful.

"Very well. I don't mind heading into this world," I said.

Everyone else in the family said they would go in. I guess nobody wanted to be the only one left behind.

"All right, then! Go on in~!"

Just as the crystal ball flashed—my consciousness suddenly went black.

When I came to, I was on a gray ground.

"I guess this is the world she made."

The sky was pure white. I couldn't tell if it was cloudy, or white for another reason.

At that moment, I couldn't see anything besides those two colors.

"What am I anyway?"

There were no mirrors here, so I couldn't tell.

I could move around, but the most I could do was slide around on the ground and jump. Plus, I could think, but I couldn't talk.

These creatures probably had no concept of conversation. Conversation itself was extremely high-level anyway.

"Staying still won't accomplish anything, so let's try going somewhere."

I silently moved forward.

I didn't feel tired at all, but with nothing but a flat horizon ahead of me, the place felt empty.

Now that I was this weird little creature, I couldn't really tell the passage of time, but I finally met something besides myself.

It was—a slime.

It was a normal slime. The kind I'd find around the house.

It was jumping up and down.

Was that a threat? But there was no creature weak enough to be intimidated by a slime.

Since there was nothing else around, I got closer and closer, until I finally made contact with it.

—Bwom.

Then a strange sensation overcame me, like my body had absorbed the slime—or like I had been absorbed.

The slime in front of me was gone.

"I wonder what that was? I guess that means I integrated the slime into me…?"

But I learned right away that it wasn't so simple.

"Whaaat? The slime before me, the great Flatorte, vanished."

Hmm?

"A thought that sounded a lot like Flatorte just crossed my mind."

"I felt a sensation that was like something Mistress would think! What does this mean?!"

So Flatorte *was* here!

I decided to calmly analyze the situation.

Flatorte had been aware of the slime. So had I. And now there was no slime around me.

There was only one thing I could think of.

Flatorte and I had been separate slimes, but then when we got close to each other, we combined!

Now that I thought back on it, Godly Godness did say there was only one type of creature here.

That meant this world—was a world full of nothing but slimes!

"Do you think so, Mistress? Whoa, I can read your thoughts!"

"Yeah, I can hear what you're thinking, too."

Now I understood the point of this world that Goodly Godly Godness had created.

She had made a slime world as a thought experiment, then tossed us in here to see what would happen.

As I thought about that, my body started moving forward.

Strictly speaking, it was Flatorte who was moving.

"Let's keep going, Mistress. That's the only thing we can do, after all."

"You're right. Let's go."

I was hearing Flatorte's thoughts as my own, so I was feeling a little off.

"I'm gonna smash everything that pisses me off. I'm gonna punch everything that pisses me off. I'll beat everyone who gets in my way. I, the great Flatorte, will create a path in front of me. Even if no one's done it before, I, the great Flatorte, will be the first!"

"Your thoughts are so violent!"

"But, Mistress, when you're mad, it's unhealthy to hold it all in. If it makes you angry, fight it. You've gotta pummel people who don't make any sense, right?"

"That might be the right way to think for dragons, but I wish you'd calm down, just a bit…"

I didn't know how much time passed, but as we kept going—

—a slime appeared before us.

"I wonder who it is this time. Or maybe it's a slime native to this world?"

"Yeeeaaah! Let's beat 'em!" The hotheaded Flatorte rushed forward!

"I'm telling you, be more careful! Observing is just as important!"

"Mistress, it's better to ask forgiveness than permission! First, we step up to the challenge!"

"I know those words sound cool together, but your head is just empty!"

Our slime collided with the other slime.

—Bwom!

There was that feeling again of mutual absorption.

"Oh my, the slime before me has vanished. I wonder where it went? It rushed right at me..."

"This inner voice sounds like Laika's."

I couldn't hear the actual sound aloud, but I could tell who it was by her ladylike manner of speech.

"Hmm? Was that slime you, Lady Azusa?"

So we did indeed combine with a slimeified Laika. But that brought some big trouble.

"Why do I, the great Flatorte, need to be combined with Laika?! This is the worst!"

Flatorte was raging!

"Ugh! Flatorte is here, too...? Please let me leave!"

"That's what I *was* going to say! Get out!"

The slime was wiggling every which way!

"Argh, our body's twisting everywhere! Stop, stop!"

We were twisting in all sorts of weird directions!

"What are you doing?! Flatorte, please do not behave so oddly!"

"Shut up! I'm *trying* to get you out of here!"

"We've already combined, so I don't think it's going to work..."

The slime, which included me, was hopping all over the place and squishing flat on the ground. I guess this is what happens when you have one body, but three minds!

After a little while, both Laika and Flatorte settled down.

It was just a guess, but they were probably tired. I was in the same body, so I could feel it, too. Apparently that's what happened after going through these weird motions over and over again.

"I don't know how to get you out of here…"

"I don't seem to have the option of cutting you out, Flatorte… I am not even sure where I stop and you begin."

Yeah, exactly. We were all one slime right now. I couldn't differentiate which part was me, which part was Flatorte, and which part was Laika.

"Essentially, I am one with Lady Azusa right now…" Laika was blushing—at least, that's what it felt like. "Wh-what an honor! An honor more than I deserve!"

"Is that something to be happy about…?"

"Yes! Though this may not be the real world, I am very happy!"

Yeah, it'd be a tragedy if something like this happened in real life. I guess I should be glad I got to experience something so weird personally.

But one of us didn't think that way.

"Waaah! I was one with Mistress, but then Laika got involved! She's a contaminant! What a waste of this whole thing!"

Laika and I sharing a body meant Flatorte and Laika were sharing a body.

Flatorte seemed to recognize that again.

Oh no, another fight was about to start…

"Please get along, you two… Even if you don't, we're still sharing a body, which means your arguments won't accomplish anything…"

"If you say so, Lady Azusa…"

"Then I'll obey…"

I tried thinking about how much of us was the master and how much wasn't, but then I quickly realized that was too difficult.

But they could probably hear my thoughts…

There wasn't a whole lot of common sense in this world.

And so we the slime traveled across the wasteland.

I don't know if slimes understand the concept of travel, though.

Also, I say *wasteland*, but the only thing in this world was this empty field.

Just as Goodly Godly Godness had explained, plants probably didn't exist here.

We moved forward, sometimes rolling, sometimes hopping.

"Hey, do you know how much time has passed?"

"I have absolutely no idea. It does appear the sun neither sets nor rises in this world."

Maybe a slime didn't have much sense of time.

As for food, we were probably absorbing something from the wasteland or the air. Or maybe the concept of nutrition hadn't been set up in this world.

"*Just sleep when you're sleepy and eat when you're hungry. I don't feel like doing either right now.*"

I had a feeling that this world was best suited to Flatorte.

As we moved straight forward—we encountered a massive slime.

This was probably because several slimes had already combined there.

"We do, in fact, have the option to run. What should we do?"

"Mistress, we can't run—that's embarrassing! I, Flatorte, am going to fight!"

"Lady Azusa, one cannot retreat without beginning the fight. We must first engage; otherwise, we are not running. We are simply not doing anything."

With a good hop, step, and a jump, we managed to get right on top of the slime.

However, the moment we made contact, I felt that unique sensation again, but I didn't go unconscious.

"Wow, Falfa can hear so many people thinking! Amazing!"

"Mom is here. This is a miraculous experience."

"It's a lot louder now. But I'll hold my tongue. Plants are good at that."

Wait, could this be…?

* * *

"*Gasp!* I've merged with my daughters!"

I could barely contain myself, so I hopped in place.

Apparently, if anyone wanted to move, even if everyone inside wasn't on the same page, the slime would move.

"There is nothing more miraculous than becoming wholly a part of my daughters. What an amazing experience! Thank you, Goodly Godly Godness! This is the best, the absolute best! I can feel how sweet and good you all are! Is feel the right word when we're all the same?!"

"Calm down, Mommy, calm down."

"I believe she is temporarily excited due to this unique experience. She will relax eventually."

"Argh, you're all so loud! Animals don't know how to sit still!"

My daughters were very blasé about all this, and that made me a little sad. Maybe I had overreacted.

Oh yeah—back in college, I did hear a mother could truly smother a child with love, so I guess this was something similar...

If a parent can't separate from the child, then the child can't develop independence... This was difficult... But they were all like children to me, so I guess they would still let me smother them a little bit as their mother.

"Shalsha has not learned enough about this. I cannot say anything about this."

"I don't think anyone has ever pinned down how to define a child, after all~"

"You really like those difficult topics, don't you...?"

My daughters sure were levelheaded...

"But Falfa is very happy to be the same as you, Mommy!"

"Thank you! That's what I wanted to hear!"

"Shalsha is happy, too. But I am uncertain whether to conclude this is love for another, or love for the self."

"This is a really difficult topic considering this slime form we're in... Well, think hard and think lots... Thinking hard is a good way to study anyway."

"The animal world is much simpler than the plant world."

"Sandra, I am not entirely sure if slimes are animals."

Meanwhile, Laika and Flatorte were having their own conversation:

"We've gotten quite big."

"Let's keep going and be the biggest in the world!"

Everyone could hear everyone else's thoughts, but it seemed like we could have individual conversations among ourselves.

Afterward, we just kept going forward, forward, forward.

I wondered how far we had come—but it couldn't have been too far. We were moving at a slime's pace, after all.

But we moved forward.

There was nothing else to do. This wasn't a figure of speech or anything; there really wasn't anything else to do.

I seriously wanted to know what enjoyment slimes got out of life... Or maybe this was just a special case because the slimes were the only ones here, and slimes in our original world had more to think about?

But we could use our knowledge from our original world, so—

"I'll take it with my knight."

"Then I will move my sentry into the space in front of it."

Shalsha and Laika were playing some chess-like game.

I didn't know who was better, but I bet it was a good match.

—And finally, we absorbed the Halkara-and-Rosalie slime.

That meant the whole family was in one slime now.

"My body feels heavier with you, Madam Teacher... Oh, this is rather sexy..."

"Halkara, no funny ideas."

Was *sexy* even a concept in this world?

"I've felt heavier before... Is there something weird about that?"

"Miss Rosalie, that is simply because your ghost body was passing through a person's body..."

Halkara pointed out the inconsistency.

We were now one big happy family, but that didn't mean we'd "won" somehow. Our only choice next was to keep going forward...

* * *

I thought there might not be any slimes left in this world, but that wasn't entirely true.

We discovered some other native slimes that weren't a part of our family.

But as our slime got bigger, the way we thought changed.

I was starting to sense that everyone couldn't say what they were thinking anymore. Like their personal opinions had dwindled. I guess it was because the local slimes didn't have any of their own thoughts.

We had to absorb more.

We needed to absorb more.

We…*I* must absorb…

And I moved forth.

…

……

I proceeded through the world, doing nothing else.

When I found a slime, I approached and absorbed it into myself. That was my goal, an act that would bring us to some decisive conclusion.

At some point, I was made of over one thousand slimes.

And eventually, I stopped finding them.

At last, I stopped seeing any other slimes.

That was not all—the ground and sky I was once aware of no longer existed.

I could infer why that was. I was so great, so large, that I had absorbed them all.

At one decisive moment, I came to the following conclusion:

I was now the entire world.

* * *

Slimes, ground, sky—the "other" no longer existed in this world. Everything was now contained within "me." In essence, I was "one," and I was "all."

I stopped in place.

Perhaps it was fair to say I no longer was aware of the concept of movement.

I would exist here forever!

Suddenly, an entity within me thought:

"Even if the whole of this world is within me, what would happen if there are other worlds besides this one? Would I still be able to call myself one and all?"

Another within me responded:

"This is an interesting thought experiment, but it is a paradox. If I am not one and all, then I would be able to move. But If I am indeed one and all, then there exists no place for me to move. I am already this entire world itself, and therefore, I have stopped."

My immobility was proof that all existence was already contained within me.

Therefore, other worlds could not logically exist.

However, there were entities with counterarguments within me.

"This simply means I am incorporated with this world. So long as I am within this world, there is no separate entity to observe me moving, which is seen as being unmoving. But that does not prove there is no outside."

"Wait, what does that mean…?"

"Apologies. Things have gotten so complicated, I'm not sure anymore… My essence seems to have been bad at studying…"

"Let me build a metaphor for you. Say this world is a ball, and I am the ball itself. The ball will ostensibly seem to be permanently frozen in space. That is because there is nothing but the ball."

"That's easier to understand now!"

"But then say the ball eventually collides with a wall, breaks the wall, and enters the outside. In that case, whoever is on the outside will then be cognizant of my movement. This is just a possibility, of course."

It sounded like the point was that there might be worlds out there besides me.

I agreed. If there was even the slightest chance that I was the whole of everything, then I should be able to move.

Then when I find this other entity, I will incorporate it into myself.

However, in order to be cognizant of my movement, I must enter another world. Until then, I could not tell the difference between moving and staying still.

But in my perception, I intended to be in motion.

Then, after a long, long time passed, I sensed an "other" for the first time in an eternity—something akin to a wall collided into me!

Oh...I finally found it...

I was not all. There were other things that still existed!

I would break this wall and absorb everything in the world outside!

"Now it is time to incorporate everything into.......... Huh...? Oh, it was a dream..."

I was collapsed on the dining room floor. Other members of my family were also lying on the floor, or asleep at the table.

But we started waking up all at the same time.

All except Godly Godness, who sat with a crystal-ball-like world on the table, sipping on tea.

"Well done, everyone. Thank you for participating in my experiment."

"All I can remember is dreaming about being a slime..."

I felt like we were talking about something grand and philosophical at one point, but I couldn't really recall.

"Yes. I made a world of only slimes, but to be quite honest, it was a bust. The slimes absorbed one another and eventually became the world itself."

Shalsha crossed her arms, closed her eyes, and nodded. She was acting as though she understood.

"That is already a problem, but it was even looking to leap into worlds outside its own," said Godly Godness. "And if it incorporated other worlds into itself—"

"Then it would have become a kind of abyss sucking in everything. If such a thing existed, many worlds would come to be destroyed, and even space itself would vanish. There was a risk of every single world turning to nothing." Shalsha put together the rest.

"That's terrifying, Shalsha."

"To put it in a way you understand, Azusa, if there was a world that was nothing but slimes, it would eventually become a black hole and end up absorbing everything, including other planets~"

Black holes were really scary.

No, maybe slimes were the true terror?

A little while later, I would shiver whenever I killed a slime.

"How awful it would be if this world was all slime…"

I was so glad there were things here besides slimes. So glad for all the different things in my world.

"What's wrong, Mommy?"

"I can tell you are on edge."

Falfa and Shalsha, who had come along with me, were worried about me.

When I looked at their faces, a switch flipped in me.

"I'm so glad slimes exist!"

Because if they didn't, then I wouldn't have my little slime spirits!

"I love both of you!" I squeezed them both in a tight hug.

"Falfa loves Mommy, too~!"

"Shalsha does not need to speak of this."

It was a good thing that nothing was in extremes—moderation, moderation!

I CUT MY HAIR **TOO SHORT**

"Your hair is so long, Azusa."

I was at Momma Yufufu's house to hang out when she made this remark to me.

"Huh, you think so? I don't really pay attention to it."

"Yes, it's gotten a bit longer. I can really tell when you lie on the couch like that."

Oh… I was lazing around on the couch now. This was embarrassing.

"Then I'll go get it cut soon. I didn't know it was that long…"

"Oh, I've got a great idea! ♪" It sounded like her voice went an octave higher. "Yes. I'll cut your hair. I have scissors. Hee-hee-hee~"

Momma Yufufu went straight to a small drawer and began searching for her scissors.

"Wait, hold on! I didn't say you could cut it just yet!"

"Don't worry. I've been a droplet spirit for a long time. Cutting hair is the least I can do."

"That has absolutely nothing to do with cutting hair."

It wasn't like I was doubting Momma Yufufu, but I didn't know what she'd do to my hair; I wasn't sure if I should let her near it.

"I cut my own hair, see." Momma Yufufu brushed her fingers through her hair.

"I see. Then I guess you're okay…"

She was generally fashionable. In my opinion, she was one of the fanciest spirits I'd seen.

But given the aesthetics of Curalina, the wandering artist, spirit fashion was still a mystery to me.

Even when we went to the World Spirit Summit, there were a certain number of male spirits walking around shirtless, showing off their muscles. If they empathized their physique over fashion, then hairstyles wouldn't mean much…

"I've always dreamed of cutting my own daughter's hair~" Momma Yufufu said dreamily.

Oh no, look at her face! A daughter just can't say no to that!

"Fine. Cut my hair, Momma Yufufu! Just hack it all off!" I replied with a thumbs-up. Time to bring a smile to my momma's face!

"Oh, no~ I won't hack it off. I'll be a little more careful than that."

And so Momma Yufufu was getting ready to give me a haircut.

I sat in a chair, and she wrapped a cloth around my front. I looked like a little rain charm.

This was just a regular house, not a beauty salon, so there was no mirror. It made me nervous, but as long as Momma Yufufu could see, this would probably turn out okay.

"All right, I'm getting started. First, I'll have to wet your hair. There, I just have to touch it."

Maybe she really was cut out for hairdressing work.

"All right, here we go!"

Snip! Snap! Kshrt!

For such a gentle spirit, Momma Yufufu sure was going ham with those scissors.

Kshnap! Snap! Fzzzt!

The more violent the noises got, the more anxious I became.

"Hey, Momma? Could you be just a little more, y'know, gentle…?"

"It's all right. I decided to be a little bold— Oh dear. I may have cut off a little too much."

"What?! It's been, like, ten seconds since you started! You're freaking me out…"

"Don't worry. I may have cut too much, but this is level-one overcutting. I can easily recover from this. A drop of jelly cake!"

I guess that was the expression for *a piece of cake* in this world.

"Fine. I trust you, Momma."

"Yes, leave it to me. I won't make any more mistakes."

"Did you just say *mistakes*…?"

Snip, snip, snap!

Ahhh, the cutting noises are more measured than they were earlier.

"Oh my, I've cut too much again~"

"Momma Yufufu?! Are you sure you're okay with this?! Are you sure things aren't getting worse?!"

"Yes, it's all right. You look very chic."

"That's what friends say when you have a bad haircut! Are you seriously, *seriously* okay with this?!"

"Trust me, Azusa. I can't turn back now. If we stop here, you'll look very strange. This is about a level-fifty-three overcut."

"That's quite a level up!"

How many experience points did it get in that short of a time?!

"Well, if I had to say whether we were in the safe zone or danger zone, I'd say we are safe, but leaning toward danger."

That would probably rank in a list of top five things you never want to hear at a salon.

"All I need to do now is not make any more errors. Yes, I can do this! …Oh dear, it's level fifty-six."

My overcut level shot up by three!

"I can do this. I can do this. Here, and here. All right. This, and this… Yes, this is certainly the danger zone, but we're still a little safe yet."

"We're in *danger* now?!"

I want to see a mirror! No, actually, I don't!

"Trust your momma, Azusa. A mother's love is genuine."

"Momma Yufufu, the problem right now is my hair. You know that, right? This has nothing to do with love or any spiritual concepts."

I was starting to wonder if this was her way of sweeping her mistakes under the rug.

"Well, I said it's in the danger zone, but it's really only level-thirty-one danger. I can get this down to a level fifteen."

"What were you saying about level fifty-three earlier, then?"

"That was the overcut level; this is the danger level."

"Level thirty-one is kind of high. That's the level of an experienced adventurer."

"That's what I mean; I'm going to get it down to level fifteen. Like an adventurer who has been relatively active for about three years."

"It's still bad either way!"

—The entire time afterward, I was in a state of terror.

I kept hearing disturbing snippets like, "Level-sixty-three danger," "Midlevel overcut," "This isn't my fault; it's the scissors'," "Don't worry about it, don't worry about it," but I started shutting it out.

"There, finished! I'm just going to say it's finished!"

Just say it's done!

"Here you go, Azusa. This is what it looks like."

Momma Yufufu brought me a looking glass.

My hair was much shorter, and I now had my hair in a bob cut.

"It's not *not* cute, right? I think it looks nice. It's stylish."

"It might be stylish, but I wanted something a little more conservative…"

I definitely remember women having hairstyles like this in my past life. This would work well for super-stylish people.

But if I had to define it, then I'd say this look went better with shorter girls. I wasn't exactly sure if this was meant for me…

"Azusa, I have short hair, so I could only cut to shorter hairstyles. It's only now that I realize this."

Hold on, Momma—your hair is plenty long!

Benio

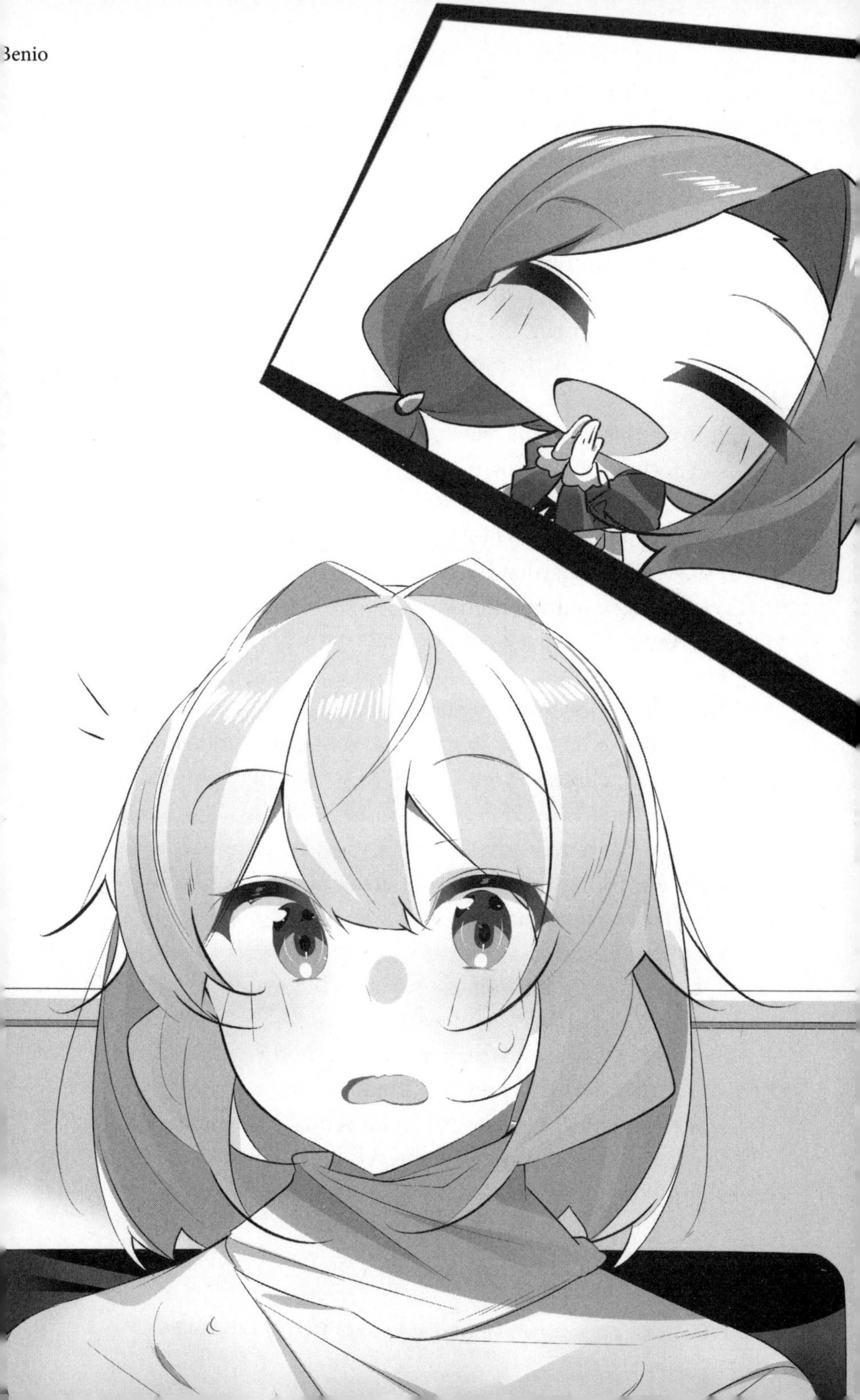

Well, it was too late now.

There was no point in complaining to Momma Yufufu now, so I went home to the house in the highlands.

In her defense (well, in my own defense; let's be honest), it was trendy enough. It wasn't deathly unnatural. If I saw someone walking around with this haircut, I'd probably think it was cute.

Just compared with my previous hairstyle, it was a whole lot shorter now.

If I insisted it was a makeover, then it would probably work out somehow. And my hair would grow back anyway. Yeah, this was fine. If I thought about the no-problem level of the whole thing, it was probably a level 3.

When I got home, the first one I came across was Sandra. Well, she was in the vegetable garden right outside the house, so strictly speaking, it was right before coming home.

"Oh, Azusa. You cut a lot of hair off. Did you break up with someone?"

"No."

That assumption was completely unnecessary.

"Well, that's good. You look really fashionable and confident with that style. If you changed your clothes to something lighter, I think you could really own it."

She gave me better advice than I was expecting. I guess she had been alive for a long time, after all, and only looked like a child. But didn't she live in a dormant state for a long time? Could she say anything at all about fashion…?

I see. If I changed my hair dramatically but wore the same clothes, it would just make it seem even more out of place.

The clothes I'd been wearing so far were for witches, so some of them were fairly dramatic and only kind of chic.

Now that my hair was short, I could probably seem like I was at the cutting edge of fashion if I also lightened up my clothes a bit. Wa'evah, dunna, innit (to quote Her Ghostly Majesty, Queen Muu).

* * *

My determination only grew when I opened the door to my house and formally returned home.

Falfa was in the dining room reading another difficult book. It looked like there were more math formulas in it than letters.

"Oh, Mommy! Wow, Mommy! Amazing!" Falfa's eyes were glittering. My new haircut sure was going over well!

"You think so? Do I look good? Oh, I'm so glad to hear it."

I'm a simple girl; the moment my daughter approved, that was enough to send my excitement through the roof. All thanks to Momma Yufufu~

But an even more important piece of information came out of Falfa's mouth.

"Mommy, you have the same hairstyle as Falfa and Shalsha now!"

Say *what*?! I hadn't thought about that.

I looked in the mirror again, and—

"Hey, you're right. It's really similar to both of yours…"

Obviously, we didn't look exactly the same—and good thing, because the height difference would make it a little strange if our hair really was identical. At most, we looked similar now.

But still, compared with the hairstyle I used to have, there was no doubt that my current one was a lot closer to theirs.

Then Shalsha came in.

"Sis, it's almost time for our stroll of the— Oh, Mom…"

Shalsha looked at me, and it seemed she was quite nonplussed at this unusual new sight.

"Mom, what did you do? You…you are cuter."

I internally took a victory pose. *My daughter said I was cute! Yay, yay! I'm so happy! Today is a good day!*

"Man, you're super cute now, Big Sis."

Then Rosalie appeared from the wall, which would have been pretty spooky if it didn't happen to us every day. When she pops out of the floor, though—that'll give you a fright.

"When you three and your similar hairstyles stand together like that, **you look less like a mom and her kids, and more like sisters.** You could honestly pass as siblings."

There came another important statement. Almost as though it were underlined in pink marker, like a keyword phrase in a textbook.

"Say that again, Rosalie."

"Huh? Say what again? That **you look less like a mom and her kids, and more like sisters?**"

"Yes, that!"

Thinking back on it, I'd lived as Falfa and Shalsha's mother figure up until now. There was absolutely no problem with that. It's been a wonderful thing.

But in terms of looks, Falfa, Shalsha, and I naturally looked more like sisters.

I guess it wouldn't be so bad if we acted like sisters every once in a while. Yeah, not bad.

Actually, I wanted to.

"Falfa, Shalsha, why don't we go travel to another town sometime soon?"

"Okay! Falfa will come along!"

"Traveling offers perspective on things one paid little mind to previously," said Shalsha. "It is through the past that we learn new things. By looking outward, we take notice of what is inward."

I didn't really need all that complicated logic myself—I just wanted to spend time with the two as sisters.

By the way, my new haircut was generally well received by the rest of the family—except their comments were all a little strange.

"Oh, that looks great, Mistress. Your hair won't get in the way when you're sparring with someone!" Flatorte was thinking of battle above everything else.

"Does this mean long hair gets in the way of training, Lady Azusa? I believe you look wonderful with short hair!" I had a feeling that Laika's thoughts were very close to Flatorte's. Must be a dragon thing.

"Madam Teacher, did someone break your heart? When did you

even give your heart away?" Halkara was thinking about romance. "Who dumped you?! Where is she?!"

"Please explain why I can only date women."

"Because I've never seen a man anywhere near you, Madam Teacher~"

I dunno, I was getting irritated… She wasn't saying anything particularly odd to me, but it was rubbing me the wrong way…

But it was all good in general. I had to let Momma Yufufu know that she hadn't totally failed me with her haircut.

The only problem was that the more romantic-minded people saw my short hair and assumed I'd been through a rough breakup…

Once I hit the town with my daughters—no, my little sisters, I was going to find clothes that matched my hair.

On a particularly sunny day, I took Falfa and Shalsha to the provincial capital of Vitamei.

Laika took us partway there. I felt bad having her escort us on a day she had cooking duty, but apparently to her, flying over to Vitamei was just a quick stop.

And so the three of us walked through town.

"It's so lively~ Falfa is more excited than usual! Falfa hopes they sell candy!"

"Ah, the hustle and bustle of a capital city. Those who gain enlightenment while surrounded by distractions are true sages. Those who say they reached nirvana in secluded lands, devoid of everything but the sound of deer and bugs, are not truly worthy of the title."

I had a feeling their differences were clearer for every mile we traveled.

"We'll of course visit any stores you want to go to. But first, I want to pick out some clothes, so do you mind waiting?"

"Okay!"

"Shalsha will wait three years upon a stone, nine years facing a wall."

That might be a little too long.

Oh, and there was another important rule here.

"And listen, you two: Today, I don't want you to call me Mommy. Call me Big Sis, okay?"

It was kind of embarrassing saying it myself, but I had to speak with confidence so it wouldn't be awkward.

"Okay! Big Sis! Big Sis Azusa!"

"Well done, Falfa!"

I sure brought up an obedient kid!

Wait, no. That was a maternal train of thought. No breaking character!

"B-Big Sis Azusa... That makes me somewhat uncomfortable...," Shalsha said, hiding her mouth with her hand. It looked like she was more opposed to it.

"I know it might be a little weird, Shalsha, but just for today, okay?"

"Okay, Mo... Big Sis Azusa..."

I didn't mind that she was a little shy about it.

Honestly, my daughters were so cute, they could say it however they wanted.

Well, now that I had my daughters'—er, sisters' approval, it was time to buy some clothes.

I went on a little adventure (and not the dungeon-crawling type).

I bought rather luxurious clothes and changed in the store.

I decided to go with a skirt a little on the shorter side. I even bought a scrunchie as an accent.

I think I've unconsciously leaned more toward subtle, unobtrusive clothing thus far, possibly because I'm a mom and head of the household and whatnot. And a witch by trade.

Actually, even when I lived alone, my life really only consisted of going back and forth between my house and Flatta, so I never really paid much attention to fashion.

Even in my past life, someone wearing Harajuku-style clothes in a bear-riddled countryside would absolutely get some weird looks. But if you wore gaudy clothes, then you were less at risk of getting shot by a hunter…

Well, past-life talk aside...

I've looked like a seventeen-year-old—a high school girl, basically—for a long time, but I never dressed like one. Had my looks been wasted on me?

Today, I was going to be more like a high school girl!

"Well? What do you think of your big sis's clothes?!"

"Wooow, they're so pretty, Mommy... Er, Big Sis Azusa!"

"You're radiant, Big Sis Mom. Like an angel."

They weren't quite seeing me as a big sister yet... Shalsha was even calling me Big Sis Mom. It made me think of a somber household, where the real mom was no longer around, and the big sister had to play the part.

I guess we'd just have to get used to it, little by little.

In any event, I was ready. It was time for us sisters to go out on the town!

First, at Falfa's request, we went to a candy store.

"If there's anything you want, your big sis'll buy it for you!"

"Ooh, I want this, and that! And that one, too!"

"Shalsha will have the same as Sis Falfa."

"C'mon, be a little more independent... You can get anything you want for yourself, Shalsha."

"The grass is greener on the other side. Shalsha will undoubtedly regret choosing something different. As such, I will simply choose the same to start with."

Sure...I guess.

"Your little sisters are adorable," said one of the staff members. "Are they twins?"

Yes, they thought we were sisters! Mission success.

What kind of mission is it? I'm not quite sure, but it's a success in my mind.

We walked around town eating our candy.

To my left was Falfa, and on my right was Shalsha.

"Big Sis Azusa, this candy is delicious!"

"Right? But this whole day out is way more delicious for me~"

On my other side, Shalsha was quietly nibbling at her sweets. Probably because it was good manners to stay silent while eating.

I could hear little comments as we passed by: "They're so cute~ Look at the twins!"

Right? Aren't they adorable?

Someone else said, "They're twins. They look exactly the same!"

They sure do. Their personalities are totally different, though.

But everyone was paying attention to the twins, and not me. I guess twin sisters had a much bigger impact.

That might've been a miscalculation on my part... I underestimated the power of twins.

Well, now I just have to walk around town until I get a reaction!

I heard a voice that said, "Hey, look at those sisters all walking together!"

Yes, yes! We are a lovely trio of sisters!

"You're right, look at the twins~" came a voice afterward...

Just Falfa and Shalsha again? Include me please! I look like their big sister, right?! We're three peas in a pod!

"Mo— Big Sis Azusa, there's a shop Shalsha wants to go to."

"Sure, where is it? We'll go anywhere you want~"

"The used bookstore." Shalsha pointed to an aged, delicate-looking building.

The sign out front read VITAMEI SPRING OF WISDOM BOOKSTORE.

That sure was a sober place... Not really a hangout for sisters to spend a day on the town...

I guess that was because despite how cute Shalsha was, her hobbies didn't really lend themselves to showing off our sisterly bond... But I was going to do all I could for them. If they had requests, I'd do my best to fulfill them.

"Sure. Let's go into the bookstore together."

"There aren't any shops like this around the house in the highlands. Shalsha is happy."

Shalsha jogged off toward the store.

Then Falfa also seemed to show some interest—"I hope they have some essays on heavenly bodies~!"—and rushed after her.

Hmm, I was the odd one out here!

I wanted us to behave more like sisters would, but I had a feeling we were just acting like we normally did!

But then a voice of salvation came to me.

"That young lady must have her hands full with two little sisters."

"Caring for two little ones is always difficult, even for a big sister."

Hey, people were talking about us as a trio of siblings!

That's right! We are three beautiful sisters!

Wait, they didn't say *beautiful*? Oh, don't mind that part.

Now that I felt better, I bought several grimoires at the used bookstore.

As we walked, I heard some more comments:

"All three of those sisters have the same hairstyle~"

"They look so good!"

You might think I was hearing *a lot* about us, but I wasn't hallucinating or anything. They really were saying these things about us.

With my stats, I could hear a whole ton if I concentrated on listening. That's why I could catch snippets of conversations that most people wouldn't be able to.

Right, don't we look good? A beautiful trio of sisters, we are!

"Big Sis Azusa, I'm having fun! ♪"

"You can tell, Falfa? You can, right? Yes, I'm having a lot of fun, too~"

I felt more energetic than usual, probably because my hair and clothes were new.

Fashion didn't just change how someone looked—it was the starting point for a change in action.

"Oh, Shalsha, reading while walking isn't very safe… You might run into someone…"

She looked kind of like the philosopher Kinjiro Ninomiya like that...

"I couldn't help myself. I will read it over thoroughly when we get home."

"Falfa, is there anywhere you want to go to next?"

"Hmm...the library!"

The twins sure loved to study, huh?!

That said, it wasn't like there were amusement parks in this world, and we could still see plenty of wildflowers growing around the house in the highlands, even if we didn't have a large flower garden. Of course, if we came to a big enough city, they'd go after the books...

This library, however, wasn't like Japan's public libraries; it was a private one where we paid an entry fee. That's how it goes in the provincial capital.

"Sure. We'll go to the library..."

"Yay! I love you, Big Sis Mommy!"

"Big Sis Mom, you care so much about your little sisters' education. You're setting a good example."

I just can't escape the mom part of me, can I...?

Wandering around in the library in my fashionable clothes was kind of pointless, but that's exactly what I did.

As I perused books on herbs with my brightly colored clothes, some more witchy types came by. I was so out of place...

—And before I knew it, an hour and a half had passed.

Hanging out with the bookworm twins had made the day go by super fast. It was almost a waste.

"Um...if possible, I want to go somewhere else... Got any other ideas?"

"Shalsha wants to go to the harbor and watch the boats come in."

"Boats, eh? Not a bad idea."

Kids sure did love their modes of transport.

This harbor was not by the sea, but by the river that flowed through Vitamei.

Nanterre Province didn't connect to the ocean at all. But there was a river, thin and narrow though it was, that served as a channel for cargo ships. Smaller ones, at least—there were some spots where people had to forcibly pull the boat along.

We went to a spot that had a good view of the boats coming and going and sat down on a set of rough-hewn steps.

"Shalsha, look, a boat's coming in. Look~"

Shalsha had her nose stuck in a book. She wasn't watching at all.

"A boat's coming, look!"

"Oh…yes, a boat. A harbor bustling with the sounds of unloading cargo and sailors calling. Some are accented with the dialects of far-off lands. People from so many places mix together here. How fascinating."

"You really have glum ways of having fun…"

"And as I listen to the sounds, I read at my leisure. This is a splendid way to use my time."

She was just going to read anyway!

Dammit… I want to run around, play, have fun more like sisters, but Shalsha is too elderly…

Falfa's probably getting excited about the boats, though, right?

That's what I thought, but Falfa's eyes were glittering as she read the book she'd just bought.

I guess the vessels couldn't win out against the excitement of reading.

"Boy, I guess I'm happy to have daughters so interested in studying…" I sighed in defeat.

I was putting an end to my plan to act like sisters.

And that's when it hit me again.

It wasn't just my own fault that they were so used to me as a mother.

They really were well-raised girls, so when I forgot myself and started acting childish, it was hard to tell who the adult was here.

At the very least, Falfa and Shalsha were more adultlike than any random seventeen-year-old. Of course, they were still childlike in some ways—they did chase grasshoppers around sometimes—but they were mature enough to seek out books they couldn't get in Flatta.

Ah well. I was going to make sure I stayed a good mother to them from now on.

"Oh, another boat," Shalsha murmured as she looked over the harbor.

Sure enough, people were disembarking from the newest arrival.

"It really is lively down there."

But this boat was somehow unlike all the others, and alarm bells were going off in my mind.

"Your Majesty, why did you decide to go out of your way to take a boat here…?"

"To see if the trade ships are in operation, Miss Beelzebub. This is part of my work, too, you know. I am not here for fun."

Two of the people who stepped out of the boat were Beelzebub and Pecora!

Why are they here?! Wait, I just overheard their reasons why.

They were probably going to start selling goods from the demon lands or something. Even though the kingdom and the demons didn't have any formal relations, trade was still an option.

But seeing these two here today was not a good thing.

They would definitely laugh at me if they saw me with almost the same haircut as Falfa and Shalsha…

I could already see how it'd go in my mind.

Pecora would say something like *I see you have a playful side, Elder Sister~ ♪ Please match my hairstyle next time, okay~?* She always tries to mess with me somehow…

Beelzebub would say something like *You may have a similar hairstyle to the girls, but I am not interested in adopting you.* I can already hear her now. I didn't want her to adopt me anyway.

I was just going to let them pass.

Beelzebub could very well show up at the house in the highlands tonight, but…the most important thing now was getting through this.

"Your Majesty, there is nothing here. Let us return home."

Yes, go home. Now. No need to do any overtime here.

"But we are considerably closer to Elder Sister's house~ Miss Beelzebub, why don't we drop by since we've made it this far?"

"Then I will have to purchase some gifts for the girls."

They were both planning on going to the house in the highlands.

Okay, change of plans.

I would spend time here in Vitamei. So when they went to my house, we'd be like, *Oh no, we just missed each other.*

They wouldn't be coming to stay the night, I didn't think, so we'd be in good shape.

—But then.

At the worst possible moment, there came the comments I'd been hoping for.

"Omigosh, those three girls sitting there are so cute!"

"Gorgeous sisters!"

"The big sister and little sisters all have the same haircut. They must be close."

The boat passengers were talking about us.

"That lady really has an eye for fashion. She looks like a city girl."

"Well, this *is* the provincial capital."

"What a lovely picture those three sisters make together."

I'm really happy about this, but please don't be too loud about it! They'll notice!

"Oh? Three beautiful sisters?" Beelzebub said. "Where are they? I doubt they are anywhere near as gorgeous as I am."

"I am more on the cuter side, so I suppose I'd be outclassed in your category~" Pecora added.

Well, crap.

Pecora looked straight at me.

I bet she had a sixth sense for my panic, specifically.

"Oh my, oh my~ If it isn't my elder sister~ And she seems to have had herself a little makeover~" Pecora came right at us with the speed of a predator chasing its prey. "How lovely, Elder Sister. What a nice thing to do. How wonderful it is to try out the fashions you like and try to keep them secret from me!"

"Are you sure that's what's going on...?"

"Then perhaps I, too, shall get my hair cut the same way as yours. And then why don't we walk the town together? Oh yes, what a wonderful idea! What days are you free next week?"

"Stop making plans up on your own!"

Of course the demon king would force us into something...

"Well, if it isn't Azusa and the girls. Fancy meeting you here. What happened to you, by the way? Have you gone mad...?"

"Rude! It doesn't *look that* bad on me!"

Have some tact, Beelzebub!

"No, it's not that it looks bad on you, but you are trying to force yourself to match the age you appear to be. It's upsetting. Your mental age is not that young..."

"Don't just stand there and analyze me!"

"Inside, you are quite old. 'Tis why this looks so strange. Your garish outfit is like a costume."

"Please stop saying such hurtful things. And if we're talking mental age, then Falfa and Shalsha aren't exactly young, either!"

Why was the one dressed as an evil executive saying this stuff to me? She was way cringier than me with that outfit.

Yes, yes, I was a corporate slave on the inside. I was living as these two girls' mothers.

But it didn't seem like I would be the only victim here. We were with Pecora, after all.

You're next, Beelzebub.

My predictions were correct.

Pecora's eyes glinted devilishly, and a wicked smile crossed her lips.

I knew what she was thinking: *It is time for a scheme worthy of my title as the demon king.*

"Well, since we're all here, why don't you have a bit of a makeover yourself, Miss Beelzebub?" Pecora shoved Beelzebub from behind.

"Eep! I quite like my hairstyle, so I have no intentions of changing it!"

"Oh, you can keep your hairstyle~ But wearing clothes that make you look like a proper young lady might not be so terrible from time to time~"

"No, no such outfit would look good on... Er, where are we going...?"

"Oh, it's all right~ Please leave it to me, just leave it to me~ ♪"

Pecora steered Beelzebub away from the harbor and to the city center.

It was hard to tell just by looking, but Pecora was pushing with unbelievable force, fitting for the demon king. Beelzebub could scarcely fight back.

"Heh-heh-heh. Oh, this is funny. Should we follow them? Are you two coming along?"

"Big Sis Mom, I would describe you as *guileful*."

"Big Sis Mommy, you look like a villain~"

Well, I'm not just a pure saint, you know. And you don't have to tack Big Sis *on there anymore.*

Both of them were just calling me Mom anyway...

I had nothing to lose now.

I guess it was time to get a good look as Beelzebub got turned into Pecora's plaything.

I followed after Pecora and a very panicked demon minister.

Beelzebub had been brought to a shop that was selling really expensive dresses.

She probably could have escaped on her own, but given the glint in the demon king's eyes, that wouldn't be possible. (Not that her eyes ever *weren't* glinting.)

"Yes, now I will pick out some clothes for you, Miss Beelzebub, to turn you into a proper young lady. Get changed in the dressing room, please~"

"Er, Your Majesty, I'm afraid this might not have anything to do with work..."

"I am the demon king. And you should follow what your sovereign says, okay?"

She was abusing her power—and it was hilarious. I wanted her to do it.

"Look, little Falfa and Shalsha want to watch, too."

"I wonder what Miss Beelzebub will look like!"

"Indeed, I am intrigued," Shalsha said without looking up from her book.

She really likes that book, huh...?

"Fine! I shall wear it! I shall wear whatever you want!"

I wasn't sure if she should have said *whatever you want* in front of Pecora. Beelzebub was getting desperate. Even though this was a losing fight, she had to put in the effort to minimize the damages.

Thus began the Beelzebub fashion show.

"All right, first, we have a dress for a lady!"

Pecora was the MC, and she pulled back the dressing-room curtain.

Beelzebub emerged wearing a glamorous dress studded with jewels.

"Ooh...this is embarrassing..."

Embarrassing? I personally thought her normal outfit was way more embarrassing, but maybe she was more used to wearing that.

Falfa and Shalsha both cooed in amazement. Beelzebub could pull this off surprisingly well.

"You look good, but you seem like you're plotting to give me a poisoned apple..."

"You did not have to say that!"

"All right, why don't you try on the next dress? Black is the basic theme of the next piece. It is truly chic—you could wear it to a funeral~" Pecora explained preemptively.

And so Beelzebub showed off this black dress. "Yes, this one is much more comfortable. 'Tis not as odd." She didn't seem all that dissatisfied with it, but—

"Elder Sister, your thoughts?"

"You totally look like a boss character. If there was a cabal of ten superpowerful demons, you'd be one of them."

"That was not a compliment, I presume?"

Nope. I'm here to enjoy the show.

"Indeed~ She looks as though she would be the seventh defeated out of a group of ten~ She deals quite a lot of damage to her opponent but ultimately loses when she leaves herself open for one fateful moment."

"Please stop thinking about my defeat! You too, Your Majesty!"

Pecora's mischief accelerated with the next outfit. "This is my personal recommendation! Here we go!"

When the dressing-room curtain opened...Beelzebub was wearing a pink dress covered in frills and frippery from head to toe. She even had a hood on that made her look like Little Red Riding Hood.

The look was so intense, I felt like we'd suddenly warped to Harajuku...

"Your Majesty... A demon should not be wearing this..."

Beelzebub's face was bright red; she knew this was weird.

"What? Yes, they should! I love it!"

"This would be another one of the ten demons. One who's super girly. And eating candy the whole time or something."

"I do not want to hear any compliments from you, either, Azusa!"

Wow, this is so relaxing when it's happening to someone else. I want Beelzebub to show up at the house in the highlands dressed like that sometime.

But I had made a grave miscalculation.

Misery loves company.

I was in no position to be laughing at the misery of someone else...

As this whole thing was going on, misery had sneaked up on me...

"You're next, Elder Sister. ♪"

"Huh? What do you mean?"

"Well, now that your hair is short, I picked out an outfit to match! Come now, get changed!"

So the fire wasn't on the opposite shore, huh? It sparked on my side...

I got shoved into the dressing room next to Beelzebub.

With no other choice, I changed into the clothes Pecora prepared for me.

What she had brought was…a white suit for guys… A princely outfit…

I wore that and stood next to Beelzebub in her Lolita outfit.

"Oh yes! When the two of you are standing together, your power levels double!"

"What power levels?!"

"What do you mean by *power levels*?!"

Both Beelzebub and I were complaining. *This is grueling! What series are we cosplaying from anyway?!*

But Falfa and Shalsha were clearly happy about this.

"Wow, Mommy, you look so cool!"

"You look more gallant than ever before, Mom."

Hey, that was more complimentary than I expected…

"Miss Beelzebub is pretty, too!"

"These sorts of clothes draw out the secrets of the wearer."

"Oh, you think so? You two have quite sharp eyes, but I knew that already. I suppose I've now shown you another facet of myself." Beelzebub always immediately played along the second my daughters flattered her.

"Could you two perhaps strike some poses for me? Like a prince protecting a princess. Here we go!" Pecora really sounded like she was making a request to some cosplayers.

But I could also tell that Falfa and Shalsha were looking forward to this. As their mother, I couldn't betray their hopes.

"We're doing this, Beelzebub."

"I shall do anything for my girls."

"They're not *your* girls."

"I shall do anything for my *adorable* girls."

She was stubbornly adding adjectives.

Afterward, Beelzebub and I spent a little while striking some fitting poses.

- The knight protecting the noble young lady
- The knight vowing loyalty to the noble young lady
- And the knight carrying the noble young lady, bridal-style

* * *

Oh, come on, anyone can see this is too much!

"Wonderful, wonderful! ♪ I of course love it when you carry me bridal-style, Elder Sister, but it is just as well to toy with you like this every so often~ ♪"

"If you're going to be so spiteful, you could at least have the decency not to grin at me the whole time."

But there was no doubt that Falfa and Shalsha's smiles were the brightest they had been the whole day at that moment.

"You're super cool, Mommy!"

"We have not seen this from you before, but it is an excellent quality. I almost wish to emulate you."

Right. I felt like I'd done the right thing as a mother.

"I suppose I shall let you carry me if it will make the girls happy," said Beelzebub.

Something about that irritated me.

"Yeah, I can carry you to make *my* girls happy, too."

I suppose opportunities like this weren't so bad every once in a while.

But…no more than that, please.

I USED **HAIR GROWTH MAGIC**

"By the way, do you plan on keeping your hair short from now on?" Beelzebub asked once we were done being Pecora's dress-up dolls.

"No, not really, but it takes a while for hair to grow back. It'll be a long struggle."

Momma Yufufu sure had chopped a bunch off. Even though I had insanely high stats, my hair wasn't exactly going to grow back insanely fast. If it did, then I would have to cut my hair all the time, and it would just be a pain.

"I see. In that case, I have the perfect spell for you," Beelzebub said breezily. "Muum Muum had once arrogantly claimed her ancient civilization had a magnificent spell for growing hair."

"That ancient civilization sure is amazing! They have everything!"

I knew the development of their civilization was a bit on the strange side, but I had no idea they had studied hair growth.

"If you would like your hair to grow back, I suggest going to the Thursa Thursa Kingdom to see her. You would be treated well there, of course."

"Yeah, you're right. Once I've had my fun with this haircut, I'll head out to Muu's."

"But 'tis not a bad haircut you have there." Beelzebub stared hard at my face—or my hair, rather. It was kind of embarrassing.

"Aye, 'tis good. Fresh. Almost endearing."

"Whoa, what are you talking about? You're exaggerating… Flattery will get you nowhere."

"You almost resemble Falfa and Shalsha. Excellent, indeed."

"…Oh, that's what you mean."

It seemed like Beelzebub judged everything based off how similar it was to Falfa and Shalsha.

"Your cuteness is absolutely no match for either of them, however."

"You don't have to go over every detail. And don't look so smug when you talk about how cute my daughters are."

It was a little weird to act like their mom in front of me when I'm their mom.

And so once I had my fill of having short hair, I headed for the ancient kingdom of ghosts.

"I see. So you would like to grow your hair out again," Laika said, flying in her dragon form.

Right now, I was riding on her back on our way to the Thursa Thursa Kingdom.

Rosalie was with me, too. I wanted to make sure she got to see Muu.

"Long hair is certainly more fitting to your image. The people of Flatta seemed to have been somewhat bewildered as of late."

"Oh really…? I didn't hear anything like that."

I guess it was hard to share your negative opinions with the subject of those opinions.

"They have said things like 'The Great Witch looks nice like this' and 'It feels like the Great Witch has descended among the mortals from afar…like we could be friends…or even more than that…' and whatnot."

"Yeah, that scares me, so I'm growing it out!"

But I guess it was normal for people to react if you drastically changed your image.

"Aren't you gonna grow your hair out, Big Sis Laika?" Rosalie asked, the lower half of her body buried in the dragon. I guess that stabilized her.

"Yeah, if you grew your hair out, Laika, you'd seem even more ladylike!"

"No, I am more comfortable with this length... And long hair will get in the way when I fight. I would not be surprised if I was considered an idler for growing my hair out as a mere trainee."

She sure was an earnest girl. I doubted anyone would call her an idler, though.

"Either way, I will stay as I am. I am more tempted to ask if you are going to keep your hair as is, Miss Rosalie."

"Ha-ha-ha! That's a funny thing to ask! I'm a ghost; I can't grow my hair! The only spiritual beings who can grow their hair out are cursed dolls!"

I wondered if that was indeed something to laugh about, but it was funny enough for Rosalie.

"Evil ghosts are spirits who stay behind in the mortal world, attached to the past. They can't just go and keep changing their hair and clothes; that's against the rules. People'd be like, *So are you attached or aren't you?!*"

"Oh, I see."

When Rosalie spelled it out for me like that, it made sense to me.

Ghosts were supposed to be frozen in time in their own way. Rosalie herself had been cooped up in the same building for a long while, too.

I figured it would get boring before long, but I've lived the same life with no change for three hundred years, so I'm not much to talk.

"But Big Sis's magic does let me change my clothes sometimes, and I think that's more than enough for me. I'll reincarnate if things get any more luxurious. Ha-ha-ha!"

I guess that was supposed to be funny, too... The ghost life sure was hard.

Finally, Laika's speed and altitude began to drop as we approached the Thursa Thursa Kingdom.

* * *

We came to the heart of the kingdom, which had an impressive array of pyramid-like structures. If UNESCO existed in this world, it would absolutely be a World Heritage site.

When she sensed us, head-maid-slash-minister Nahna Nahna came to us.

"Long time no see, everyone. What brings you here today? Her Majesty is currently developing the dungeon, so I believe it will be a while before she arrives—and what happened to your hair?"

Nahna Nahna wasn't the type to wear her emotions on her face, but she sure seemed curious about my hair.

I wondered if she was going to ask about a breakup, too. Everyone wants to talk about romance the moment someone gets a haircut.

"Aha, I suppose you made a cursed doll that used real hair."

"No!"

"You could make five with how much you cut off. In that case, I can introduce you to a cursed-doll-making master, a national treasure in the human lands."

"No, thank you. I have no intentions of doing anything like that."

But it was true we were here about the hair.

"I got it cut too short. I came here because I heard you had a spell that could grow it out again."

"Ah... It seems Her Majesty has gotten carried away and spoken too much again, I see..."

Uh-oh. Nahna Nahna's expression seemed somewhat troubled.

"Did something bad happen?"

"That spell is classified as an A-plus trade secret. More specifically, the existence of the magic itself is not to be spoken of, much less what it can do."

"It's that strictly hidden...?"

"That is because once word gets out about it, many people will want to use it. Yet it is very cumbersome to use. It could easily destroy ten, twenty small elf-villages."

Yikes!

"However, there is nothing I can do now that you know about it. I shall tell Her Majesty off once she arrives. She honestly needs a better sense of restraint."

I sensed no respect at all for own queen, but Muu didn't seem to like stiff relationships, so maybe this worked for them.

"Her Majesty should be here soon. Let us wait here at these outdoor tables for a while. I shall provide desserts made with local fruits."

Sure, might as well enjoy the wait.

Three hours later...

"Is she still not here yet, Miss Nahna Nahna...?"

She was taking way more time to show up than I thought.

"I apologize. She insisted she would arrive at the surface on her own and would not take no for an answer. She is rather weak, so it seems she is taking an extremely long time," Nahna Nahna said casually.

Right—Muu had a physical body, so she couldn't immediately appear here...

"That is all right. Let us relax while we wait, Lady Azusa. Oh, may I have another serving of sweets, please?" Laika had good manners, but she was asking for seconds over and over again.

As we sat and chilled out, Muu finally appeared.

"*Huff, huff...* I finally got 'ere...all on me own... I made it..."

She was acting like an athlete reaching the finish line!

"Goal...!" When Muu got to our table, she flopped over on her back.

"Congratulations, Your Majesty. You made it under three hours. Two hours, fifty-nine minutes, three seconds."

"Get in! I finally beat free hours!"

Was this a marathon?!

"But I still got a ways to go... I needa fink 'bout me form an' not push meself... I gotta beat two hours, forty-five minute next..."

I didn't think there was much to do for her form if she didn't seriously consider building up some strength first. I bet one of us wouldn't even take fifteen minutes to walk that distance.

"My apologies, Your Majesty, but our objective today is not to improve your physical strength. Please hear what request those of the house in the highlands have."

"Oh, hey... I can do anyfin' you want. Wa'evah, dunna, innit."

Not sure why the catchphrase came in there, but sure, I guess.

"Hey, so you've probably noticed, but I cut my hair too short. You have magic that can grow it back, right? I want to use that to get it back to normal again."

"'Air Growf magic...? Oh, no. I told Pecora durin' our game o' Kings..."

Kings with two sovereigns? Seriously?

"Please refrain from sharing A-plus secrets, Your Majesty."

"Before I told 'er, I says, 'You better not tell *anyone*.' But sorry anyway."

That would guarantee she tells *everyone*.

"'Air Growf magic, 'ey? I mean, we do 'ave that."

Hmm, did that mean it wasn't what I thought it was?

"This country's just filled wiv dead people, yeah? So it's set to work for dead people. We're gonna need to fiddle wiv it to make it work for the livin'."

A skill just for dead people felt kind of surreal.

That's when I got an idea. "Then could you get our ghostly Rosalie to grow her hair out?"

"Easy peasy! Give 'er a few tweaks, an' Bob's your uncle."

If Muu said so, then I'd trust her.

"Well, you heard her, Rosalie. Why not grow out your hair? This opportunity doesn't come up all that often."

"Not a bad idea, 'ey. We could make plenty o' tweaks on a dead person to get it workin' for livin' people. Let's do that, yeah? We should do that."

Well, that was easy!

"Wait, wait, what? Me?" Rosalie pointed to herself and blinked, but she didn't seem that upset about it. Everyone wants to look stylish, don't they?

"Lovely jubbly, then let's 'ead off to the ruin wiv a magic circle in it!" Muu said. Still lying on the ground.

"Your Majesty, are you able to get up on your own?"

"Obviously! Hrrrgh! Oof... I pull'd a muscle... I pull'd a muscle in me left leg...an' in me right knee..."

I suspected this would take forever if she walked on her own, so I just picked her up and carried her.

The ruin with the magic circle was a somewhat quiet place.

There wasn't much on the first floor besides the entrance, but there was a staircase that went underground, which had a wide-open space at the bottom.

"We 'ide A-plus spells like this so they don't get out. We can't 'ave people knowin' 'bout spells like this, now can we?"

"Except we know. Is that okay?"

"Well, can't take away what you've already found out... Hey, Rosalie, luv, get to the center of the circle."

There was a unique-looking magic circle drawn in the center of the room. It looked nothing like the magic of modern humans or demon magic.

"Uh, okay... Going in..." Rosalie fearfully floated into the middle of the circle.

"All right, guess we just leave 'is to the 'air-Growf-magic technicians now."

"Yes, I have already arranged for them," Nahna Nahna said.

Some ghosts came in and formed a ring around the table in front of the magic circle. On the table was an array of stone tablets. I guess that's how they activated the spell.

But there was one thing I wanted to point out—

—all the ghost technicians were bald guys...

"I am Dan Dan, chief technician for A-plus magics. This ghost will have more hair than she knows what to do with," one of the technicians said.

His head was so smooth, I almost didn't believe him!

"Just to let you know, we are not that interested in hair. That is why we have been able to objectively carry out our research on this magic."

I mean, I guess, but at the same time, it didn't add up. I didn't know what to make of it...

"Dan Dan, don't bova wiv all 'at, yeah? Just grow out Rosalie's hair."

Muu was generally impatient—despite selfishly making us wait three hours.

"Yes, understood. Let's go!"

The bald guys (ghosts, actually, but I'm just going to call them guys) started poking at the stone tablets. From afar, it simply looked like they were operating computers.

They looked intense—this had to be really high-level magic.

"Locks lifted!"

"Systems activated!"

"Magic-circle operations normal!"

The staff was yelling.

Then the magic circle finally started glowing.

"Okay, Hair Growth magic activate!" Dan Dan yelled.

Then Rosalie's hair slowly started lengthening.

"H-hey...it's almost at my neck!"

She was clearly feeling the difference. This was a first for her, so the look on her face was a mix of excitement and anxiety.

Her hair grew more and more, until it definitely fell in the *long* category.

Yes! This was a huge success!

—But that was when the problems started.

Rosalie's hair wouldn't stop growing!

"Gah! I can't see through my bangs!"

"Ahhh! Now you *really* look like a ghost!"

Some ghosts have their faces totally hidden by their bangs, don't they...?

And it wasn't just her bangs. All the rest of her hair kept growing, and she was soon buried in it!

"This seems like a failure," Nahna Nahna remarked quietly. Her reaction was surprisingly neutral, given the circumstances, but we needed calm people at a time like this.

"You absolute plonkers! Do somefin'! Can't you restore this now?!"

"I'm sorry! We made a mistake in the settings!" Dan Dan apologized. "I shave my hair, so I am not entirely sure how strong it should be…"

Then this was a total failure starting right from the technicians they chose! They *definitely* needed people with hair to be technicians!

To get to the point, Rosalie now looked completely like a ghost with that trademark long hair.

"Ghost hair doesn't feel heavy at all, but this would weigh a ton if I were alive… Long hair always gets in the way…"

"Why not make the best of it and scare some humans around the world?" Nahna Nahna was really acting like this had nothing to do with her…

"Put it back, you lot. She looks like an evil ghost. She'd be terrifyin' if she walk'd round town like 'at!"

She looked just like a scary ghost. She'd make us jump out of our skin at the house in the highlands if she lived like that.

But among us was someone who really liked pranks.

Nahna Nahna pulled Rosalie's hand.

"It is times like this that we should get the absolute most entertainment out of what's happened. Let us proceed outside."

She was going to go show her off!

"Hey! Those kinds of pranks aren't really—"

But Nahna Nahna slipped through the building and floated upward toward the surface.

"Gah! She has those tricks up her sleeves because she's a ghost!"

"I wonder what the people are gonna fink 'bout this one… She's right rotten, she is. Like a poltergeist."

I bet Muu had been waiting to make that joke, but I was going to ignore it.

"Hey, Muu, you're the queen here. Don't let your ministers run around and do what they want."

"Yeah, Nahna Nahna's only a minister, but she secretly finks she's better'n me, so nofin' I say'll get to 'er."

"And you're okay with that? Aren't you the queen?"

"I fink it's better if the ruler's someone relatable. I wanna be the kin'a queen who'll see a limited-time, 'alf-price sale at the market an' panic."

"That's too much."

She also just went for cheap stuff in general, far as I could tell.

"I wanna be the kind who says, *'Ey, how much you fink I got this for? Three 'undred fifty* gitan? *Nah, bruv, it was a 'undred fifty* gitan, y'know wha' I mean?"

She was just a penny-pincher who wanted to brag about her cheap deals.

"Lady Azusa, we cannot neglect Miss Rosalie, so let us go up to the surface," Laika suggested. She was the most decent of all of us.

"You're right. I don't think this will lead to a big incident, but we shouldn't ignore it."

We went up the long, long staircase back to the surface.

We could immediately hear screams coming from every which way.

"Gaaah! An evil spirit!"

"Help me!"

"Don't look at it, or you'll die!"

"I thought *I* was a ghost, but that's the real thing!"

It was a considerable commotion.

"I heard a loud scream from over there! Let us go!"

Laika and I headed toward the voice, and there, we found Rosalie wandering around, her obnoxiously long hair covering her face.

"Oof, I can't see!"

Nahna Nahna was pushing Rosalie along. "Now let us make our way toward those graves over there. There are plenty of citizens we have not yet spooked."

"Oh, come on," Rosalie complained. "People are way too scared of someone whose hair is just a little too long…"

And from my point of view, Rosalie was appropriately horrendous.

I never knew hair alone could change someone's aura so drastically…

Plenty of ghosts afterward saw Rosalie and screamed.

"I feel like they're bigger scaredy-cats than I am."

"Perhaps evil spirits do not usually meet other evil spirits, so their tolerance to one another is quite low."

I see. I guess they rarely saw other ghosts (who weren't themselves or their friends).

Wait, hold on.

That meant ghosts were also afraid of ghosts. They were the same as me. I'd always been afraid of unseen visitors myself, so that gave me a small feeling of familiarity.

—Ten minutes later.

"The joke has run its course, I believe."

Nahna Nahna stopped pushing Rosalie, and the whole commotion came to an end.

Afterward, we safely managed to shorten Rosalie's hair from scary-ghost length to just normal long hair.

They could also shorten hair, so the technique was a little more flexible than just "hair growth."

"Yes! Long hair is cute, too!" I said.

"I believe it would look lovely on you!" Laika agreed.

But Rosalie herself didn't seem like a fan.

"I dunno, I'm not really feeling it. I like how it was originally. Long hair just gets in the way. And I don't want more incidents like what just happened…"

This sounded like a question of habit; someone who always kept their hair short wouldn't find long hair very fitting.

Rosalie returned her hair to its original state. I wish I could've shown the rest of the family, but we wouldn't be able to cut Rosalie's hair back at the house in the highlands. Oh well.

Now, I was supposed to be next in line, but—

"Hey, since we're here, why not grow your hair out a bit, Laika?"

"What are you talking about, Lady Azusa?!"

Laika was awfully surprised. It didn't seem like she ever thought she would come up as an option. Her guard was down, no excuses.

"Well, I wanna see what you look like with long hair, too, Laika. It's fiiine. Seems like we can put your hair back the way it was anyway."

I decided to play the status card and be a little selfish just this once.

"Mmm... Well, if you say so, Lady Azusa..." Laika gave in and stepped into the magic circle.

The technicians were much more serious than they had been previously.

Muu had her arms folded as she watched on, so she was probably nervous, too.

"We'll make no more mistakes, you hear me?"

"We will succeed, even with a living specimen!"

"Our pride rests on this!"

"Voluminous without the weight!"

I just wanted to know why everyone saying this was all bald.

"Listen to me, you fail this, an' I'll make ya grow 'air an' wear the worst styles! Old stuff, an' *not* vintage!"

Her threats were hair-related, too.

But still, Rosalie was—and if you'll excuse my word choice—the test subject here already, so I didn't think there could be any more big failures.

On the other hand, Laika was growing tenser and tenser standing in the magic circle. Anyone would be frightened there.

"Everything is in order!"

"Same here!"

"Give the order anytime!"

"Begin!"

The magic circle lit up again.

How was it going to turn out this time? *Please succeed!*

It wasn't as dramatic as Rosalie's turn, but Laika's hair was slowly starting to grow out.

And then it stopped right at the short end of what I'd call long. It was an exquisite length.

The texture of her hair was also smooth, so it didn't feel like it was just a longer version of her normal hair.

She was such a proper young lady!

"Um, what do you think, Lady Azusa…?" Laika asked, playing with her new hair.

I instinctively covered my mouth. "Oh, Laika… You're so pretty… So pretty, it pains me."

What the heck was this? She couldn't be a dragon, could she? She was definitely an angel. This wasn't just elite-class-tier nonsense. This was heavenly. What incredible power she held!

"I am in awe—I can't believe such a cute girl is my apprentice! I almost want to *ask* you to be my apprentice!"

"Lady Azusa, please do not praise me so… It makes me uncomfortable…"

But it was so cute how she got so flustered like that, so I couldn't not do it.

No matter what expression she made right now, it would just destroy me. Like the goddess of destruction.

"My, my. She has more majesty to her than Her Majesty."

"You right, she's way more— Oy, that's rude, Nahna Nahna!"

This master-and-servant duo was starting to get their banter down. It was also possible that Nahna Nahna had been appointed minister because she could keep up with the retorts. Muu didn't trust people who didn't tease her.

That said, it seemed as though the ghosts were appreciating the scale of Laika's cuteness, too.

The technicians, with their bald, shiny heads, sang her praises:

"She's so cute!"

"I'm ascending!"

Please don't ascend to heaven! It'll be like we killed you!

Rosalie was looking away for some reason.

"She's too bright. It's like she's gleaming! A ghost like me can't look at her directly!"

She was less of a dragon, and more like a goddess now.

"E-everyone, please stop! Y-you're teasing me too much…"

Laika was, of course, bright red. That was the obvious reaction.

But no one here was teasing her.

"You're really incredible, Laika. You might be the most beautiful girl in the world."

"Lady Azusa, please stop!"

Afterward, we returned Laika's hair to normal.

I was sad to see it go, but I felt like if she stayed in the house in the highlands with that haircut, her cuteness would just create more trouble, so I guess we had to… And we didn't want her to end up with stalkers.

And I got my hair safely returned to its original length.

"Yeah, I think this hairstyle is perfect for me. And it matches my hat."

Makeovers were fun, but a standard style was also important.

"I like you best this way, Lady Azusa." Laika accepted my normal everyday self with a gentle smile.

"Yeah, I agree."

Now that I had others who loved me, I had a feeling that I liked myself way more now than when I was alone.

"I wish you hadn't gotten rid of your long hair so quick."

"Please, *please* do not say that!"

Laika had been like a goddess, and so I was going to keep a clear memory of the image in my head.

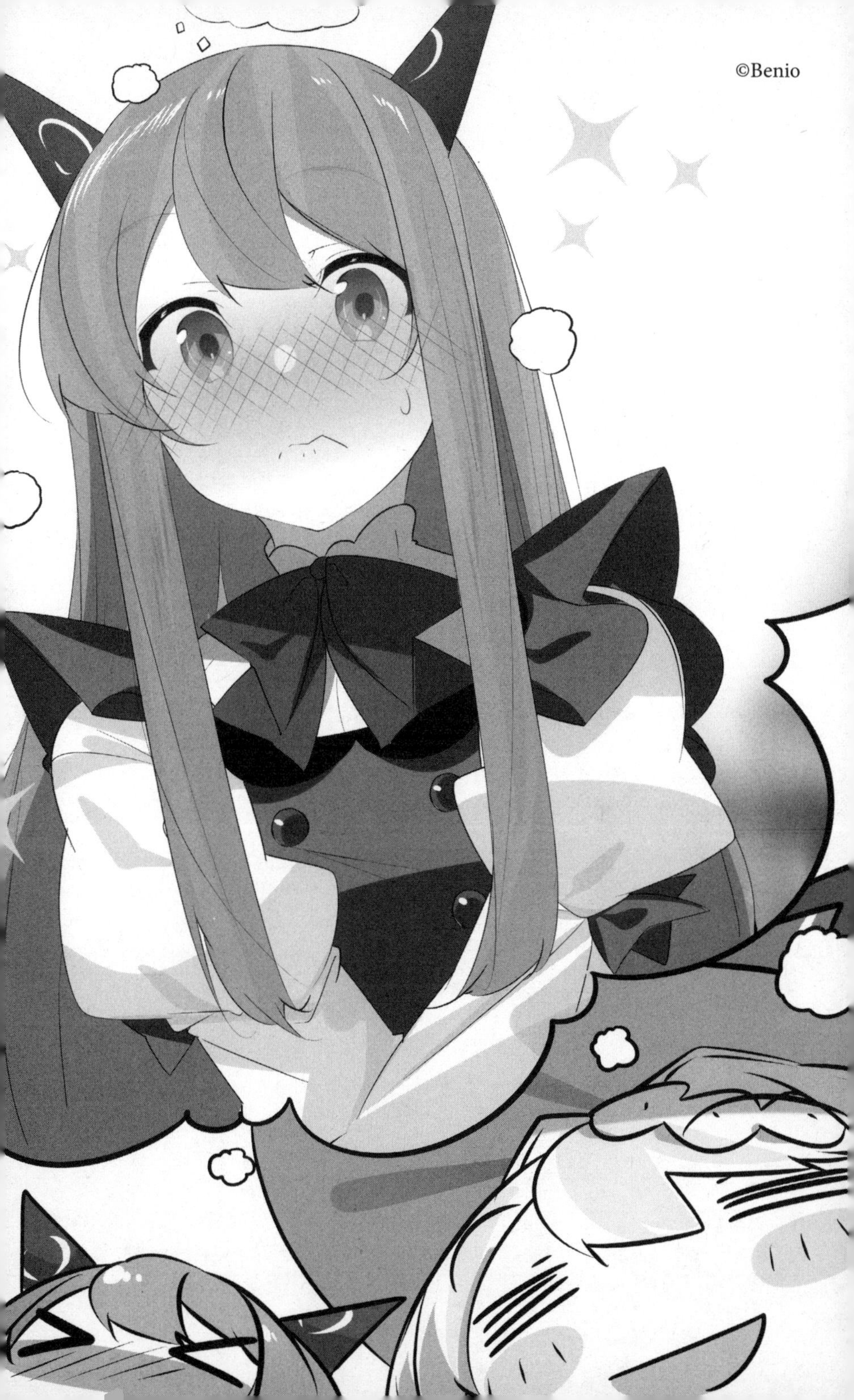

WE WENT TO A **MEAT FESTIVAL**

"*Yaaaaaaawn.*"

"How unbecoming, Flatorte. If you *must* yawn, then at least cover your mouth with your hand."

Laika admonished Flatorte for her loud yawn during breakfast.

The yawn was certainly dramatic enough that I was almost worried she'd dislocated her jaw.

"What are you talking about? Yawning is natural. What I mean is that I, the great Flatorte, am not at fault here. I should be able to get all my yawning done at once."

Flatorte always talked back whenever Laika criticized her, but that was a very Flatorte-esque response.

"Yet despite that, we still have a little thing called manners. And yours are awful."

"It's not like I'm using my Cold Breath with my yawn or anything. It shouldn't be bothering you. Life's so much harder when you let all the little things get to you. Life should be easygoing—that's what peace looks like!"

I saw Laika glance in my direction. Her face read, *What do you think, Lady Azusa?*

"Hmm… It doesn't really bother me… I think this is fine. I actually think you could stand to be a little more carefree sometimes, Laika."

"Personally, I find this irresponsible lifestyle brings me much more stress, and then my health suffers..." Laika sighed.

"I see. I guess telling a serious person to suddenly just take things as they come is cruel in its own way." After all, you're still asking them to change their basic outlook on life.

"And it is strange to hear the word *peace* coming out of your mouth, Flatorte. Blue dragons want to fight all the time, do they not?"

"You're probably right..."

When I went to visit her hometown, all they ever did was ask me to fight.

—Then Flatorte suddenly went pale, and her hands started shaking. And was her skin turning blue?

"Ooooh... Th-this is bad..."

"What is it? A sudden illness? Should we take you to the doctor?"

I couldn't really imagine a dragon getting sick, but I bet they did feel under the weather sometimes. Flatorte, especially, struck me as someone who would eat stuff off the floor...

"I-it's peaceful..."

What does that mean?

"It's been so peaceful recently that my body craves battle..."

I had no idea her addiction to battle would give her withdrawal symptoms!

"Mistress, I need a spar... I want to go to Flatta and spar with all the humans there, one by one..."

"No, no! That'd kill all the villagers!"

"Oh, but I don't have to fight. I want to see someone fighting someone else—someone evenly matched!"

"Evenly matched? Hmm..."

Those words didn't really match this relaxing area.

Then there came a knock at the door.

I opened it, and there was a mail-carrying wyvern, meaning this matter was demon-related.

"You must be Azusa, Witch of the Highlands, yes? This is from Lady Beelzebub."

The wyvern handed me a letter. I opened it right away. The first thing that caught my eye was a flyer.

"A bullfighting festival…? Minotaurs are the demons with bull faces, right?"

The other sheet of paper was a letter from Beelzebub. It basically invited us to come check out the bullfighting festival if we had free time.

"Please hold on a second, wyvern."

I took a pad of paper and scrawled out the following:

To Beelzebub: Okay.

"Please give this to the minister of agriculture. Or you could send it to the ministry itself."

The wyvern took the paper and flew off.

I didn't pay any postage fees, but I guess Beelzebub would take care of the payment once she got it.

But the timing of the invitation was actually perfect.

I went over to Flatorte and showed her the flyer.

"This event should be pretty neat, Flatorte. You can eat some meat, too. Look at this!"

"Yesss! Now I can let off some steam!"

Flatorte, still gripping her knife and fork, shot up out of her chair. It was like a declaration of victory.

"Manners, Flatorte!" Laika was getting irritated again.

I was sure that Laika would enjoy it, too, so I hoped she would just be patient with Flatorte...

Looked like the food would be substantial, too.

And by the way, when I looked at the flyer again, I found a lot of weird little things.

Was bullfighting a part of minotaur culture or something?

And should minotaurs be serving beef dishes? Wasn't that cannibalism...?

Well, it was totally natural for big fish to eat small fish, and big birds sometimes gobbled up little birds, so maybe it was the same. Humans didn't understand those values. If it was fine with the minotaurs, then that was that.

I guess I'd ask Beelzebub when we went. She'd probably be showing us around anyway.

Afterward, another message came from Beelzebub. It basically said she would have Fatla come pick us up in her leviathan form.

That meant we'd be able to eat Vania's cooking. Her food was exquisite, so that was another thing to look forward to on this trip.

But at about six in the evening on the day before we were supposed to leave—

—a shadow passed across the darkened sky, and that's when Fatla and Vania finally arrived at the house.

One of them had probably been in her leviathan form, but I'm pretty sure they were one day early, right?

"My apologies; we wanted to be certain we would not be late, but as a result, we have come much too early. Would you allow us to stay?" Fatla politely bowed her head.

"Come on, I told you we could've left a little later! You're too uptight, Sis~"

It was surprising to see Vania annoyed with her sister rather than the other way around.

These two sisters were on the extreme opposite ends of the serious-careless scale.

"Yeah, sure, you can stay…"

Now that they were here, I decided to ask the leviathan sisters about the bullfighting festival and the minotaurs.

"Is it safe for minotaurs to eat beef?"

Unlike elves and dwarves, minotaurs didn't really live in human society, so I didn't know much about their culture.

"A minotaur's home-cooked meal always has beef," Vania informed me, calling on her extensive culinary knowledge.

"I see… Don't they feel like it's cannibalism?"

That was my greatest concern.

"Hmm, I do occasionally hear of minotaurs who oppose it, but they also keep bulls as pets. And those pet bulls are the ones they enter in bullfighting events."

"That doesn't sit right with me, either…"

"Minotaurs from the west tend to eat the meat, and minotaurs from the east tend to keep them as pets."

I see. I guess if the culture differed between areas, then of course they'd hold both a meat festival and a bullfighting competition.

"From what I learned in school as a student, it is apparently unknown if minotaurs and bulls are even related. It is possible the similarities are purely surface-level." Fatla gave an academic supplement.

"I don't think it would be an accidental resemblance… But when you wonder how the species came to be, there are a lot of mysteries…"

I wondered how the evolution of living things worked in a fantasy world.

On Earth, I think the first time minotaurs were mentioned was in

Greek myth, but the east must have had something halfway between human and cow somewhere.

I didn't know too much about it, but I knew about Gozu, or "ox head"—a guardian of hell whose name aptly described his physique.

But that wasn't about this world, so I couldn't look it up anyway.

"Mom, this demon encyclopedia says little is known about the minotaur. It seems no one has come to a conclusion about their origins yet." Shalsha came in holding a thick book.

"I see. I didn't know you had a book on the demons."

"Beelzebub gave it to Shalsha. I read through it carefully."

At least Beelzebub was helping with the girls' education, too, instead of just being the aunt who spoiled them.

"Miss Azusa, though they are labeled as minotaurs, they are still normal people. We would most appreciate it if you relax and enjoy the festivities."

"What Sis says. That, and I think the boss wants an excuse to invite you over."

The leviathan sisters were on the same page here.

All the previous events we'd been to weren't all that formal, and we got to treat them like a vacation. But there was one family member who was on an entirely different energy level.

"Bullfighting! I've always wanted to see it for myself! I wanna see their horns clash until I can't take it anymore!"

Flatorte was as excited as an elementary school kid on the day before a field trip.

She had just been lamenting how peaceful it'd been, so this was perfect. We could watch bullfighting all day, and Flatorte wouldn't get hurt, so it was perfectly safe, too.

"Miss Flatorte, you mustn't expect too much from this. From a dragon's perspective, a fight between bulls is of no importance. It's practically child's play."

Fatla must have sensed incoming trouble, so she was trying to lower the bar...

This was definitely on a much lesser scale than a battle between dragons was.

"No need to worry! Even the littlest animals can fight tooth and nail in their own way! I'm happy enough with that!"

I guess bulls were among the "littlest animals" to a dragon…

But we had leviathans, supermassive creatures, right in front of us, so…all right, I guess.

The next day, the whole family hopped on Fatla and made our way to the town around Vanzeld Castle.

We were all used to riding on the leviathans now.

When Fatla landed at the leviathan landing zone near the castle town—aka the airport—Beelzebub was waiting for us.

"You made it. I figured you'd not seen a minotaur bullfighting festival, so I decided to invite you."

"Thanks, Beelzebub. One of us is really looking forward to it, so it was perfect timing."

Flatorte was practicing her punches and kicks, as if she were the one going to be fighting. Maybe that's how she lets off steam.

Even though she was older than me, there was nothing big-sisterlike about her. She probably didn't even think of herself as older, either.

"I really wanna know what kind of bulls they're gonna show. The pitch-black ones are the strongest, right? No, the reddish ones are gonna be more violent, right? No, I bet there's going to be a surprise, and a pure-white bull is gonna appear!"

"Oh, her… She may be a bit too excited for this. It is just a bull fight…"

It didn't seem like Beelzebub could keep up with Flatorte's excitement. But the way Beelzebub described this—that it's *just* a bullfight—seemed kind of rude to the bullfighters. Maybe this wasn't much more than side entertainment to the demons.

"We told her it wasn't a big deal, boss, but she wouldn't listen to us…"

"Lady Beelzebub, I believe the image she has in her head of bullfights was established long ago."

The leviathans were defending their own innocence.

But still, I wondered why the demons were so fully intent on downplaying the bullfights. I was starting to feel bad for the bulls that were entering.

"Well, 'tis all well and good. The meat festival begins before the bullfighting. Why not have a meal there?"

We made our way to the coliseum.

Outside it were rows and rows of food stalls serving steak and skewers—there was probably every kind of meat dish there.

"Yes! This is fantastic! My blood is burning, and my appetite is growing!"

"Oh, this is delightful!"

Our two dragons were beyond excited.

"Laika, I'm going to start on the left side here. You start on the right."

"Understood. Be careful not to end up carrying more than you can hold and dropping everything."

The two went through each stall one by one on their respective sides and bought their food. They worked together at times like this and never any other time…

"They're not even going to choose. They're going to conquer every last dish here."

Some people go for broke at food festivals; for them, this is standard procedure.

"You can purchase all that you like, too, Azusa," Beelzebub urged me. We were full-blown guests today.

"You're right. Okay, then I may as well get a steak."

I went to the stall and placed my order, and the steak I received looked beautiful. It was also a half a kilogram…

"I can't eat this much... Wait, aren't stalls at food festivals like this supposed to give out just a little bit so you can walk around and eat...?"

"What? That is hardly a meal. Are you feeling ill?" Beelzebub genuinely asked me. I had underestimated the demons' standards.

"Hey, everyone, would you like to have some?" I ended up sharing with Falfa and Shalsha.

"Ooh, thank you! I love steak! I can eat so much more!"

"Meat is amazing. It brings activity to the mind. A wise sage once said, *If there is meat, one must eat.*"

Did a sage really say that?

"Falfa, Shalsha, if either of you wants a more generous portion, I will buy as much as you like for you! Ask me for anything you want!"

"They'll stuff themselves full! So don't get any funny ideas, Beelzebub!"

I was trying to think of a way they could eat without leaving leftovers, but she was getting in the way. Nobody likes getting more assignments right when you think you're done with your work.

"In the event they cannot finish, then simply toss it. Foolishness is another way of enjoying festivals."

"I get the logic, but I'm not really down with teaching the girls to waste food. That is education, too."

In any case, I could see they could eat their way through this. My daughters weren't particularly big eaters, but I knew they'd be happy to have meat.

I felt a little bad since Sandra couldn't have any, but—

"Hmph. Cows and humans that eat grasses are fated to be eaten by demons. How pitiful."

—she was smiling dauntlessly, like she had just defeated her sworn enemy, so I guess we were all right. Apparently, she saw all herbivores as her enemy.

"Oh yeah, do you want some steak, Halkara?"

"Madam Teacher... Please help me eat..."

Halkara was holding a plate full of meat skewers, piled so high that it hid her face.

"Hey, Halkara! Do you even understand what *moderation* means?!"

"No, that's not what's happening! I don't believe I can eat this on my own, either!"

Halkara was making an excuse, but I couldn't see her face behind the skewers, so it looked like the skewers were talking.

"I entered a lottery for these. If you lost, you got one skewer; if you got fourth prize, you got two skewers—the number of skewers you could win at the stall was basically up to chance…"

There were places like that back in Japan, too. Almost all of them would give you just one if you lost.

"And I got the special prize."

"Why is your luck so good?!"

"But I didn't think I'd get one hundred…"

"That's too many!"

That was enough to bury anyone.

"I was so happy the moment I won. But then the plate came out, and that was when the reality of the situation hit me. *How am I going to eat all this?* I thought. And the portion on each skewer is so big…"

"It really is demon-sized… Okay, let's find some open seats where we can sit and eat…"

There were tables underneath a temporary tent near the food stalls. Just like you'd expect to see at a meat festival.

"Ooh! It's so spicy! This would go great with a drink! Elves may be generally vegetarian, but we'll make an exception for meat dishes that go well with a drink!"

Halkara downed some alcohol as she ate her skewers.

"Uh, let me just say…don't get blackout drunk before we go to watch the bullfighting, okay?"

"No, one must get intoxicated at a big festival! I don't make the rules~"

She knew what she was doing and was going to get drunk anyway!

"Okay, but if you get too drunk to walk, I reserve the right to just leave you."

"Heh-heh, that's all part of the fun."

That was very charismatic of her, but if she drank enough to black out, then she wouldn't remember anything she said.

Also, Falfa and Shalsha had been quiet this whole time, but that was because they were concentrating on eating the meat.

"Hom, hom…"

"Num, num…"

That tasty, huh? It was almost like I wasn't feeding them enough at home…

Then it seemed as though the dragons had finished their mission of splitting up and ordering enough for two from every stall; now they were devouring their food at an empty table. Were they competitive eaters or something?

Rosalie sat alongside the two. She couldn't eat, so maybe she was observing the dragons' way of life.

"This event is quite well attended. What a relief."

Beelzebub was having something that looked like barbecue and was drinking milk. I've never thought those two would go well together, but they are both from cows, I guess. There were stalls selling milk, too.

The leviathan sisters also sat beside her, concentrating on their beef.

Fatla struck me as someone who would have a small appetite, but that wasn't the case at all. A demon's appetite was a formidable thing.

"I guess the reason you invited us, Beelzebub, is because the Ministry of Agriculture was involved, right?"

There had been a list of supporting organizations on a sign, and I saw the Ministry of Agriculture on there. This event certainly was relevant to the agriculture, forestry, and fishing industry.

"Indeed, that is part of it. 'Twas originally just the bullfighting, but attendance has been falling year after year. That was where the ministry came in, and we added a meat festival alongside it."

"Bullfighting really isn't that popular, is it…? It sounds like it'd be wild and exciting, though…"

That said, there were plenty of events, even ones that seemed they should be popular, that lost attendance year after year, so maybe bullfighting just got unlucky.

"Well, we can support events that have been on the decline for a while now without taking much responsibility for them, which is something we are grateful for. That means we can experiment," Fatla said as she wiped her mouth.

"Cutting right to the point… But I get how you feel."

"Changing the bullfighting event is not easy, considering the tradition behind it~ That is why we decided to add a portion where we eat meat. We gathered a lot of well-known meat restaurants run by minotaurs. My judgments were correct." Vania was proud of herself. When it came to food, her skills were the real deal.

"This is my first time seeing all this, but I think it's going well. You're doing a great job, Ministry of Agriculture." I praised them with a smile, although the three of them didn't seem all that happy about it.

But not everything was going perfectly.

Halkara had stopped eating. "My stomach suddenly told me, *I'm finished; don't eat any more…*"

Told you so!

"I ate it all so rapidly, my stomach did not alert me until it was far too late. To think I would fall victim to a trap like this… *Urp…*"

"It's not a conspiracy. This is one hundred percent your fault, Halkara."

She was like someone who gave up on an eating contest partway through. She was a pharmacist—why didn't she take care of herself? But then again, I got the impression that a lot of doctors were unhealthy.

"There's still plenty of time. Fawn over the little cows, at least. Heh-heh-heh, even the herbivores are fated to be eaten."

Sandra was in a good mood today—or a sadistic mood, rather. Did she really hate cows and bulls that much?

The topic of Halkara aside—

"I've gotten to see a lot of minotaurs here. They sure are a diverse bunch."

Some of the minotaurs looked like the fantasy and mythological illustrations I saw back when I lived in Japan, where their heads were entirely that of a bull, and some just had bull horns and tails, but practically human faces.

And there were some minotaurs who were kind of in-between.

"That is because while some demons live in insular communities, others live in towns and mix with other species. Some have less pronounced minotaur features, while others have more."

"Now that I think about it, demons really are diverse... Well done keeping it so peaceful."

As someone who knew how messy Earth was, I was a little embarrassed.

But Vania was shaking her head.

Fatla finished chewing and swallowing the meat, then spoke up.

"It is not like that at all. There have been a number of fights in the past. That hasn't changed, even when the current demon king assumed power."

"Oh, I see... It doesn't feel like that at all to me, though..."

"We have faced our own set of hardships as well. It is different with each nation. There have been problems within the Ministry of Agriculture as well..."

Beelzebub gazed off into the distance. She must be thinking profoundly on some memories.

"Oh, how many times have I had to go and apologize for Vania's mistakes...?"

"Hey! Boss! It's a little weird to bring that up now!"

Vania was the problem?!

"Twelve times for the major incidents. If we include the smaller incidents, the total is fifty-three times."

"Please don't just count everything, Sis! I'm telling you, it wasn't that much! I only remember eight big mistakes!"

That was still a lot, though, wasn't it? But I guess for demons, who worked for a very long time, maybe it wasn't. I don't know.

Laika, Flatorte, and Rosalie then came back.

Laika's and Flatorte's skin was glistening.

"We ate everything! Gosh, meat really does fill you with energy, doesn't it? I feel ready for all my training in the days to come!"

"All the stalls hit the hat trick—delicious, fast, and cheap! It was fantastic! None of them were bad!"

"Of course they were good, Flatorte; they're food stalls."

"No, no, there are a lot of places where that's not a given. I say the minotaurs are doing good work!"

Rosalie whispered in my ear, "Big Sis, I think the dragons have gotten a little closer now."

Bonded through meat...

Back when I was a corporate drone, we used to talk about people who communicated best when they were drunk. I guess that could be the same for them, but with meat. Dragons understood one another through meat.

I doubted there were many people who wanted to conquer all the stalls at a meat festival, so of course their friendship would develop as they went around by themselves.

"A wise man once said, *A close friendship is forged around the meal pot*."

This wise man Shalsha kept talking about today didn't seem to think about very lofty things.

"Mommy, the bullfighting is starting soon~" Falfa said, eyeing the crowd.

She was right. People were starting to head into the coliseum.

"Bulls are gonna wham other bulls! Falfa is excited~!"

I was pretty sure things were going to be a little harsher than just *wham*, but Falfa's expression was adorable. Maybe I could just rename bullfighting into *bull wham*.

"Those people will be sitting in the general seating. We will be in reserved seats, so there is no reason to rush," Beelzebub explained.

"That's the VIP treatment. We've gotten our fill of the meat, so let's get moving. We shouldn't wait so long that we end up rushing."

I wanted to leave plenty of time between events. If you kept cutting out all your extra time, you might suddenly die one day, after all...

"Shall we go in, then? I personally would rather wait until the second half, though."

"Indeed. The bar of expectations has been raised so high, I believe a betrayal of those expectations may be a serious letdown. You may treat the bullfighting as a cute extra to the meat festival."

Did Beelzebub and Fatla hate bullfighting for some reason...?

"It is just bullfighting, after all. Please feel free to fall asleep if you get bored. At least we'll be sitting in the sun." Even Vania expressed her disapproval.

We made our way inside as the three demons mercilessly insulted the sport we'd come to watch.

Meanwhile, Halkara still hadn't finished her mountain of meat skewers.

"Um... I'll be bringing this with me, so everyone please feel free to snack on them..."

The skewers themselves were delicious, so I would take bites here and there.

When I saw that Halkara's hundred skewers had barely been chipped away, I remembered once again that moderation was important for everything.

In the worst case, Laika and Flatorte could easily finish them for us.

WE WATCHED BULLFIGHTING

The reserved seating in the coliseum had a great view of the stage in the center.

"Man, I'm so pumped! Bulls, fight till you're bloody!"

Flatorte, enough with the violence.

But I had a feeling that long ago, people watched bullfighting with the same excitement back on Earth. I think it was really intense, and it wasn't unusual for the bulls themselves to die. And I think the matadors killed bulls, too…

"Here is the match list, everyone. It has been translated into the human language."

Fatla passed a piece of paper around to everyone.

"This is sumo!!"

The whole list went on and on. There were so, so many matches.

"Sumo? Oh, you mean that form of freestyle wrestling. Yes, bullfighting is indeed freestyle wrestling."

Fatla understood the word *sumo*.

That aside, would this really be sumo? All the cow names sounded like professional sumo names and everything.

"'Tis exactly why I told you we should have come in partway through. All the opening matches are so dull. 'Twould be perfectly well enough if we came to watch the top twenty fights."

In sumo terms, that would be about the number of matches for the *makuuchi*, or senior-grade wrestlers…

"I think we should at least watch from forty onward, boss."

It seemed like Vania had a different opinion than Beelzebub.

But we'd be watching another twenty matches before the *juryo*, or junior-grade wrestlers, even entered the ring. We were seriously here to watch professional sumo.

"I will explain for all our non-demon guests. Grading is divided into six ranks, and from greatest to least, they are the gold class, silver class, copper class, bronze class, chrome class, and cloth class."

What Fatla was explaining to us sounded a lot like the six ranks of sumo: *makuuchi*, *juryo*, *makushita*, *sandanme*, *jonidan*, and *jonokuchi*…

"Matches start with the cloth class. There are twenty when you add the silver and copper classes, then once you also add the gold classes, there are about forty."

So gold class was literally *makuuchi*, silver class was literally *juryo*, and copper class was literally *makushita*.

"Bulls from the gold and silver classes wear the cloth of the warrior. They'll pace fully around the circular stage once, giving them the chance to show off their figures to the audience."

That *was* just how they entered the ring! That was only something people in the *makuuchi* and *juryo* ranks did—this really was turning out to be sumo!

Why was it so much like professional sumo, though? I was almost starting to wonder if this was a joke... And no one seemed to really notice it besides me, which felt weird...

"Lady Beelzebub," said Fatla, "according to the association's announcement, the event is now sold out. We are enhancing the Ministry of Agriculture's prestige."

"Indeed," Beelzebub replied. "The numbers certainly fell when they began to suspect match fixing, but it seems we have made up for it wonderfully."

I felt like I'd heard this conversation somewhere before, too!

"But there have been many more bulls getting injured when they start seriously clashing. I believe it was also a necessity."

"That might be true, Fatla; if they found out that the result was previously determined, even if the fight was real, some will grow very angry."

"Well, the most notable matches of the past were true fights, either way."

"And the increase in injuries was not simply because they were all fighting seriously in every match. The bulls are much heavier compared with how they were in the past. That is why more are getting injured. The bulls of yore were more muscular, but when competitors found out that the heavier ones had an advantage, they all became heavyweights."

It was starting to feel like Fatla and Beelzebub were in on the joke now.

"It seems there are more minotaur guests, too. I am glad to see them return."

"'Tis because there were many minotaurs who said the bullfighting name was sullied back when doubts arose about match fixing, and they stopped coming to watch. This trend must have just started to die down."

It was starting to feel like I was in the Ryogoku Sumo Hall…

"But, Lady Beelzebub, there are many bulls belonging to other demons besides minotaurs; perhaps it is the times. The most chivalrous spirit depends on the owner, after all."

"There are alraunes entering bulls, too. Like this one, Cownokusa. I believe it won't be long until the era when humans start entering cows arrives."

That sort of felt like a discussion about the globalization of sumo.

"But bullfighting is a festival before it is a sport. All the sacred rituals can rather complicate the process."

"Bullfighting has not quite taken roots among the demon world. Perhaps that is why."

Sumo used to be a Shinto ritual, too…

"Yeah… No matter what any of you say, this is professional sumo… Sumo wrestling…"

"Azusa, this is not wrestling. 'Tis bullfighting. They have only surface similarities."

But they were still *way* too similar!

"Oh, the cloth-class matches are starting!" Flatorte's innocent gaze was fixed on the stage.

I wanted to enjoy this like Flatorte was… I wanted to be able to watch without making needless mental commentary… To be honest, I couldn't concentrate!

Representatives from both the east and west brought out the bulls.

Then, when the bulls came to face each other, the representatives stepped back.

Fight!

"Moo~" "Moooo~" "Mooooooooooooooooo~" "…Oom~"

The bulls stood inches apart and started licking each other's faces.

This was super…serene…

* * *

The judge then stepped forward and declared both bulls the winner. I didn't mind, but I really wanted to know how they decided who won or lost. They were just licking each other.

"...That was pointless." Flatorte immediately disapproved!

"'Tis what it is—this is the cloth class. It will be like this for a little while."

It was very possible that we came into the coliseum at the wrong time.

The matches afterward were so easygoing; they could hardly even be called bullfighting.

They were really just putting two bulls in a ring together. None of the bulls seemed like they wanted to fight, either.

Sometimes, people who looked like senior-ranking judges would get together and deliberate over a judgment, but the standards of judging were a mystery to me.

"Hey, Beelzebub, when does the bullfighting end anyway?"

"We ended up coming in at around nine in the morning. Well, the gold class will be wrapping up at around six in the evening."

"That is waaay too long!"

"Hence why there was no need for us to enter so early. 'Twould have been perfectly all right if we came in around two twenty to watch the silver-class matches."

I guess the reason Beelzebub and the others weren't so into it was because there were so many stupid matches like this at the beginning...

"There are also other events after the bullfighting, so watching it all would put us at nine in the evening."

I guess this was way longer than professional sumo. That usually ended at six.

"Can we come and go as we please, then...?"

"Aye, so long as you keep your ticket on you, you are free to do so."

Maybe I would go back to the meat festival and buy something later...

The bullfighting went on for so long, the three kids all fell asleep.

Of course they would. Anyone would pass out watching this. The first three matches were nice because the bulls were cute, but the parade of nothing but bulls was getting a little boring. Hopefully, no dragons would be entering the ring.

During the whole thing, I went out to the meat festival to buy some barbecue. I asked for half a portion.

And then it was a little after two in the afternoon.

"Oh, they will soon be presenting the silver-class bulls," Beelzebub said.

All the bulls that had their name called came out in order, with every one led by a colorful cloth that was wrapped around each of them.

"Oh, it's the *juryo* ceremonial entrance."

"There you go with the strange words again. 'Tis the silver-class presentation."

Maybe the same god had influenced Japan and this world... Or maybe a reincarnated somebody was the one doing the influencing. This was just way too similar.

But there was one thing different about the silver-class ceremonial entrance.

A huge image was projected onto the coliseum board!

"*Hello and welcome, bullfighting fans! We are tentatively using brand-new magic technology to bring you announcements over a magic stream~ I, the demon king, Provato Pecora Ariés, will be your play-by-play commentator today~ ♪*"

They were making good use of ancient wisdom!

"*Our commentator today will be the fighter Miss Fighsly. Miss Fighsly, if you please~ ♪*"

Fighsly was next to her!

"I am Fighsly. I'm looking forward to the matches today. Please contact me with any work requests."

"*Oh, this is a public magic stream, so please refrain from making advertisements~ ♪*"

This was seriously like a TV broadcast now...

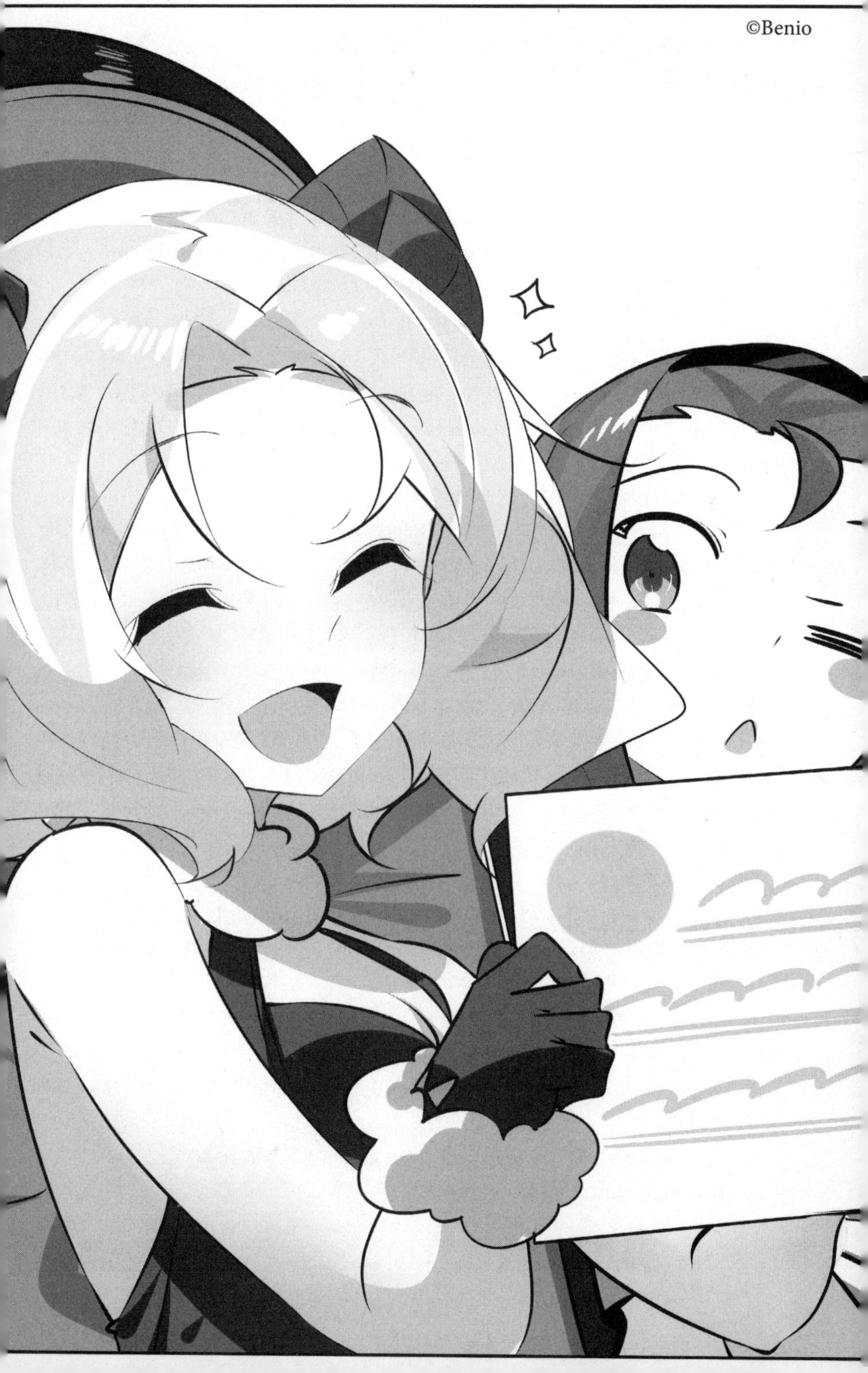

"Miss Fighsly, what would you say is the most enjoyable part of bullfighting?"

"Betting money really gets me going—even if it isn't exactly legal."

"This is a public stream, so please refrain from mentioning anything against the law~ ♪"

This was already turning into a full broadcast accident.

"Our next match will be between Daiseicow and Cowayate. What do you think will be the highlights of this matchup?"

"In terms of weight, Daiseicow is the heavier one here. So the question is, will Cowayate be able to wrap around quickly to the side and pressure him from there? Once a heavy bull gets knocked into the air, the effect of gravity is weakened, you see. Which would then make his weight disadvantageous."

Hey, so she could do a proper analysis.

"Well then, it's almost time! Daiseicow is pushing! He is pushing! Oh, but Cowayate knew what was coming! He is attacking back from the side! Push, push! Oh, and the winner is—Cowayate!"

Now that this whole thing had reached a higher level, it finally felt way more like sumo.

Oh, not sumo. Bullfighting... This was complicated...

"Well! That was exactly the sort of match we were expecting from Cowayate. Daiseicow had a good attack there at the beginning, but he was unable to follow through and ended up taking a break. And then Cowayate took the rest from there."

"They both put up a wonderful fight. ♪ Everyone will shine if we all keep going, so we just need to do our best and aim for the top. ♪"

Her commentary sounded like lyrics to a pop song. But that aside—

"Pecora looks like she's having fun."

"Her Majesty generally likes attention, you know. She simply could not let an event like this happen without her."

I suppose it was natural for the demon king to want to be the center of attention.

That was about when the sleeping girls finally awoke.

"It was so loud, Falfa woke up..."

"This event is supposed to be loud, though…"

"How noisy… How can I get a good nap like this?!" And Sandra was even getting angry at the whole thing.

Shalsha was still asleep.

I guess some people slept better with the perfect amount of white noise.

Also, Flatorte was starting to get wild—her tail was whipping back and forth everywhere.

"Yes! Push 'im, Cowdaijin! Use your horns, throw 'im up in the air and get in there! Then you can push 'im out all in one go!"

Even though it was a little different than the bullfighting we imagined at first, I was still glad to see her enjoying herself.

Laika and Halkara were also looking on eagerly. I guess that was because the definitely-not-*juryo* matches were more intense.

I never got to see sumo live, so it was perfect for me.

And I know this makes me sound like Halkara, but…I bet it would be more fun to watch with a drink. *Maybe I'll go grab one during break time…*

"Taiyocow has moved around to the back without making any contact! And he attacks with his horns! That will make him the winner~! Oh dear, the stadium has gone quiet. Perhaps that was seen as unfair. What do you think, Miss Fighsly, our analyst?"

"*I would prefer if he had taken this fight properly and head-on, but this is still a battle for victory. I believe the bulls must keep that in mind while they remember the rules. And bulls change a lot, you see, so they need to think of this when they come into contact. It might have been a little easy for the opponent here.*"

I didn't know if sumo commentary was actually like this, but this definitely felt like sumo commentary.

"Well, it's already time for our next match. *This is a roller coaster of offense and defense! Things are becoming so complicated! After some deliberation, the judge has announced victory for the west!*"

"It seems that called for some discussion."

"Indeed. The stablemasters—the minotaur judging committee—are gathering on stage."

Stablemasters were what they were called in sumo, too…

After a set of exciting matches, the gold-class matches started.

"What would you say is the biggest difference between the gold and silver classes, Miss Fighsly?"

"The prize money for the gold classes is awarded by the company, so bull owners who can win against the popular bulls get very rich. At the most, I'd say about twenty awards will be given. It's quite a lot. I am jealous."

No need to get so precise about the money, Fighsly.

The house really was sold out—every seat was filled.

Then a wyvern came and unfurled some kind of banner over the stage.

ALL SEATS SOLD. THANK YOU!

They had those in sumo halls, too!

"Seems as though the ticket-holders who were spending time at the meat festival are finally coming in. This is where the real event starts."

Beelzebub, of course, was taking in the scene.

Wait, she was talking so much about bullfighting with Fatla—wouldn't she know a lot about this competition, too?

Bulls with huge horns were clashing in the ring.

"Yeeeaaah! This is what I came for! Go! Get 'em!" Flatorte was waving her hands and yelling.

"This *is* bullfighting!"

Somewhere along the way, the event had become the bullfighting I knew well. I felt a little strange, almost as though a spell had been cast over me. Even the kids were cheering and using the bulls' names.

This was a thrilling match! Especially when the smaller bull beat the bigger one!

By the time I realized it, we'd finally reached the last match of the day.

"*Cowow and Cowryu have made contact! Their horns are interlocked! They cannot move! They are at a total standstill! Are we looking at a stalemate~?!*"

"Well, once they come to a stop, I would say Cowow is at an advantage here. Given time to think, the battle-hardened Cowow will turn this in his favor. If Cowryu can pull off a decisive maneuver—"

"Oh, with a twist of the neck, Cowow has flipped Cowryu! Cowow is the winner!"

The entire coliseum was filled with shouts, both happy and sad. The latter belonged to Cowryu's fans.

"What a wonderful match. The owner of the winner will be getting a considerable sum of prize money. Wow, that's tempting! Maybe I should buy a bull. But the expenses might not be worth it."

This sports analyst was spending too much time analyzing money.

"We sure had a fantastic time with our bullfights today~ I was truly impressed! Our bullfighting tour schedule is already available, so please attend one of those if you are interested~ ♪ We will have events where you can meet and pet the fighting bulls~ ♪"

Pecora was honestly pretty good at commentating. Her status as the demon king must have gotten her used to talking.

Then out of nowhere came the *boom bo-boom, boom bo-boom* of *taiko* drums.

"Those are the great drums that signal the end of the bullfighting. It is an old tradition," Fatla informed me.

Just like sumo, to the very end.

Now, the bullfighting festival should have ended there, but—

—not many people were getting up from their seats. There were probably more new people coming in to sit down.

"The second part will be beginning now," Beelzebub said.

"Oh yeah, you did mention there would be another three hours…"

What was going to happen in these three hours? I was only thinking about the bullfighting, so I didn't really look into the details.

"There is not much of a big difference, really. Honestly, you could call this Minotaur Day. It all has to do with the minotaurs."

"The meat festival is over, so what's happening now?"

After a little while, there came a bugle sounding a fanfare.

Then the bulls came out again.

Every one had numbered cloths on them.

"Now it is time for bullracing. I, the demon king, Provato Pecora Ariés, will continue to provide the play-by-play!"

"And I, Fighsly, will be your color commentator."

They appeared on the screen again!

I guess bullracing is like horse racing...?

"Fighsly, which bull do you think will win?"

"Well gee, to be honest, I don't know because I don't really care. The gambling system is rigged to get the bookies most of the money."

Then don't be an analyst!

"But this job does earn me some money. So I'll do what I can, considering I don't know anything!"

If you don't know anything, then you should turn down the job! That's a job for a professional!

"Thunderbolt, number five at the gate, is the most popular one this time around~ ♪"

"What a cool-looking bull. The pattern on it reminds me of a bird taking flight."

What a stupid analysis!

"The second most popular is number eight, Dune of the Vampire."

"My guess is that the fourth most popular will take first place. No real reason—just a gut feeling."

Seriously, fire this analyst.

"Miss Azusa, bullracing was started here at this very bullfighting festival through a partnership between the Ministry of Agriculture and the sports agency. We are allowing bets to take place. We believed people would grow tired of bullfighting alone, so we decided to incorporate elements of other sports."

"Thanks for the explanation, Fatla... You should've been the analyst instead of Fighsly..."

"No. It is not good for a public servant to work as an analyst."

I thought about how the very head of state was providing play-by-play commentary, but I decided not to let the little things bother me… The demon king usually did whatever she wanted, after all.

Some other members of the family were getting heated over this, and I noticed Halkara had several betting tickets in her hand.

"Yes, Nethervoid! Nethervoid! Or Oceanic Creator, it doesn't matter!"

"She's getting into betting!"

I'd sensed she was interested in gambling before, so I guess I was right…

"Madam Teacher, this is part of helping the bullfighting festival. Philanthropy, essentially!"

That sounded like the logic of someone who really liked horse racing.

"Well, it's not like you're going to be losing millions of gold in one day, so enjoy it. You're earning money at your company anyway."

"But, Azusa, this is not the last race. There are five races today," Beelzebub said.

Oh, she'll lose way more money than I thought.

"Halkara, I'm capping how much you can bet."

"Whaaat?!"

Wait, how much money was she planning on betting anyway?

She should just own a bull. Her company was doing well, so she could pull it off.

And then a bull race that was suspiciously like a horse race began.

"Nethervoid! My hopes are on you! Make up ground on the outside! You can do it! You! Can! Do it! I believe in you!" Halkara's excitement over this was getting excessive.

"Sheesh, you're cheering like you've got a friend in the race."

"Nethervoid, if even a little of my hopes and dreams for you can reach you, it'll be enough! Please win!"

But all the rest of the family was watching the race seriously.

Even Sandra, who had been watching the whole event with vengeful delight, was yelling, "You can do better than that!" The bulls were running along the track, so I guess that was just as interesting.

Bullracing was a sport that the whole family could enjoy.

We Watched Bullfighting

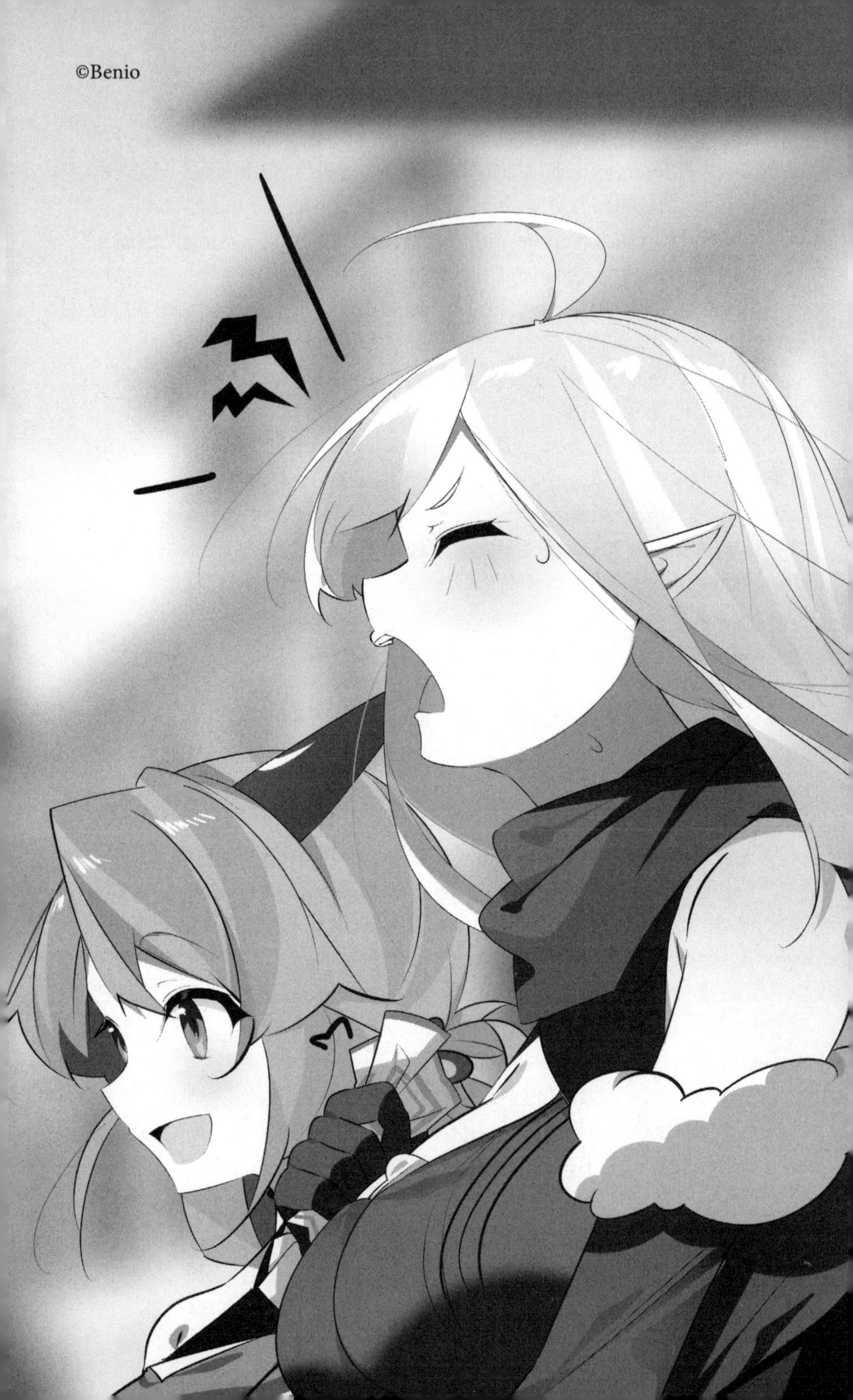
©Benio

* * *

But starting from the fourth race, there was another change.

Out came minotaurs, numbers pinned to their clothes.

"What? The minotaurs themselves are going to run?"

"Minotaurs are quite fast. Many of them find successful careers in sports," Beelzebub explained.

I had a feeling that this was going to be much more popular than the bulls. I could hear people screaming some of the racers' names.

"Some are essentially idols—among other minotaurs, at least."

"I wonder what makes a cow face more or less attractive…"

Now that the minotaurs were lined up, it felt more and more like a track meet.

The bright lights lit up the coliseum, so we could still see the races during nighttime.

"Crandahd! Number nine, Crandahd! Don't lose!"

Even in the minotaur race, Halkara was betting like always…

"Miss Halkara is so enthusiastic about this… As officials from the Ministry of Agriculture, we are touched…"

Vania was impressed, but I wasn't sure if she was having the right sentiment here…

But once the race started, I got super enthusiastic about it, too, so I wasn't much different from Halkara.

The minotaurs were *incredibly* fast. It almost felt like the wind was even reaching the audience.

And all thanks to the ancient magic, we could see close-ups of the runners' faces on the screen.

This was practically like modern day!

Well, since Halkara was already cheering for Crandahd, I would, too.

"Go! Get ahead! Crandahd! Push forward! Yes, he did it! We won!"

"We did it, Madam Teacher!"

In our excitement, Halkara and I hugged each other tightly. It's so exciting when the person you cheer for wins!

After a little while…I thought we had been hugging a little too much.

"Hey, Halkara, sorry, but...you can let me go now..."

"No, now that we're here, I thought maybe...you and I could go for an extended rendezvous...or something like that..." Halkara wasn't letting go.

"What are you talking about, Halkara?!"

"See, I believe I said it before, but I am heteroflexible."

"First I've heard it!" I quickly escaped Halkara's clutches.

The last and fifth race was a relay race, which heated the entire coliseum with excitement.

By the way, I had to stop Halkara before she sank her entire savings into the fourth race. The minotaur she'd bet on ended up stalling partway through...

"Halkara, you know that stereotype about people who ruin themselves gambling? That's you."

"Life itself is a gamble, isn't it, Madam Teacher?"

Don't say it like a proverb!

The cheers hadn't even finished echoing through the coliseum as the demons started heading home.

"Phew. I would say 'twas quite successful, so that is a relief." Beelzebub looked like her work was over. She wasn't here for fun—that meant it was genuine ministry work.

And as someone who'd watched the entire thing, I knew that well.

"Beelzebub, Fatla, Vania, well done, all of you."

I had to praise all of them. I knew very well what hard work felt like.

"Mmm. 'Tis no big deal when it comes to us."

I was kind of hoping they'd be happier about it, but it was true that it was a small thing compared with all the work Beelzebub had done previously.

"Well done, Miss Beelzebub!"

"Oh, Falfa, thank you! Now I'm not tired at all!"

"Hey... You treat me way differently than Falfa..."

"Why must I treat you and the girls the same?"

True, but it did irritate me a little.

"Shalsha has never had much interest in sports, but I learned a lot today. Attaining knowledge on subjects one does not know is the fundamental joy of learning. Thank you for offering us this opportunity, Miss Beelzebub." As I thought, Shalsha's thank-you was stiff.

But it was her own way of expressing her gratitude.

"Of course, I am going to do all I can for my girls~"

"You know they're not *yours*, right…? I don't mind overlooking it a few times, but you sure use *my* a lot."

"Hmph, they might one day truly be *my* girls. Heh-heh-heh…" Beelzebub smiled dauntlessly.

"She's a demon… This demon is showing her true colors…"

If I wasn't careful, we might cross a point of no return.

But in the opposite sense, this meant we all enjoyed the bullfighting festival, and my daughters even loved it.

WE VISITED THE GREAT SLIME

Falfa and Shalsha were helping Sandra study in front of me as I drank my afternoon tea in the dining room.

"Okay, did I get this right?"

"Wooow! Very good! You got sixty percent right!"

"Okay, then I got a lot wrong. You said 'wow,' so I thought I got more than that."

I guess a positive-reinforcement style of teaching could sometimes give the learner premature joy…

"That's not true. These are simplified questions from university entrance exams. That means you can take pride in solving over half of them."

"R-really? Well…I did photosynthesize a lot of nutrients to work hard and study into the night, after all. That's why!"

Sandra was getting smarter and smarter right under my nose.

Actually, she was solving really difficult problems.

When she came to the house, she scarcely had a grasp on how to write.

It was fun watching my daughters grow. I mean, it was also my daughters helping her grow, so… Oh well.

If someone's own kid became a professor, then it would be normal for the kid to be smarter than the parent. Falfa and Shalsha were at a high enough level to teach at a university.

"Sandra, I'm impressed you want to study into the night, but don't stay up too late, okay? It's bad for you."

There was no need for her to cram all night like a student preparing for a test. That was my educational policy. It's not like cramming gave me a happy adult life last time, after all.

"That's the standard for an animal, though, right? So long as I photosynthesize during the day, I can stay up to study."

"Oh, okay... If you say so..."

I still wasn't completely familiar with the plants' point of view. It was about time I got used to my daughters' sense of values.

"Still, you spirit sisters are really smart. I admire that." Sandra never really said anything nice outright, but even she was praising them.

Maybe now that she herself had gotten smarter, she could grasp how amazing Falfa and Shalsha were.

"There weren't many things to play with in the forest where Falfa and Shalsha used to live. But if we went to the nearby town and said we were going to study, then many shops would lend us books."

"Many people let things slide because we were children. Shalsha is truly thankful. Our gratitude knows no bounds."

Oh yeah, they did say the orphanage had given them clothes and other life essentials. Their lives had been in the good care of many people.

Now that they mention it... I've never gone and said hello to any of those people...

"Hey, I want to go and thank all the institutions that helped you two, so could you tell me where they are?"

It felt a little on the late side for that, but I still thought I should bring over some edible slimes or something.

"Mommy, the orphanage director passed away already."

"He was already old when we first met him. We attended his funeral, and every year that we lived in the forest, we visited his grave."

I forgot we were so long-lived. And still, Falfa and Shalsha were doing all the things they should be doing. They really were good kids.

"But it might be a good idea to see all the people who took care of us, right, Shalsha?" Falfa's expression was more serious than usual—she was talking as an older sister.

"See, there's someone in the forest who watched over you, right? The Great Slime, was it? Maybe it's about time we go say hello."

Sandra was confused, and I could almost see her thoughts on her face, as if she was thinking, *Great Slime? What's that?*

It was a pretty unique concept, so I understood how she felt.

"So the Great Slime is…"

Actually, how *was* I supposed to explain this?

"…The Great Slime is a great big slime."

"Azusa, you're talking down to me just because I look like a kid, aren't you?"

Sandra glared at me. *I didn't mean anything by it. I'll think of a good explanation, so just hang tight for a little longer.*

"The Great Slime is made up of a collection of what you could call the slimes' thoughts. You could call it, like…the head slime, maybe."

I had met the Great Slime once before.

But that was back before Rosalie was family, so now there were more of us here who'd never seen the Great Slime.

"I see slimes go through a strange evolution, too. I doubted they were even animals, but they're nothing to laugh at, either."

Now that she brought it up, what kind of category of creature would slimes fall under anyway? They were vaguely like monsters, but that was a broad category.

"Okay, then let's have the whole family go say hi to the Great Slime. It'll be like a homecoming for Falfa and Shalsha."

The Great Slime was probably going to be around semipermanently, but we should still drop by every once in a while.

"Okay. Thank you, Mommy!" Falfa responded with great enthusiasm, so we all took off on a day Halkara didn't have to work.

We all hopped on Laika and Flatorte and headed to Falfa and Shalsha's hometown. It was three hours one way on a dragon.

The two dragons had a bit of trouble finding a place to land, but we managed. We could move pretty quickly anyway.

"This area has poisonous gas… We must be careful…"

"Yeah, you especially, Halkara…"

Poisonous gas spouted from the ground in the Forest of Belgria, where the Great Slime lived. It was dangerous, but not deadly enough to put either Laika or me in danger. And for slime spirits Falfa and Shalsha, it wasn't a problem at all.

Also, I didn't see any withered plants in the area, so Sandra was probably going to be okay.

That was why, for all practical purposes, the only one who had to be careful was Halkara.

"This is a dark forest. The tall trees are taking all the light. They're so greedy!"

Sandra was indignant for the most unique reasons, but it certainly was eerie—it felt like night was approaching here in the forest even during the daytime.

Finally, we spotted something deeper in the forest sitting quietly, something that looked like a massive jewel at a glance.

"That's one huge sapphire! What a treasure!"

Flatorte was overjoyed and ran off.

Even blue dragons, who had sloppy lifestyles and probably not enough money to last them one night, still got excited over treasure like any other dragon would.

Except it wasn't treasure.

"Oh, Flatorte, wait, wait!"

Before I could stop her, Flatorte—

Bwump!

—gently ran into the treasure and bounced off it.

"What? This is way too soft to be a jewel. It's so squishy…"

Flatorte was poking the not-jewel with her finger.

"That's the Great Slime, Flatorte."

"What? This? Do slimes get this big, Mistress?"

It wasn't surprising that Flatorte was surprised, but... *Wait a second, I explained this all before we left. Wasn't she listening?*

"It's a great big slime, which is why it's called the Great Slime. It looks like a regular slime, but it's closer to a spirit, like Falfa and Shalsha."

"Huh, this world is full of surprises."

Rosalie seemed frustrated ("Big Sis already talked about this..."), so Flatorte really wasn't listening.

"You can take off your shoes and climb up it if you want. It'll talk to you if you do."

"Oh, I wasn't wearing shoes when we left."

Well, you should! You're way too wild!

Flatorte first climbed up to the top of the Great Slime. "Weird—it's so jiggly. I bet it'd be fun to jump on, though!"

That was exactly how Falfa and Shalsha used to play, apparently.

Falfa and Shalsha were born here precisely because this was a place that brought about the birth of the Great Slime.

This forest apparently made it very easy for slime thoughts or souls or what have you to gather.

"You are Flatorte. Greetings, I am the Great Slime."

A human form appeared from the Great Slime's main body. This was the form it took on when it communicated.

"Gah! Something popped out!" Flatorte was shocked. *But I'm pretty sure I told her about that, too...*

"Welcome to the Great Slime— Well, it might be a little funny for me to welcome you to myself. But I suppose once I've gotten this large, I am a bit like a place of my own. I see there are others here I've never met before."

"It's a lot like me," said Rosalie. "But with an actual body."

I see. I guess it was like our resident ghost, too.

"I am Sandra, the mandragora. You sure do well for a slime."

Sandra was mysteriously condescending, but I guess that wasn't too weird, since she was another unique being.

"It's been a while!"

"We are home for a visit. Nothing has changed about the forest." Falfa was jumping on the Great Slime like it was a trampoline, and for some reason, Shalsha was sitting with her legs folded underneath her. They had very different ways of interacting with the Great Slime.

"The forest itself has not changed, but the areas outside have gone through surprisingly big transformations. Oh yes, there are so many more people now. It's worth scoring them."

The Great Slime had a habit (?) of giving anyone who visited it a number grade.

I was curious about these big changes, but the Great Slime seemed to put more value in giving its scores.

"First, Falfa and Shalsha—ninety-nine points."

Falfa and Shalsha were delighted to have such a high score.

Even though Shalsha sat still, her legs folded neatly underneath her, Mom could tell she was happy.

"Both of you have grown to be such upstanding girls. You don't get a full score because I look forward to seeing how you will develop even further in the future."

The Great Slime was also kind of like a guardian to Falfa and Shalsha, so that score made me happy. And if I was this happy, then the girls must be overjoyed about it.

"Next, let's go with Laika."

"O-oh, yes!"

For some reason, Laika stood up straight at attention, like a student being called by a teacher.

"You are also at ninety-nine, Laika. Very well done."

"Thank you!" Laika bowed politely. I wasn't sure of the rubric, but it was a good score.

"Now, Azusa."

I felt like I stood up a little straighter when the Great Slime said my name.

"In addition to your ninety-seven-point total, you have twenty bonus points."

"What are the rules here?!" *What do you need to do to get bonus points?*

"You have made valuable contributions in many areas, Azusa. Thus, the extra twenty points."

"So by default, I lose to Falfa, Shalsha, and Laika by two points. You might want to check your math."

"Oh, the ninety-seven was fairly arbitrary."

"Please do a real screening! Stop giving people whatever numbers you like!"

I wasn't just going to be happy with any high score.

"I suppose I'm next…" A bead of sweat dripped down Halkara's cheek. She got a low score last time…

But the Great Slime also seemed somewhat uncomfortable and looked away.

Another low score?

"Halkara gets…a score I cannot disclose!"

No way! It isn't going to tell us?!

"What?! That's so bizarre! I don't mind a low score; please just tell me!" Halkara rushed right up to the slime. I understood how she felt.

The Great Slime (or rather, its human form) slid backward without moving its legs. Its figure could appear anywhere on the body of the slime itself…

"My apologies, but I will not disclose this score… I cannot tell you, Halkara!"

"That doesn't make any sense! Then what were everyone else's scores?"

The Great Slime glanced over to Rosalie. "Rosalie is at eighty-two. She is working toward improving herself every day as a ghost."

"Hey, I got a good score, too!"

Yep, that's a number to be proud of.

The Great Slime then went on to look at Flatorte and Sandra. Its eyes were clearly swimming with worry.

"I cannot disclose Flatorte's and Sandra's scores!"

Don't tell me it just decided not to say failing grades…?

"This is unacceptable! Say it! Don't underestimate me just because I'm a plant!" Sandra joined Halkara and drew up close to the Great Slime.

"No! Not this, I can't…!"

"Why are you hesitating?! We have scores, don't we? Please tell me, too! Wait, is there corruption in the grading system?! Are you subtracting ten points from those whose grades were bad in the past~?"

"No, there's no corruption here! I cannot disclose them!"

"Then at least tell us why you can't tell us!"

"I cannot do that, either! I'm sorry!"

The Great Slime was under a lot of pressure. This was getting weird…

Well, there was an 89 percent chance that it was refusing to say any failing scores.

On the other hand, Flatorte yawned lazily. "I don't care what score it came up with."

I had a feeling that was the right attitude to take, in a way.

In the end, the Great Slime never announced their scores.

Halkara and Sandra still resented it for that, but the Great Slime stubbornly refused to tell them anything.

The Great Slime casually made its way over to Falfa and Shalsha. For how special it was, it sure acted human…

Oh right, there was something I was curious about—I should ask before I forget.

"Hey, you said there were some big changes nearby. What happened?"

"Oh yes, something unusual happened since the last time you were here."

When I brought up the subject, the Great Slime looked a little relieved to be talking about any topic besides the scores.

I wonder what had happened? Everything looked exactly the same, at least on the outside.

"What could it be~? Is the poison gas gone now?"

"Of all the possible changes, the poison gas is the only thing I can think of."

Like the twins they were, Falfa and Shalsha arrived at the same conclusion. Even having lived here for so long, the two of them didn't seem to know, either. Apparently, there was a strong association between the Forest of Belgria and poison gas.

"No, that's not it. Also, you should know that at the current gas density, Halkara has about another hour to live."

"Oh, that's a relief— Wait, isn't it dangerous for me to be here, then?!" Halkara went pale. She was the only one who wasn't physically OP in one way or another.

"I'm certain you all are most uneasy. But I assure you, you have plenty of time. Please relax."

"I appreciate the sentiment, but I am still a little scared. I'm the type to get lost in a conversation and forget the time."

Halkara sure was aware of the mistakes she tended to make. She'd matured, too. Even though she probably failed the Great Slime's arbitrary test…

"I always tell myself, *One more drink!* and yet I always end up drinking five more for some reason. That's happened hundreds of times now, and I can't seem to cure myself."

Maybe the Great Slime didn't disclose her score because of that.

"Miss Halkara, if you start feeling ill, I will take you to a place with fresh air, all right?" Laika was being careful, too. As long as they had this arrangement, I'm sure things would work out before it got too bad.

"Thank you, I appreciate it… Also, even without the poisonous gas, this forest still gives me the shivers… I'm afraid this might be rude to Falfa and Shalsha, but as an elf, I can sense something strange about this place. I didn't feel like this last time…"

Halkara was cautious today. I guess she'd been through a lot of terrible things in the past.

"Ha-ha-ha! You're a coward, Halkara!" Flatorte, the member of the family who rarely ever thought ahead, burst out laughing.

"This is nothing!" said Sandra. "Elves are so miserable. It's just dark; there's nothing wrong with it. Actually, I'd say it's better the population is so sparse here, if that's because of the poisonous gas. If only we could spread this poisonous gas throughout the world."

Sandra, are you suggesting we destroy humanity...?

"No, it truly feels strange here! I don't think you can describe this through dragon or plant standards..."

I think it would be best to trust Halkara here. Elves were specialists of the forests.

"I feel a chill on my spine, like something's going to pop out at me!"

"Big Sis Halkara, you see ghosts every day—I'm a ghost! You're getting too frightened! A good majority of evil spirits can't even do any evil, and they don't cause any harm to humans anyway!"

"...I am the most normal of this family. Common sense doesn't work with the rest of you!"

I'm with Halkara on this.

"But there aren't any spooky spirits here, so that won't be a problem. I'd bet my head on it."

I wondered if Rosalie could actually remove her head. I'm pretty sure she couldn't. And if she could, I hoped she wouldn't...

In that case, maybe the change the Great Slime was talking about was an increase of a new type of plant in the forest, or something else like that.

"The big change I was talking about is—"

The Great Slime calmly began talking again.

"—a girl who would count as Falfa and Shalsha's younger sister was born."

Whaaaaaaaaaaaaaaaaaaaaaaaaaaaaaaaaaaaaaaaaaaaaaaaaaaaa aaaaat?!!!!!

That wasn't just unexpected; it was at least five miles above my expectations—it was *that* big of a shock.

Everyone reacted differently. Laika and Halkara mirrored my own internal reaction, screaming, ""Whaaaaaaat?!""

Meanwhile, Falfa and Shalsha kept blinking, as though they were trying to process the information in their minds. It was like the impact was so great that they froze.

"To be more precise, another slime spirit was born," the Great Slime quickly explained, as though it was surprised by our shock. "Since Falfa and Shalsha were born as slime spirits first, I called her their 'little sister' for convenience's sake. Of course, they are not related by blood; you could say she's your junior cohort."

The Great Slime calmly unpacked the meaning of *little sister* for us, but Falfa, Shalsha, and I were still reeling from the impact of the word.

We couldn't pretend this was a stranger, at least.

"Sis… What do we do…? There's a younger slime spirit…"

"What should we do…? At times like this, we should count prime numbers to calm down…"

I'd honestly never seen the two so bewildered.

Not to mention I had no idea how I should treat this new "sister," myself.

Whether she was their little sister or "junior cohort" or whatever, if she was a slime spirit—

—she was my daughter.

The souls of the slimes I'd killed had come together to give birth to Falfa and Shalsha. By that logic, that meant another girl born from the collection of slime souls like them would make her my daughter.

Plus, I've been taking care of the first two as my daughters, so it would be cruel to treat the third as a stranger. Maybe I'd feel differently if there'd been hundreds of slime spirits, but…this was only the third.

I had to accept her!

"Oh, you don't have to think of her as your daughter. She was born from the souls of slimes killed all across the world, so her connection to you is quite thin. At least, I don't think she considers you her mother."

Slimes were being killed all over the world?

That was a bit of a relief, but it was also a little sad.

Anyway, we should first start with getting information about this girl.

"So, Great Slime, what's her name?"

Considering this was Falfa and Shalsha's younger sister, she was probably called something like Nyalnya.

"This spirit's name is Margrave Wynona of Idell."

"Well, that sure is a fancy-pants name!"

If I walked up to her and told her I was her mother, she would probably think I was a stranger trying to suck up to her... But wait, could you get a title like *margrave* so soon after being born? Was she adopted by the previous one?

"Also, she only calls herself the margrave of Idell—she has no actual noble title."

That's what she *calls herself*...? Can you really just call yourself something like that? Maybe it doesn't happen often enough to be worth making it an enforceable rule.

"Idell is the name of a small region where Falfa and Shalsha used to live, in fact. She is likely trying to say she is the lord of that land."

"She sure is self-assertive..."

Halkara was going pale. *Wait, is this because of the poison gas? Should I get Laika to take her up into the air?*

We should wrap this up, then... We'd just get the information we needed.

"So where does this Wynona girl live?" Falfa was digging for information on her little sister, too.

"She has remodeled the hut where you and Shalsha used to stay. That's where she is."

At least she was making good use of past items.

"Mom, now that we've heard about this, we must go. We should go to the hut," Shalsha said, staring straight into my eyes.

"No parent would say no to that," I replied with a smile.

I was a part of this, too—it wasn't just Falfa and Shalsha.

"But...let's go somewhere with clean air for a bit for Halkara first. After that, though."

Halkara's lips were turning purple.

She really couldn't handle the air here...

I GOT A **NEW DAUGHTER**

It was easy to get back to the house on the highlands by dragon, so I put Halkara on Flatorte and sent her home to rest.

But Halkara kept warning me to be careful: "I believe the source of this terrible sense I have is from that Wynona girl."

She was hypothesizing that Wynona had greatly changed the forest somehow, but there was no way to tell whether that was true or not.

I didn't want to overwhelm Wynona by appearing suddenly with the entire family, so only four of us went—Falfa, Shalsha, me, and Laika, who took us there.

We walked down a long, narrow mountain path. There wasn't much room to move; this wasn't a place anyone visited very often. The trees around us had grown in densely, so it was hard to see ahead. There wasn't as much poison gas here compared with where the Great Slime was, but getting lost in here would be extremely dangerous.

"Falfa wonders what she's like. Do you think she's like us~?"

"I cannot say. We should not get our hopes up. It is unclear if she even has a human form."

I didn't think whatever way she would greet us would be as ridiculous as Shalsha was imagining (she was calling herself a margrave, after all), but it was true that we didn't know anything about her personality.

"I hope we will be able to have a friendly chat." Laika, unsurprisingly, seemed a bit anxious. "Our only precedent here is Falfa and Shalsha, so we have no choice but to come face-to-face with her."

"Either way, we'll know when we meet her. That's for sure," I said, as much for my benefit as hers.

"We should be at our hut soon," Falfa said.

"Sis and I lived a modest life there."

We were getting close to our destination.

We rounded a corner, and a magnificent sight greeted us.

There in the forest stood a splendiferous, chalk-white manor.

"Oh my god!" I couldn't help but shout aloud in wonder.

Hadn't they called it a *hut*? This was a manor fit for nobility…

"Whoa…," Falfa said in shock. "Our hut is a mansion now… What happened…?"

That would shock anyone. I'd never even lived here before, and I was surprised.

"Margrave Wynona of Idell should be inside. This is not the time to be intimidated." Shalsha was ready to go.

"But, Shalsha, someone really important must live here. You think it's okay for us to say hello without making an appointment or something? We're not going to be chased out?"

We weren't in the right mental state to meet the little sister.

That said, we couldn't back down now. We had to look into this mystery.

"She's a slime spirit. She will understand. We will go in first, and we will figure out the rest. Dialogue is important." Shalsha briskly made her way toward the manor.

She really was into it today!

But then a massive white dog emerged from the side of the manor gates. It stopped in front of Shalsha and barked.

"Grrrrrrr~ Woof!"

I guess it was a guard dog.

"...Strategic retreats also have their place."

And Shalsha whirled right back around to us. Yeah, dogs were pretty scary.

This was my chance to show off my strength as a parent.

"Leave this to me, Shalsha." I stepped in front of the white dog and stared straight at it.

"*Woof, woof!*" it said.

Staaare.

"*Woof... Woof, woof...*"

Staaare.

"*Awooo...*"

The dog then flopped over to show its belly, a sign of obedience.

Phew, solved that one. Aww, good puppies are so cute.

Animals could sense another person's abilities, so I guess it understood I wasn't someone to tangle with.

"Wow! That's so cool, Mommy! You'd never lose to a doggy!"

"Even the gods of destruction will turn back before you."

Was that something you said to compliment a parent? Well, whatever...

"All right, now we can keep going."

I knocked on the door.

I didn't know if this would catch the attention of anyone living in such a big house, but it was also rude to just walk in.

No response. Guess I was right; she wasn't going to see us so easily.

"Mommy, there's a sign on the side here that says, NO SOLICITORS, NO UNAUTHORIZED ENTRY, BEWARE OF DOG. NUISANCES WILL BE REPORTED."

Yeah, she wasn't going to see us.

"It doesn't matter. We're not selling anything. Yep, doesn't look like it's locked, so let's go in."

I opened the door, and a white tiger immediately leaped at us.

"*Roooaaar!!*"

The white tiger growled at us.

"I'm surprised she managed to get one of these in here!"

Either way, I was going to avoid fighting with this animal the same way I did the last one.

I stared hard at the white tiger.

It growled at me for a while, but twenty seconds later—

"...Mrow~ Mrow!"

—the white tiger rubbed its face against my legs.

Solved. Power is justice. Justice is power.

"Go home now. You did good. I don't think your master will blame you, either."

The white tiger went into a big box labeled MARSHMALLOW'S HOUSE, which sat inside the building. I guess it was being kept just like a cat.

Marshmallow made me think of a little dog, though...

"Wow, Mommy! Even the tiger acts cute with you!"

"You are the true king of beasts."

I didn't know how to feel about my daughters' compliments. "It looks like security's tight, but we'll just keep going. Also...Laika, could you wait outside, just in case? So you can contact the house or Beelzebub if we don't come out."

That would be safer for all of us. I was fine protecting these two alone, though.

"Yes, Lady Azusa! I will wait for you as I play with the guard dog."

Laika must really like pets...

It would be awkward to make her wait with nothing to do, so it was perfect.

We left Laika behind, and the three of us continued into the manor.

The narrow corridors just led deeper and deeper into the building.

This place felt like it was made to be a dungeon, or as a way to wipe out intruders. Certainly not to function as a living space.

Just as we reached a blind spot at a ninety-degree turn in the corridor, I sensed something.

I quietly peeked around the corner, and there, I saw a white snake, its tongue flicking in and out.

It didn't really try to bite us. I guess this snake was gentle.

"Why is she so into the color white?!"

It was hard to tell if they were supposed to be gatekeepers or pets at this point.

Anyway, the white snake was adorable, with its cute little eyes. Even though I wasn't the biggest snake fan, I still gave it a soft pat on the head.

At the end of the straight hallway, there was a door.

"Be careful when you open it, Mommy!"

"We cannot observe the inside of the room until you open the door. Anything could be lurking within."

She was right. Considering how things had gone so far, nothing in there would surprise me.

There was a polar bear inside.

"How did she get a *polar bear*?! That's not something you can find wandering around in a forest!"

This was the first time I'd seen one in this world.

The polar bear didn't try to attack us at all, either.

I used my ice magic to cool the room down, and it was super happy with that. *I guess they like it cold...*

"Such a big bear!"

"It has a nice coat. It seems smart. Shalsha wants one."

The polar bear was cheering the two up. I even got it to let Falfa ride on its haunches. This place was like a petting zoo— Although bears are a little too scary for your typical kid's attraction.

"Yaaay! Falfa's so high up!"

"Falfa, we're gonna keep going, so get down from the bear, okay?"

We opened the other door in the polar bear's room and found a spiral staircase leading up to the second floor. I guess we had to go through the polar bear's room in order to get to the upper floor. The first floor was literally like a dungeon.

The second floor, huh? Maybe we'd finally be able to see Wynona.

But to be honest, my enthusiasm for meeting her was going down a bit... Whoever lived here was a total weirdo.

Still, no turning back now. Even if a daughter went a little off the rails, a parent still had to be responsible for them.

But the lady of the house sure seemed to be tough on intruders.

As we were halfway up the stairs, an attack came at us from the second floor.

Something white was hurtling right at us.

I really wish they didn't underestimate my senses.

"Falfa, Shalsha, don't move."

I stood in front of the two of them and took the attack.

The object turned out to be a white boulder. It stung a bit, but not enough to have an effect on me.

"What a terrible greeting. I didn't think anyone could be more stubborn about it."

I looked up the stairs and saw a girl in a white dress standing there. Well, I say *girl*, but she didn't look much younger than me.

"What?! Why did that not kill you? What a terrifying foe..." The girl seemed somewhat panicked herself.

"You're Wynona, right? We're not here to hurt you. We just wanted to see you. Can we talk?"

"All right, very well." The girl nodded.

Good. That should settle this for now, I thought—but I was naive.

"I shall hear what you have to say within the white gaol."

A white cage appeared around us; this was relatively high-level magic, I could tell.

"You cannot use magic whatsoever within the white gaol. And now you—"

I punched the cage, and it crumbled to pieces. That must have broken the spell outright, because the cage itself vanished.

"What?! To think the white gaol would be physically broken! This is ridiculous!"

Sorry, but I know my own strength.

"Urrrgh... What a fiendish intruder!"

The girl in the white dress must have been getting really upset if she was groaning aloud about it.

But still, considering her high-level magic, I wondered if this slime spirit really had only been born recently. I had a feeling she'd been alive for centuries at least.

"We don't have any plans to harm you. Let's just talk."

"What could you possibly want? Are you here to tell me you are my mother?"

"Yeah, actually. That's exactly it."

Got it in one.

The girl in the dress stared at me blankly, as if she'd suddenly been possessed.

Phew, at least that's settled.

—But again, I was naive.

"Ahhh-ha-ha-ha! Ha-ha-ha-ha-ha! You are just a con artist! Too bad, I am a slime spirit! So I don't have a mother!"

Whoops! She just doubted us instead!

"I already know what you are going to say. *You were taken from me soon after your birth. I accidentally embezzled money from my company, and now I need thirty million gold so I don't get sued. Please lend me some money.* I won't fall for that trick!"

What was this remittance-fraud scam knockoff?!

The premise that a mother had been separated from her child her whole life was hardly useful to begin with. It was extremely unlikely that the person being targeted had a missing mother. On top of that, the embezzlement part was also hard to believe...

"My apologies; the premise of a mother embezzling money was a bit too much. Although it is most certainly the type of idea a foolish con artist might try to use."

"Wait, I mean, I think it sounds shady, too! I'm not that stupid! And I'm not scamming you!"

Not only did she think I was a scammer, she thought I was really bad at it.

"Be buried in pure-white snow. Snow Wind!"

The girl extended her right hand forward, fluidly drawing lines in the air. If she was using that as a magic circle, then it was most definitely high-level magic.

A ferocious blizzard blasted toward us.

"It's so cold, Mommy!"

"The cold hurts my ears…"

It barely affected me, but Falfa and Shalsha were in pain!

"Hide behind me!" I stepped in front of them, blocking the blizzard.

But the snow was piling up with terrifying speed.

I almost wondered if this magic was for building an artificial ski slope.

It wasn't long before the whole first floor of the spiral staircase was buried in snow, and it was starting to stick to my body, too.

Falfa and Shalsha were enduring the whole thing as well. I was glad neither of them was injured.

Oof! Snow got in my shirt! It's so cold on my back!

Damn you, Wynona! How could you do this to us?!

"Heh-heh-heh. You are all buried in pure-white snow. Ahhh, white is so beautiful. Everything should be covered in it."

I could hear her gloating.

But she couldn't see us from the snow, either.

She was really obsessed with white. Yeah, she was a weird kid.

"My dream is to one day bury this world in snow and paint it all white. White, white, white everywhere. What a blessed world it would be!"

Her ideals were way more dangerous than the demon king herself…

But maybe we'd come at just the right time.

If my daughter (assuming that was the right term) was plotting to cause others trouble, then I had to stop her.

I flew out of the mound of snow.

She looked at me as if that was the last thing she was expecting.

"Sorry, but that's not enough to freeze me."

"What?! You are such a sore loser, you scammer!"

I'm not a scammer!

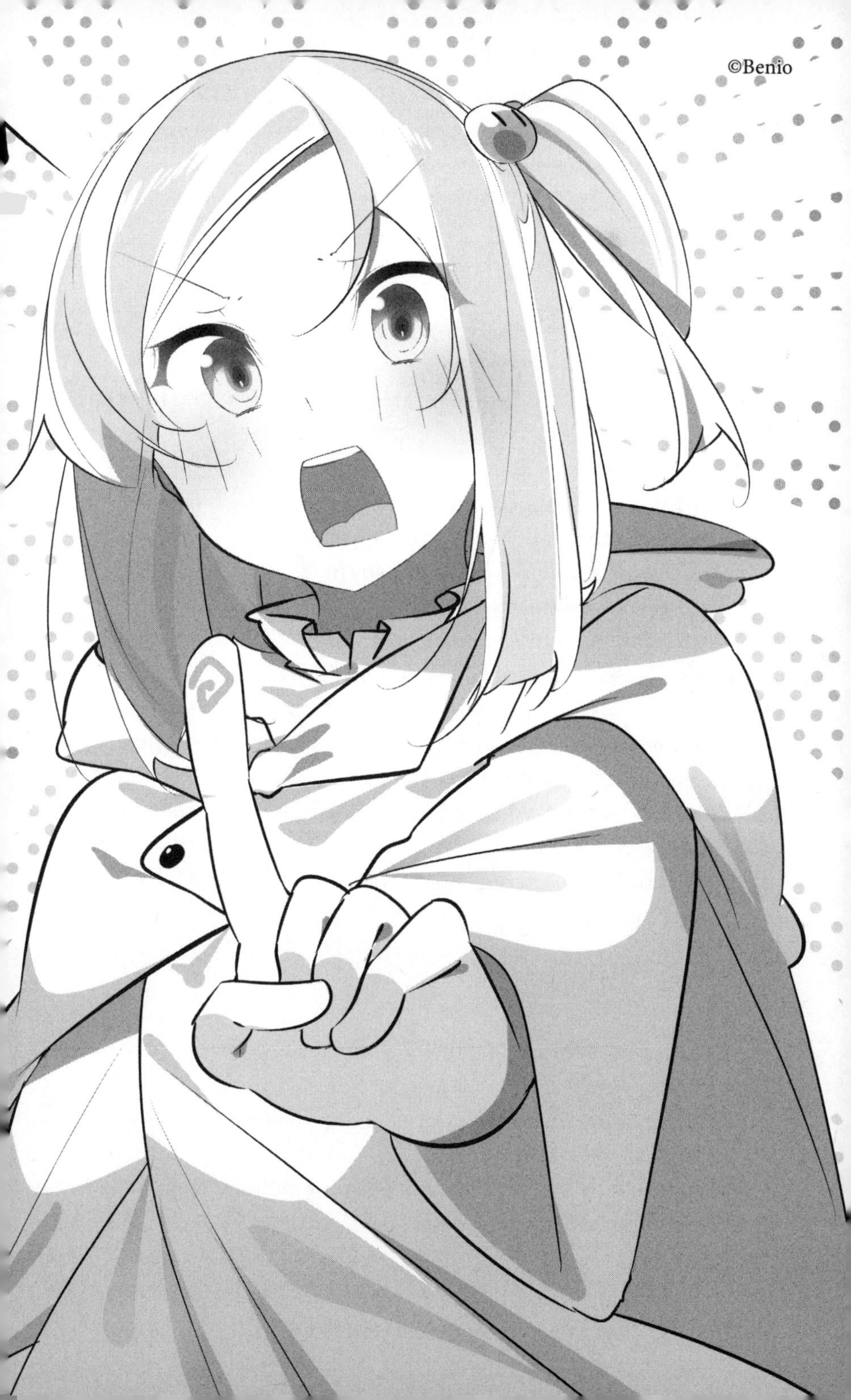
©Benio

"If it's going to be this way, then you should learn from the beautiful white egret."

Don't change the subject so quickly!

She was a wizard, which meant I could manage something if I could catch her off guard.

I landed on the ground right in front of her—and I grasped both of her shoulders.

"Say what you like, but you're going overboard. I would have been in huge trouble if I were a normal person."

"No normal person would be able to get past a white tiger or polar bear."

Okay, you have a point...

"Urrrgh... You evil scammer... Even if you defeat me here, my second and third selves will envelop this world in proper, pure white..."

I think you're talking like the evil one here.

"Just give it up already."

"All right. I, Wynona, have done all a slime spirit ought to do. I suppose it would be nice to end my life while I am unsullied and honest."

She sure had guts to talk about her terrifying ambitions like that and then call herself unsullied!

People who believed they were on the side of justice could be way more dangerous than people who thought they themselves were bad, after all. That convinced me.

"Now finish me!"

Thunk.

I butted my forehead against Wynona's. Softly, of course—no boulder cracking here.

"Think about what you've done."

"Wh...what is this...?"

Maybe she was in a little pain with me pressing against her forehead. I really was being gentle, though.

"It's because I could very well be something like your mother. Scolding you is part of my job."

"Mother…? I knew this was a daughter-help-me scam…"

Just stop with the crappy-sounding scams.

"You're a slime spirit, right? Then you're the same as Falfa and Shalsha."

Falfa then leaped out of the snow. "Shalsha and her big sister, Falfa, are slime spirits who were born before you. So that would make them your big sisters, Wynona."

"Slime spirits…? Ah, the Great Slime did say I had two elder sisters…"

Wynona finally seemed to believe us.

"I never thought I'd see the day someone would bring out the it's-me-your-slime-spirit-sisters scam."

I really wanted her to tell me who else that scam would work on besides her.

Even a guardian spirit asking for money would have more versatility.

Wynona slowly approached Falfa and Shalsha, reached out, and grasped one shoulder each.

"Yes, there is no doubt that the two of you are slime spirits." There was a weak smile on her face. "It's slight, but I still feel a little of your slime resilience."

It was a mystery how she could tell…but maybe there were some things that only fellow slime spirits could understand.

She finally believed we weren't here to swindle her.

"And that's our mommy!" Falfa reached out toward me.

"Mom has been killing slimes every day for three hundred years. And that's how Shalsha and my sis Falfa were born," Shalsha added.

"I have already heard about that from the Great Slime. I see, so that's how this works. You should have said so earlier in that case."

But you're the one who attacked us without waiting for us to explain ourselves, I thought. It took a lot of effort to keep my mouth shut.

"I apologize for the trouble I've caused, my elder sisters. I am Margrave Wynona of Idell, your younger, slime-spirit sister. I was born from a collection of souls from slimes killed all across the world. There is no doubt that you are family."

Wynona graciously introduced herself like a noble.

She tended to jump to conclusions, but there was a proper young lady in there somewhere.

"And you are—"

"Azusa, Witch of the Highlands. You've heard that name, right? I'm a witch who's been killing slimes for three hundred years."

"Yes, I know. And you are the one who led to the birth of my elder sisters, so to me, you are—"

Was this the birth of a new daughter for me?

"—my stepmother."

"What...? Your stepmother...?"

A mother was still a mother, but I still felt a bit sad. At least, I couldn't muster quite the same emotional response.

"Yes. I was born not because of the slimes you killed. That is but one fraction of countless others. That is why I cannot say my existence is a direct result of your actions. You are not my birth mother. That would make all of nature my parents."

"Yeah, I get what you mean..."

"So your we-were-born-in-the-same-universe-so-please-help scam will not work with me."

"That's not a scam; that's just emotional blackmail."

"That said..." Wynona gave a dry cough, then looked up to me with round eyes. "If you are my sisters' mother, I do not think it odd to consider you my stepmother. And so I will call you Stepmother."

Oh, part of it was because she was embarrassed. Yeah, it would be a little strange to embrace a random woman and call her Mama.

"Well, I think that's a fine point of compromise."

"Now, Elder Sisters, Stepmother—since you're here, please come with me to the parlor."

I'd been killing slimes for a little over three hundred years.

And now I had a stepdaughter.

◇

The parlor was a brilliant white.

I guess this girl wanted *everything* to be white. I doubted someone in this world with the name Wynona meant for her name to sound like the word *white*, but her interests and name did match.

Wynona served tea for us with all the manners of a girl from a noble family.

I called Laika in, too, and so the five of us sat around the table.

"Hey, so why can you use magic so well? And why do you have such a beautiful mansion?"

Now that we had the chance to chat, I had a few questions for her.

"Please ask one question at a time, Stepmother."

She was so distant with me...

"First, regarding magic, I was apprenticed to a wizard slime named Wizly, who lives in a workshop in Mount Modadiana in the province of Tomriana."

"That's where your slime network is?!"

Wizly was a wizard slime who we met when Falfa was stuck in slime form and we were searching for a way to undo it. Wizly looked like a fifteen-year-old girl, though, so I didn't really think of her as a slime.

"When I said I wanted to learn magic, the Great Slime directed me to her."

Maybe the Great Slime had all sorts of answers about slime matters...

"The snow fields I saw on my way there still remain fresh in my memory. How beautiful it was. The world should be pure white."

She was already obsessed with white even back then...

"I reached full proficiency in magic in a short amount of time under Wizly. And so I established myself as a wizard."

I Got a New Daughter

Wynona took a sip of her own tea. Even her tiniest actions were so graceful.

"So how did you build this mansion, then?"

Wynona placed a brochure on the table.

"You're a successful adventurer!"

This ADVENTURER Is AMAZING!

Newcomer Division FIRST PLACE

MARGRAVE WYNONA OF IDELL

REMARKS FROM THE JUDGES

"Her background is a mystery, but she has unquestionable skill. She will improve." (Organia Province Guild Master)

"She's simply angelic. Perhaps this will revolutionize the image of adventurers." (Royal Guild Central Committee Member)

"Her abilities are so great that I am compelled to indulge her audacity in calling herself a margrave." (Royal Guild Director)

"Ohhh, Wynona... You wear white panties, too?" (Owner of Steel Shop—An Adventurer's Mart)

I see. I guess you could make some money as an adventurer if you're good at magic. That's actually a respectable way to do it...

I had a feeling that one of those judges was kind of sketchy, but I wasn't going to touch the subject.

"I successfully earned quite a bit of money. And I used that to remodel my house all in white."

"Remodel? I feel like you just knocked the hut down and built a manor on top of it..."

"The hut was mostly empty, but I saved all the equipment that was inside. Please look over it later, Elder Sisters."

That was a nice thing to do.

"I understand. Shalsha is proud that her younger sister is an upstanding adventurer." She already seemed to have accepted Wynona as her little sister. "Treat Shalsha as your big sister in the future. It would be helpful."

Yeah, she was genuinely happy to be able to act as a big sister.

"Yeah! Same here, Wynona!"

That was exactly what I thought Falfa would say. She doesn't build walls with anyone.

"Indeed. I would like for the both of you to teach me all a slime spirit needs to know."

They looked opposite in age, so this was a little complicated.

"Oh, Wynona, your big sister Falfa has an idea!" Falfa said, her eyes glittering. "Why don't you move into the house in the highlands, too?!"

Of course, it was natural to want to live with a sibling.

There were still empty rooms in the house in the highlands, so it wasn't a big deal if we had one more.

Shalsha was looking hard at Wynona, wanting to know what her answer would be.

Nervous, I inhaled deeply.

"I already have my own house, so I will remain living here. I'm certain you would prefer to live in your home as well, Elder Sisters, Stepmother."

What a polite way of saying no!

And the title of *stepmother* was really a heavy one.

"The house in the highlands is in the province of Nanterre, no? It's too peaceful for adventuring work. It is not suited to my lifestyle."

Right, this girl already had an independent foundation.

"That is why I am unable to live with you, Stepmother."

"Could you try and not say *stepmother* so much…? Couldn't you just call me *mother*?"

It was really stressing me out. I felt even more distant from her whenever she said it.

"But I will go and visit Stepmother's house every once in a while, so fret not, my sisters."

Didn't I just tell you not to say that…? That was definitely on purpose.

But that's when I saw Wynona's expression relax a little. "Of course, I do not mind you coming to visit me, either."

"Okay! ♪"

"Understood."

The two girls replied enthusiastically.

I guess I should be happy that I have a stepdaughter now. "Sure, I'll come over when I feel like it, too."

Wynona was silent for a moment. "Fine. If you insist, Stepmother."

She was a little curt about it, but a yes was a yes.

Maybe being a stepmother came with its own delights.

On the way home, we played with the polar bear. Thanks to Wynona's snow, the bear seemed to be having a grand old time.

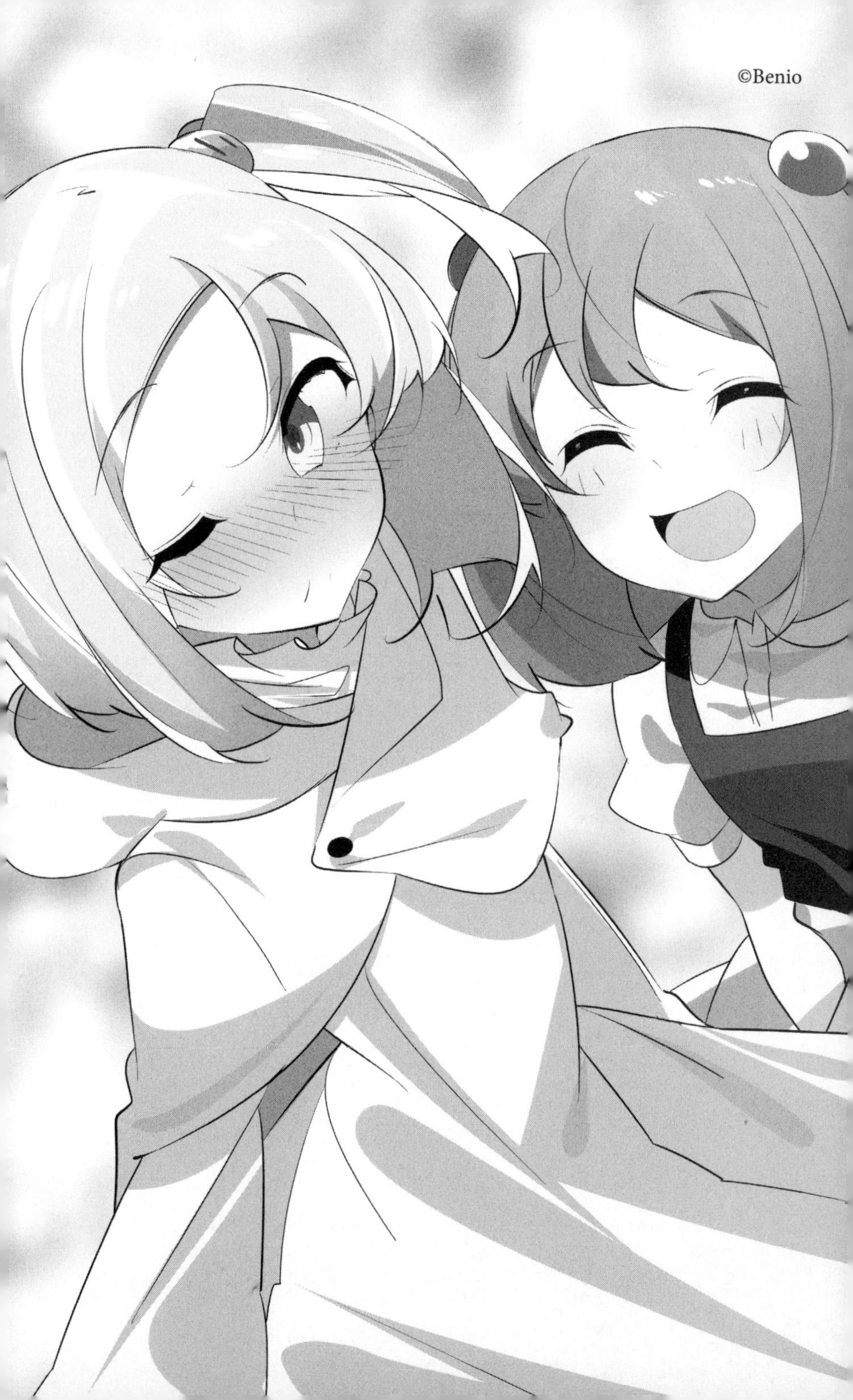
©Benio

SANDRA **SPROUTED A HAT**

Fwoooo! Pyuuuuu! Bwoooooooooom!

"Mommy, I'm scared... This storm is scary..."

"It's okay, Mommy's here. I'll keep you safe, okay, Falfa?"

Falfa clung to me, and I patted her head.

Yes—a storm had come to Nanterre.

There was nothing to block the winds battering the house on its little highland hill, so we got the full brunt of the storm.

The windows rattled, and I wasn't surprised that Falfa was scared.

But I was calm. I was used to this.

Even if a big storm came only once every fifty years, I'd still experienced it six times in my three-hundred-year lifespan. Over thirty times if that storm came once a decade.

Basically, I could tell from most storms if it was going to be the same as the strongest one from the previous year, or if it'd pass without any harm.

And as for Shalsha, the younger twin—

"Let us meditate and remove our fear," she said, sitting on the chair and closing her eyes. "The winds blow wild. Plants wither among the grasses. But the gusts bring new seeds, which take root. All things change, like the billowing winds. It is important to accept that we cannot resist change."

"It sure sounds philosophical, but should you be chatting the whole time you're meditating?"

Shalsha slowly shook her head. "It is a shallow preconception that silence brings a deeper meditative state. True hermits would be able to find answers within a crowd. That is why meditation during a conversation should be permitted."

So anything goes...?

Shalsha had to be tough to sit still in a storm like this—but there was something ominous about what she said.

She said, *"Plants wither among the grasses."*

That alone was a simple truth, but we had a plant in the family.

"Is Sandra okay...? I think she's still outside..."

She didn't have a tough physique like Laika or I did, after all. I hoped she wasn't having too much of a hard time out in those winds.

She could move, and I doubted she would try to put up with it out of pride alone, but I really should get her inside just in case.

"Oh, I went to go check on her, and she seemed fine." Rosalie the ghost came through the ceiling from the second floor.

She was peeking down headfirst. I guess the blood doesn't rush to your head when you're basically weightless.

"She said she can endure it because she can hide underground. And that wind is nothing compared with predators."

"Oh, that's good. And I'm impressed with you, too, Rosalie. You can go check outside without being affected by the wind..."

Ghosts had a lot going for them. I hoped that would be useful in the future, too.

"Big Sis, I'd say there's a bigger problem..." Rosalie went pale—and I didn't even know ghosts could do that.

"Huh? What is it? Did something happen to the house?"

I didn't think the wind was strong enough to smash our home, though. Laika even strengthened it to conform to dragon standards when she built the extension. Yeah, it should be fine...

Then Laika rushed into the room.

"We have quite the trouble in this storm, Lady Azusa!"

"Whaaat?! Is there a leak?!"

Rain that fell at an angle had an easier time of getting inside. At least, I hope that was the worst of it...

"Flatorte is playing outside!"

"What a child!"

Guess she got excited by the storm.

"Flying about in the middle of a storm will only scratch a dragon's scales. And walking about in human form will only make her clothes get dirty. I truly do not know what to do with her."

She would be soaring around right this moment yelling about how exciting it was to fly in a storm. Well, she wouldn't die, so...I guess it was okay.

Thirty minutes later, Flatorte came back inside, her hair a total mess.

"Phew, storms always make me wanna go for a flight! Why not come with me next time, Mistress?"

"Absolutely not."

She was like a surfer talking about going to the water when good waves were coming in. Or so I assumed; I'd never had a surfer friend, though.

"Flatorte, you're first in the bath. Your hair is an eighty on the bedhead scale."

Her hair was defying gravity so well, it was almost impressive.

"I'll aim for an even higher score next time!"

Don't.

Also, I was next to take a bath after Flatorte, but—

"There's grass and leaves everywhere..."

—the changing room was a catastrophe. There were even some leaves stuck to the wall, as if she'd flung her clothes off. This wasn't an open-air bath; these natural elements didn't belong in here.

The tub also had leaves and grasses floating in it, like an herbal bath.

I did check just in case, but they didn't have any medicinal properties, so this was more of a weed bath.

"I'm going to make Flatorte clean this tomorrow. This is her fault…"

After all was said and done, the storm did indeed end up harming our house.

There were so many leaves floating in the bath, which meant… Ugh, I didn't want to believe it, but had she been running outside naked? Well…I'll just assume she flew around in her dragon form, then turned back into her human form. I'm sure the leaves just stayed stuck on her body after that. Yeah…

But the storm also brought a nice thing. It was getting worse when it was time for bed, so Falfa wanted to sleep with me. Yay!

"Mommy, the whole house is rattling…"

"It makes you worry, doesn't it? Let's count some sheep slowly, okay? Well, maybe you'd want to count slimes instead."

"Okay, I'll do that. One slime, two slime, but it merges with the previous slime, so one slime, and then another one comes, and they merge, so one slime again."

"The number is just going to be one forever, isn't it…?"

Falfa had her eyes closed, but the rest of her was tense, like she was still a little anxious. But at some point, I knew she was going to calm down.

"Shalsha fell asleep while she was meditating—it was amazing. Falfa can't do that."

I think she just dozed off in the middle of it, but who knows…?

Shalsha had fallen asleep before Flatorte came back inside, so I took her straight to her bed in her room.

In a way, that meant she'd beaten her fear of the storm, so I guess I should compliment her for how amazing that was.

In the end, after about fifteen minutes, Falfa started snoring softly and cutely, too. It seemed like her sleepiness had been stronger than her fear.

"Yeah, that's good. The storm should be gone tomorrow."

I wanted to watch her sleep forever, but staying up all night wasn't good for my complexion, so I decided to sleep, too.

◇

The next morning—

—I woke up to a brilliant morning sun.

It seemed the storm had gone sometime in the night. It was exactly as I'd predicted. A storm like that would pass fairly quickly.

"I bet a walk today would feel really nice. The air should be all clear from the storm winds now."

I felt a little extra weight on my body, and then I saw Falfa clinging to me.

I didn't mind having her relying on me. It's actually what I wanted as her mother.

"Falfa, wake up. It's morning. It's so nice outside." I slowly shook Falfa.

"Oh, Mommy…where's the storm?"

"Look outside, and you'll see."

"The wind is…gone! It's sunny!" Falfa stood on the bed and started jumping in place with her arms over her head, as if she'd won something. "Falfa feels like she just solved a really difficult proof! I'm going outside! I'm gonna catch a praying mantis!"

"Sure, go ahead."

That distinct mixture of child and adult belonged to no one else but Falfa. It's an important thing to be yourself.

"It'll be a little while until food is done, so go play. Things might seem different when you go out and play early in the morning, so that might be fun."

"Yeah, I'll go get Shalsha, and we'll head out together! Sandra… might hate praying mantises, actually, so it'll just be the two of us!"

Sandra the plant often hated bugs.

But just two minutes after Falfa dashed out of my room, she came back. She seemed a little deflated, so I guess there was a problem.

"What is it? Shalsha still asleep?"

"Shalsha said she's doing early-morning meditation…"

"Meditating must be her thing now…"

I started worrying—what if she told me she was going to join a monastery?

Shalsha wasn't the type to play like Falfa did, but Falfa still enthusiastically went outside.

All right, today for breakfast, I'm going to fry up some delicious sausage for Falfa. I bet she'll be hungry after playing.

However, as I stood in the kitchen, getting ready to cook—

"Waaaaah, Mommy! Help! I dunno what to do!" Falfa flew into the house again.

"What is it? Did the wind bring something horrible?"

"No, that's not it." Falfa waved her hand side to side.

"Sandra… Sandra, she's…"

I felt a chill. *Don't tell me Sandra got blown away by the wind…?*

I thought she had mentioned she was fine in the ground, but maybe she wasn't careful enough and left too early…

Sandra looked like a child, so she didn't weigh much. That storm the previous day was strong enough to blow her away if she didn't watch out.

No, I had to stay calm at times like this. If I started acting worried, it would only make Falfa's anxiety worse.

I decided to hear what Falfa was going to say. I couldn't do anything until I knew what was going on.

"Sandra…sprouted a hat!"

"What?"

If I had the choice to say whether I understood or not, I'd say I had no idea what that meant.

I would understand if she was *wearing* a hat.

But what does *sprouting a hat* even mean?

I tested the most reasonable interpretation.

"Did Sandra start wearing a hat that blew in from somewhere?"

It was entirely possible that the storm brought in a hat.

"No. Sandra sprouted her own hat."

Nope, logic lost this fight.

It sounded like she'd actually sprouted a hat—this was no metaphor.

It was hard to believe right away… I didn't want to doubt Falfa, but hats didn't *sprout*. In my three hundred years of life, I'd never seen this happen. My own witch hat was only something I put on my head myself; it wasn't attached. You couldn't take it off if it had sprouted.

Maybe it was one of this world's idioms that I didn't know about.

"We should go outside, okay, Mommy?"

I just needed to see Sandra, and this mystery would be solved right away. I should see it for myself.

I headed for the vegetable garden where Sandra usually rooted herself.

Now let's see what's going on here.

"Good morning, Sandra. I hope the storm yesterday didn't— *Pfft!*"

I couldn't help but snort.

Sandra really had sprouted a hat!

I don't know if *hat* was the right word, because it looked more like the braided-straw head-coverings they used to wear in the Edo period.

How did this happen? I circled around behind Sandra.

Some kind of stick was extending from her neck, supporting the hat-thing on her head. It was probably part of the mushroom family.

Now that I was closer, Sandra also noticed I'd arrived.

"Good morning, Azusa. You seem a little pale. Is that from the storm last night?"

"U-uh…I'm not worried about the storm, but I guess you could say that's why I look pale…"

"Huh. That's not a very solid answer."

"Hey—are you into hats, Sandra?"

"Not really. Why is that your first question for me this morning? I'm not really interested in them. I've never wanted one before."

So she hadn't noticed.

"Let's go take a look in the mirror, okay, Sandra?"

"What, are you telling me my leaves are all rustled by the wind? Then just say it. If this is your way of being nice, it's making me antsy."

Sandra still had a bit of the wrong idea when we went into the house. A little while later—

"I have something growing on my head!!!"

—her scream rang throughout the house.

Yep, Sandra was indeed surprised… Falfa and I had no idea what to do about it…

"Wow, this is quite an unusual mushroom you have growing on you~"

We had our local mushroom expert Halkara take a look.

Sandra sat in a chair in the dining room. Halkara was peeking above and below her at every angle, checking the hat-shaped mushroom.

"There is no doubt that this is the mushroom called mandragora hat. It is quite valuable!"

"It's named after this exact situation, huh!"

But then again, there were plants on Earth called foxglove, and some people did call mushrooms toadstools. Maybe *mandragora hat* wasn't all that unusual.

"This mushroom can only sprout from mandragoras. Mandragoras do not grow in areas like this, so normally, this mushroom would not be found here. Perhaps the storm blew in some of its spores."

"Storms bring all sorts of stuff, don't they…?"

I'd been a witch for three hundred years, but there was still a lot I didn't know about the plant world. Wait, maybe mushrooms aren't part of the plant family. But the fungal world still falls under the witch domain, so same thing.

"Hey, Halkara, what kind of influence will this mushroom have on me?" Sandra asked Halkara uneasily.

That would be the primary concern of the one infected.

"Well, the mandragora hat grows by absorbing nutrients from the mandragora, then releases spores. So, um… This is how it works in general, by the way. It's just in general, okay? It doesn't apply to your case, Sandra, okay?"

Halkara was putting a lot of emphasis on this.

"Just say it! I need to know! Grrr!" Sandra growled like an angry lion. *It's been a while since I heard her do that.*

"In the worst-case scenario, the parasite will cause the mandragora to wither."

"Eek! Mrow!"

Sandra meowed in shock!!

She leaped out of her chair to hug me; she was shivering.

"I'm scared, I'm scared… I don't want to wither…"

The mushroom was pressing against my stomach…

The previous day, Falfa had hugged me, and today, it was Sandra. But in Sandra's case, this was way more than being scared of a storm.

"That's why I said *in general*! Mandragoras like you, Sandra, can walk around freely to find sources of nutrients. You can obtain much more than the mushroom can take away from you—and you can just remove the mushroom anyway!"

"Oh, you're right."

Regular plants couldn't just pick off parasitic mushrooms. They couldn't run away, either.

Sandra would manage in that regard.

"You're right… I'll be fine… Phew…" Sandra breathed a sigh of relief.

"The reason the mandragora hat takes the shape of a hat is to block sunlight, which is required for photosynthesis, so the mandragora will wither."

"What a wicked mushroom. It's like a demon."

Maybe from Sandra's point of view, but to the mushroom, that's just its nature.

There were plenty of mushrooms that grew from the roots and stems of specific plants. It was survival of the fittest out there.

"Then let's pull this nasty, annoying mushroom out right away. And then let's sauté it or something afterward."

I don't really want to eat a mushroom that's been growing out of one of my family members.

"We can remove it, but if we forcefully pull it out, parts of the mushroom will still remain in your body, Miss Sandra. If it does, then it might grow again."

"Ugh! How disgusting..."

Sandra wanted to put her hand on her forehead, but she put it on the mushroom instead. It was, after all, a mandragora hat.

But judging by Halkara's calm attitude, it was nothing to fear.

"Also, this mushroom is poisonous, so we can't eat it. It gets bigger by absorbing the poisonous nutrients from the mandragora, after all."

"Hey! I'm not poisonous! Grrr!" Sandra snapped.

"Please calm down! The reason mandragoras are used in medicines is because one of their components can be used as a poison in higher doses! The mushroom collects a concentrate of those components!"

"I see. I have such incredible power. And if I use it incorrectly, it can also be used to poison others."

That was a high-and-mighty way of putting it, but it wasn't wrong to say her poisonous components were a form of power.

Also, it was that part of her makeup that had witches chasing her before.

"Even if we pull it out, if any mycelia remain in Miss Sandra's body, then there is a chance the mushroom will grow again. We would have to ask a specialized doctor to operate on you to remove all the mycelia, but you don't want to have surgery, do you?"

"Don't you know a lot about mushrooms, Halkara? Can't you just get it over and done with?" Sandra didn't seem happy about that.

As a witch myself, I understood why Halkara was taking such a roundabout explanation.

"I am a pro when it comes to mushrooms, but I am not much experienced in mushroom removal."

Pharmacists had all sorts of specialties, too. Just like how there were all different kinds of doctors.

"Or would you *want* me to give it a go? I can give it a pluck for you." Halkara bashfully pointed at herself.

"…Sorry, but I don't think you'd be able to pull it off."

"Ouch… I'm glad you understand, but I don't think I would fail. I'm just pulling it out."

"If you pull out this mushroom, I'll grow two hats next time."

"That's too far, Miss Sandra!"

For some reason, we ended up insulting Halkara along the way, but it seemed the option of removing the mushroom was off the table now.

"But then what are we supposed to do? Am I supposed to have a hat on my head forever? I don't want that."

"No, that won't happen. You just have to be patient until the mushroom releases its spores. Once its spores fly away, the mushroom will quickly wither. And then the mycelia should die as well. And even if another one does sprout, it won't happen over and over. They will soon stop growing on you."

Live with the new hat. That was Halkara's suggestion.

"I'm not going to have to wear this mushroom for decades or something, am I?"

"A month at the most."

"I'll be that kid with the hat for a month… That's kind of long… It'll be gone right when I'm finally used to it."

I knew how Sandra felt, but this was probably safer.

And so Sandra began her new hat life. Unsurprisingly, it drew attention from everyone.

"*Pfft!* Sure is useful, though, since you don't need an umbrella when it's raining." Flatorte immediately burst out laughing.

"What?! It's not bad! I can go shopping when it's raining to show everyone how convenient it is!"

That was a weird thing to get angry about, Sandra! But I did appreciate if that meant she would help with the groceries.

"Also, Flatorte, you need to clean the changing room and the bath. It was filled with leaves."

"What...? But the leaves and grass will dry out someday..."

"We can't wait for it like the mushroom, so no!"

The person who made the mess needed to clean it up.

Flatorte went to clean, her tail whipping back and forth. Maybe she was regretting her wild antics during the storm.

On the other hand, Falfa and Shalsha were patting Sandra's hat.

"This hat is so cute!"

"It's fairly springy. Expensive quality."

"I don't feel anything, though. And expensive? It's growing on me for free."

Surprisingly, Sandra had quickly grown used to her hat.

Sandra's hat also had a favorable reception among the people of Flatta, and some nicknamed her Little Miss Hat.

I mean, this hat was going away one day, so that nickname was going to lose its meaning pretty quickly.

If a person with a distinctive bag was called Baggy McBag, then people who didn't know where the nickname came from would be confused why this utterly normal, empty-handed person had such a weird name.

But it seemed like Sandra was turning out to be popular, so I guess it was fine.

After a few days, Sandra herself seemed to start forming an attachment to her hat.

"This little thing has been fighting to survive in a land with few mandragoras. I sympathize."

Her mushroom was really growing on her—literally and figuratively. She also kept her hand on her hat when she sat at the dining table, too.

"You're not much more than a mushroom, but you still need to do your best."

Don't discriminate against fungi...

"Here, tea is ready." Laika placed a tray with a tea set on a table for our afternoon break.

"You don't want any, right, Sandra?"

"Right. No tea for me, thanks. Water on its own is much tastier." As a general rule, Sandra didn't eat or drink. She absorbed water from her roots.

When Laika sat down, she wore an odd expression. Something was bothering her. "Mmm, Lady Azusa? Do you smell something odd?"

"I don't know. Maybe some vegetables went bad..."

I went to check in the kitchen, just in case, but none of them were so much as bruised.

In the highlands, it wasn't very hot or humid, so it was pretty safe on the sanitation front.

"Our produce looks fine, Laika."

"Is that so? Then it must not be rot...but it's not a scent I've experienced before."

Maybe dragons had a good sense of smell. "Where is it coming from anyway?"

With a bit of an awkward look, she turned her gaze to the source: Sandra's hat.

Oh, I guess Laika knew the answer from the start.

"Huh? What? Are you telling me this is my fault? Can you not make false accusations, please?" Sandra hurriedly placed both of her hands on her hat.

But I mean, our circumstantial evidence did seem to implicate it...

"Oh yeah, didn't Halkara say before that part of the mushroom exudes a smell to attract bugs that'll carry the spores around?"

"What...? Ew, I don't want bugs... Some of them will come and munch on my leaves, too..."

Even if she didn't mind the hat, a whole bunch of bugs would spell trouble for Sandra. And I didn't want bugs flying around me all the time. This mushroom sure was a problem...

Then there came a knock on the door.

"Who could that be?"

I looked to the front door. It didn't sound like an adventurer coming to challenge me, at least.

I opened the door, and there stood Nosonia, standing with her wings spread.

"Oh hey! Long time no see."

This girl was a crawler who I'd helped without even realizing, and she came to repay me much later after she'd matured and grown beautiful wings.

"Indeed! Thank you very much for having me last time. I am Nosonia from the Nosonia Project." She introduced herself like an office worker. "I am sorry for intruding so suddenly. I heard tell of someone who exudes a delightful scent here, so I came by!"

I wondered for a second what she meant by "a delightful scent," but Nosonia was already flapping toward Sandra.

"Oh yes, this! This! This is the best smell in the world! How elegant!"

Nosonia was sniffing the top of Sandra's mushroom.

"Hey, no sniffing my hat!"

"This hat is actually rather floral to my people, and I just couldn't help myself!"

"Stop sniffing!"

Sandra wriggled around, but Nosonia was quite strong, being a demon herself, so Sandra couldn't get away. Although Sandra was pretty weak to begin with, so you didn't have to be very strong to overpower her anyway.

"I see. Insects enjoy this scent..."

Laika was watching on with amazement.

I was a bit hesitant as to whether I should stop Nosonia, since it wasn't enough to bring Sandra any harm.

"But I guess a bug really did show up."

From the mushroom's perspective, its goal wasn't to provide Sandra with fashion, but to leave progeny, so of course it'd make a stink.

"My, you don't see a mandragora hat every day. I would buy this for 3,000,000 koinne. Will you sell this to me?"

Koinne was the demon currency, which was roughly equivalent to the kingdom currency, gold.

Basically, she was saying she would buy it for 3,000,000 gold.

"You'd offer 3,000,000 for it...?" Sandra blinked.

"Yes, of course! A mandragora hat needs a considerable mandragora in order to grow to such a magnificent size, so you rarely ever find one this big!"

Nosonia was enraptured. I guess it was a good smell.

"Of course, we will also remove the mycelia remaining in your neck, Miss Sandra. For that, I can hire a plant-demon doctor!"

I wonder if that meant a dryad or an alraune...

"Hmm, 3,000,000? 3,000,000... I suppose I'll think about it..." Sandra had a dishonest look on her face.

To a child, 3,000,000 was an unbelievably huge amount of money. The temptation must've been intense.

"I could get all the high-quality water and high-quality fertilizer I wanted... Heh-heh-heh, heh-heh-heh..."

"Lady Azusa, this might not be very good for Sandra... I cannot imagine having access to all that money as a child..."

It seemed the honest Laika was concerned about it. I understood where she was coming from, as Sandra's kind-of mother.

"But Sandra does have the right to sell the mushroom growing out of her."

And if all she was going to buy was water and fertilizer, even though she had the choice to live in the lap of luxury from its sale, then I had a feeling it was probably okay. I would stop her if she was just going to gamble it all away, though.

"Could you please sign this sales contract?" Nosonia instantly pulled out a document that looked like a contract written in Demon.

"You were way too prepared for this. This is why everyone thinks bugs have no principles."

Sandra, that remark sounded a little discriminatory.

"Oh, no. I am the president of the Nosonia Project, so I always have contracts on me. Write your name there, and where it says *product name*, you can just write *mandragora hat*."

I wish I could carefully read through it ahead of time, but a sales contract probably wasn't going to be any trouble.

"Fine. But the contract is written in Demon, so tell me what it says in a way I'll understand. I don't want the price to end up being 3,000 after you told me 3,000,000, you know."

Sandra was particular about the money, so she was being careful now.

She sure was being mature about the weirdest things... But it is wise to always read the fine print.

Then I heard the door opening.

There wasn't even a knock.

"Hold on a moment!" Standing there was Eno, Witch of the Grotto!

"At least knock, Eno..."

Some people seemed to forget that good manners made for good friendships.

"Sorry, Miss. I heard someone say *contract*, so I rushed in, thinking I might not make it in time."

"Sounds like you were eavesdropping—"

"We'll discuss the details later!" Eno came to stand before Sandra.

So her objective was Sandra (or rather, her mushroom) after all.

"Ugh! You're the witch who was after me... I gave you one of my leaves not too long ago, didn't I? What more do you want?" Sandra was shrinking back.

Indeed, since Eno had freely used mandragora in her medicines, she was practically the most natural of natural enemies to Sandra.

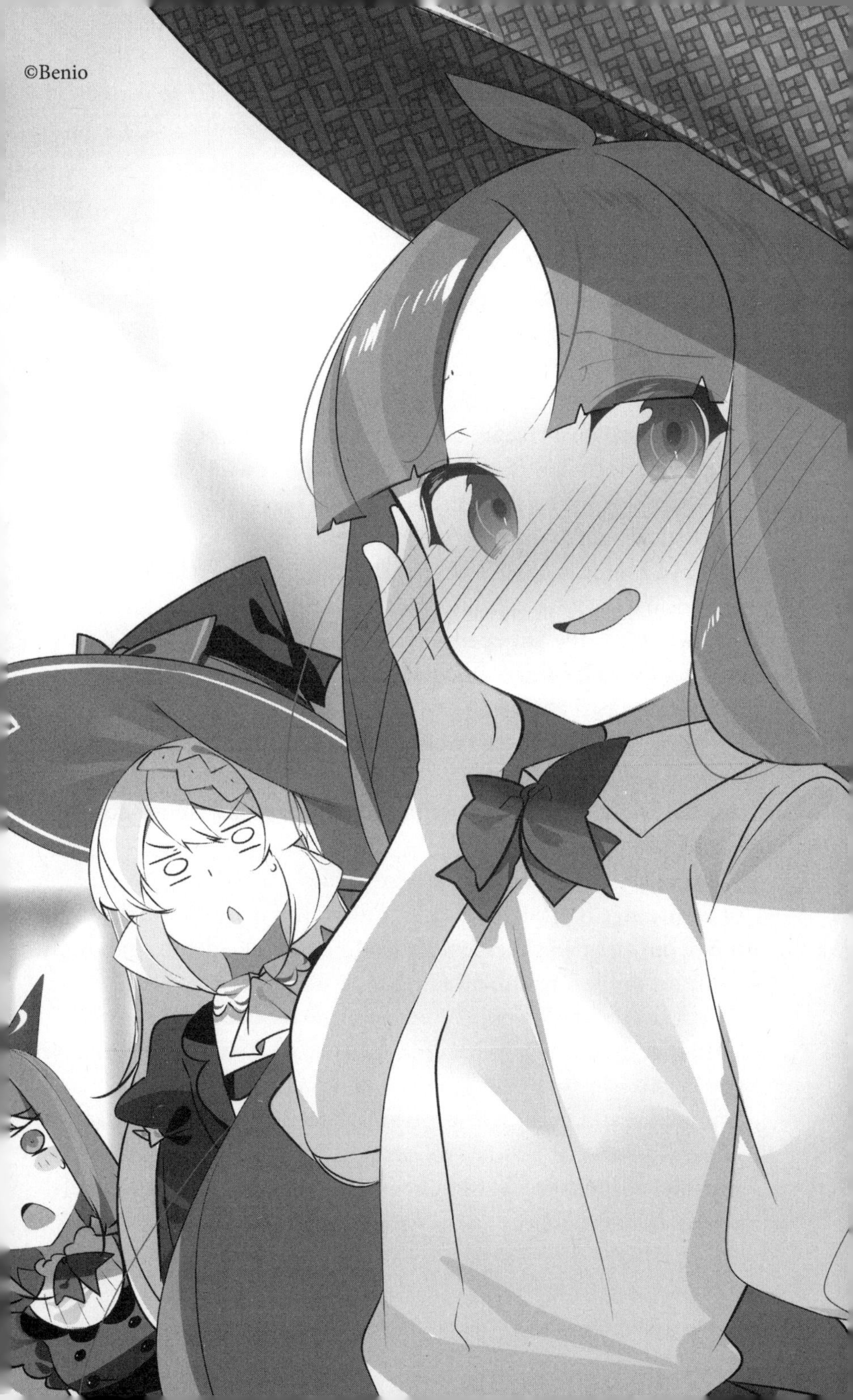

"Yes, I apologize for before. Of course, I am not here to use you in my medicines this time. What I want is that mushroom!"

Eno pointed at the mandragora hat.

"What? Stop pointing at me. That's rude."

"No, I'm pointing at the mushroom."

This was getting a little complicated.

"That mandragora hat is an extremely valuable medicinal ingredient to witches! And with it growing from a legendary mandragora, it's even more valuable! This is a premium item!"

"Hmm. So it is that valuable." I crossed my arms, nodding.

That mushroom attracted not only bugs, but witches as well.

"Did you not identify the mushroom as medicine, Lady Azusa?" Laika questioned me. I was a witch who made cures myself, after all.

Maybe I should explain. "It's not easy to turn it into medicine, and since it's not a mushroom growing in the ground, the extra work is just a pain to deal with."

We weren't really strapped for cash, so I wasn't desperate for the mushroom. I wasn't out there searching for rare plants and mushrooms with my whole heart and soul.

"I mean, if Sandra doesn't want to take it off, then we'll just have to let her be. It isn't ours; it's hers."

"Such insight, Lady Azusa. I am so impressed that money does not motivate you!"

"The bigger reason is that I can't be bothered…"

It wasn't an easy task turning an unfamiliar mushroom into medicine. Not only that, but there was no telling when I'd get my hands on this same mushroom again, so I couldn't even put that knowledge to use.

But of course, there would be witches who wanted it. Like Eno.

"Miss Sandra, I will purchase that mushroom from you for a total of 3,100,000 gold!"

She was pretty enthusiastic when she said it, but she only added 100,000 on top of what Nosonia offered.

An offer of 100,000 gold was plenty of money, but the way she said it came across as a little cheap.

"What?! How unfair of you to cut ahead of me like that, witch!" Nosonia objected, flapping her wings indignantly.

"The one who pays the most gets the prize—that is the way of things in this world! Please refrain from speaking, butterfly demon!"

But Eno was ruthless when a sale was on the line. We got a huge dose of that side of her back when we were looking for Sandra. She didn't flinch, not even when she was up against a demon.

"Very well, then. I will offer 3,110,000 koinne!"

"Then I will pay 3,111,000 gold!"

Neither of you are really raising the stakes high enough for how loud you are…

But neither party was giving way, and the price was steadily rising.

Maybe it was also hard to tell when to give up since there was only one other competitor.

Before long, 3,500,000 gold (since koinne and gold had the same value, I was just going to use gold for both) was 4,000,000 gold, and an hour later—

—it even reached 5,000,000 gold!

But it didn't seem like either of them were going to back down. Instead, it was probably even more difficult to figure out when it was time to step down now that they'd come this far. It was a lot like gambling in that regard…

"Dammit… You are quite tough for a human…"

"And I did not think much of you—but you have a lot of backbone for an insect."

*It sounds like they're in the middle of a battle manga, but they're just raising the price.

And Sandra, the very one they were fighting over, looked extremely happy.

"Heh-heh-heh, the price is going up and up. I can live with this.

Heh-heh, how wonderful. I will buy the most expensive fertilizer in the world."

Hmm, she was getting those money signs in her eyes.

"I have done nothing, but I get 5,000,000 just from selling the mushroom that has decided to grow on my head… Oh, life is full of good times!"

Oh… Even though she'd been acting like she was attached to the hat, all she could think about was money now!

"Laika, what you said earlier was entirely correct. Now that money's in the equation, I'm worried this is going to corrupt her…"

Giving a child a ridiculous sum of millions of gold would only bring trouble.

"That said, it is as you mentioned, Lady Azusa—Sandra is simply selling what she has, so we don't exactly have the right to intervene."

"Hmm… This isn't easy…"

At this point, I would just pray things would settle before the price got too high.

"Well, how about this?! 5,500,000!"

She suddenly raised the price by a lot!

"Hah! Demon attacks sure do sting…but I will not lose. I will retaliate with all my might! 6,000,000!"

"Whaaaat?! 6,000,000?! That is power befitting the name of the Witch of the Grotto, I see…"

*It sounded a lot like an intense fight, but they were just arguing over a price indoors.

"Now, what will happen next? I don't mind selling it to either of you~ ♪" Sandra was reclining arrogantly in her chair.

I had a feeling her personality had gotten a lot worse in this short amount of time…

"Oh right. While you're at it, I think I'll give more nutrients to my hat."

Sandra took some fertilizer and diluted it in a bowl. Plants who could take care of their own nutrition sure were powerful.

She then placed her bare feet (or more strictly speaking, her roots) into the bowl.

"Now grow, mushroom! Bring me money!"

The situation had turned, and the plant was now cultivating her own mushroom...

Two hours after Nosona and Eno started fighting each other by raising the price, they were still at it.

I mean, some might think this would end right away, but at some point, they started slowly and carefully saying their prices, like shogi players in the middle of a match.

"Hmm... Is that what you're going for? I see... Then I will offer...6,375,000."

"At that price, considering how much money I'd earn from selling the medicine I could make from it... I will go to the bathroom briefly and think."

I didn't really know if this was worth so much thought. I was kind of impressed.

I decided to go out and water the vegetable garden in the meantime, but the argument kept going until I came back in.

"The price should be reaching its peak soon. I suppose we'll be reaching a settlement before long." Sandra was watching the bout elegantly, her feet soaking in the bowl of fertilizer water. She had wholly transformed into a princess.

After a little while, Eno returned from the bathroom with a hard look on her face. "I have come to a conclusion, Miss Nosonia!"

"Very well, Witch. What is your offer?" Nosonia looked ready to take anything.

"This is my conclusion!" Eno slowly held out her open right hand.

What? Was she casting a spell? Direct attacks were not okay!

"Let us break for a meal! And then why don't we resume our match afterward?"

Oh, come on, really?!

Nosonia thought with her eyes closed, arms crossed for a little while. "Very well. That is all right with me. My offer sits at 6,375,000. Your turn will be next, Witch."

She seemed okay with that.

"Miss Azusa, I do apologize, but we will be eating dinner here."

"Oh, then please only prepare one extra plate. I am an insect, so I would be perfectly happy with flower nectar or something similar."

They sure were frank about all this…

"Yeah, yeah. I'll take care of you."

Laika then brought over some tea for the both of them. "Now that you are taking a break, why don't you have something to drink?"

"Oh! Thank you so much. Wow, I really appreciate all the trouble. I'll be sure to bring over my new line of clothes next time."

"Thank you very much. Please take some medicine, if you will."

We had some shameless visitors in the house, so Laika's good behavior was winning the day.

Dinner was a peaceful time of food and conversation, probably because they were in the middle of a truce.

"Young witches nowadays have no backbone. I really don't know what to do about them."

You sound like a crotchety old woman, Eno.

"But no backbone means even better peristaltic movements!"

Spoken like a true crawler!

Now dinner was over, and the battle resumed again.

The playing field was, as it always was, the dining room.

There was more of a crowd than there was last time, too. That said, it was just the family watching since they were doing this in my house. Everyone seemed relatively interested to see who was going to win Sandra's mushroom.

Falfa and Shalsha were watching as they ate some edible slime snacks.

"Who's gonna win? Falfa's so excited!"

"Shalsha hopes they fight fairly. The buds of their friendship will grow if they do."

I didn't really think this would end in friendship.

"Well then, Eno, Witch of the Grotto, will you be able to surpass my number?" Nosonia looked smug. The act of outbidding her itself was easy, though—she just had to say it.

"Certainly. This is my answer: 6,375,000 gold…and a year of fertilizer."

Now she was adding items to it!

"What? That's cheap of you. We are fighting over the price… Adding a year of fertilizer is a bit odd, don't you think?!"

Uh-oh, an objection from Nosonia.

"Is this allowed, Miss Azusa? What do you think? As a demon, I think this is unfair!"

Why was she asking me like I was some kind of judge?

"Sandra, what do you think? Is that okay?"

"It's fine. It's just adding to the terms, so I'll allow it."

The world was revolving around Sandra today.

"Yes, it's allowed! Now it's your turn, Nosonia! I doubt your industry can provide nice fertilizer, can it?!"

"W-well… In addition to the 6,375,000 koinne…I can add a grab bag I was selling when I last had a sale…"

That's just leftover clothes…

"I'm not really interested in clothes," Sandra said coolly.

She wasn't old enough to be interested in fashion! She's just a kid!

"Ooh… Th-then you wouldn't like two grab bags, would you…?"

"No. A year's worth of fertilizer is much better than that."

Nosonia's expression was tense. Had she reached an impasse? Was this Eno's win?

"No answer, Nosonia? Then I'll sell this to Eno the witch." Sandra made the last confirmation.

Was this finally the end to a long-drawn-out battle?

But then the unthinkable happened.

Plop.

Sandra's fungal hat fell to the floor.

"What? What happened to my hat...?"

As Sandra sat in bewilderment, Halkara the expert arrived on the scene.

"Oh dear~ It's gone rotten~ It's dead~"

"What?! The mushroom was all healthy today. What happened?!"

"An excess of nutrients, I believe. Did you give it a lot of fertilizer all at once?"

The whole family besides Sandra turned to look at the bowl Sandra had her feet in.

The fertilizer had backfired.

"So, Halkara, how much is the mushroom worth now...?"

"Nothing."

"Is it because it doesn't smell...?"

"The living mushroom gives off that smell to attract bugs, but it doesn't make it anymore."

Nosona and Eno were hurriedly making preparations to go home.

"Sorry, but my next job is in the demon lands, so I'll be leaving now~"

"Oh, I forgot I still have some potions I need to make today. Oopsie~! ♪"

They were acting too unnatural!

Businesspeople sure move quick when it comes to this stuff. They were already gone.

All that was left was a dumbstruck Sandra.

"But I was going to buy all the fertilizer I wanted..."

I patted Sandra's shoulder. "Greed brings out the worst in people. I hope it served a good lesson."

"I'm not a person; I'm a plant!"

The mandragora hat, by the way, totally rotted away, and Sandra was now right back to her regular schedule.

If there's anyone out there troubled by the mandragora hat growing on you, all you need to do is put your feet in some fertilizer water. If there are any other mandragora out there who need to hear it.

The End

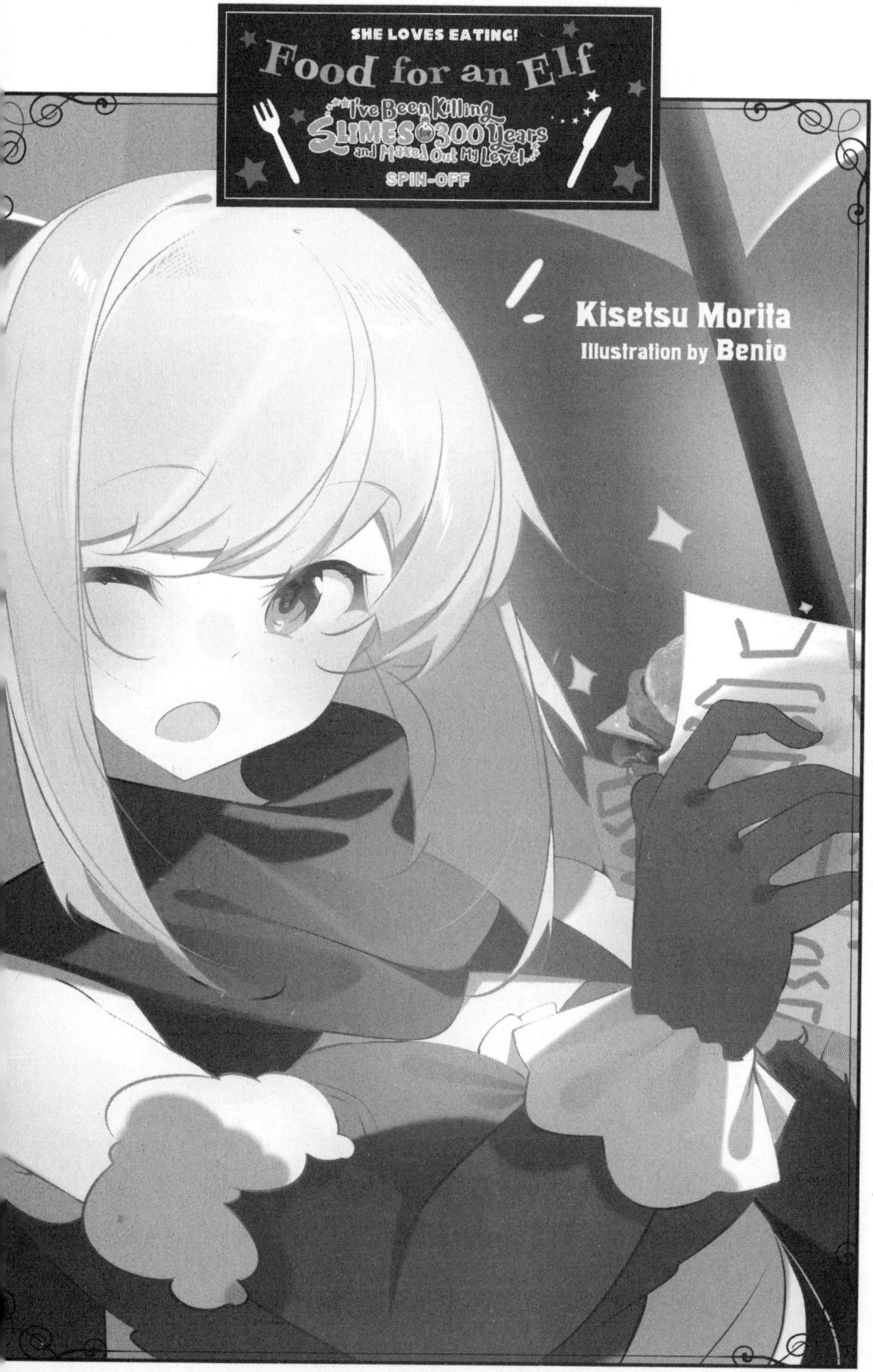
SHE LOVES EATING!
Food for an Elf
I've Been Killing Slimes for 300 Years and Maxed Out My Level
SPIN-OFF
Kisetsu Morita
Illustration by Benio

I'LL BE AT A **DRINKING PARTY UNTIL I GO HOME**, SO I SHOULD **EAT TO SOBER UP**, RIGHT?

SHE LOVES EATING!

Hello, it's me, Halkara.

Oh, it's quite late, so I suppose I should say, *Good evening, it's me, Halkara.*

Tonight, at Halkara Pharmaceuticals, we had a drinking party!

"Now, does everyone have their drinks?!"

""""Yeeeah!""""

I came to stand at the end of the table to ask my question, and I got a cheerful response.

I had fourteen employees, including both full-time and part-time workers, and today, we had a wonderful attendance rate of 100 percent!

We rented out a nearby tavern, *Mellow Revelations*, and ordered their all-you-can-eat and all-you-can-drink courses. Since we had the entire place to ourselves, we could be as loud as we wanted. As both the manager of the company and organizer of this party, I thought it was perfect.

"Thanks to all your hard work, Halkara Pharmaceuticals has been running for twenty years! Though it's been a short two decades, we've accomplished so much. And because of that, I am seriously looking into purchasing a bigger home... And that's enough! I hate long talks, too, so I'll stop there! Cheers!"

I lifted my cup, and my employees cried """"Cheeeeers!"""" in return, raising their glasses or clinking them with people around them.

And I downed my first drink still standing.

"Ahhh! They're using the Wellbranch Marquessate's good water! What an exquisite drink!"

The Wellbranch Marquessate (I know it sounds like its own state or something, but it's really just an elven, autonomous area within the province of Hrant) had rich groundwater and had specialized in brewing alcohol for a very long time. It would be nearly impossible to tell someone who was born and raised there not to drink at all.

Anyway, it was not just the alcohol!

The moment I sat down, I popped a piece of fried chicken from the massive pile on the huge plate into my mouth.

"Mmm, juicy! The chicken is good, too!"

Since this was in elven territory, cutting down trees was restricted by law.

It must be said we do use the lumber itself in all manner of ways, but we only fell trees as part of our maintenance of the forests—we take good care of them.

That said, large-scale development is difficult to carry out because of that, so there is not much livestock that need large fields, like cows and pigs.

Elves have never been much for meat, the biggest reason being those environmental restrictions. But meat does taste good when we do get a chance to eat it.

Though elves are herbivores, we can't get all the nutrients we need with plants alone. We might be long-lived, but our skin will suffer if we eat food that's bad for us.

So it's been our policy for a long time to raise chickens among the trees.

This land has been lush with trees since antiquity, so all sorts of birds live in the area. Wellbranch elves have always eaten those birds.

But most of those birds can fly and escape, so catching them is difficult.

So a wise elf once said (or not) that we must keep chickens.

Whether that myth is actually real is unclear, but to us elves, chicken dishes are a hidden but major cuisine.

There's a book called *Secret Anecdotes of the People* that even said, *Did you know the elves of the Wellbranch Marquessate love chicken?!* I don't have it with me right now, but that's what it says.

My employees were saying things like "Mmm, this is so good" and "This restaurant is great!"

Of course it is! I have my faith in this shop, after all. Everyone knows expensive food will be good.

But what was so great about taverns was that one could eat and drink to their heart's content despite the cheap price!

"Isn't it so good?! I always think so, too! Even those who don't drink won't feel like they're losing out in a place like this—I have no choice but to hold a drinking party here!"

I joined in on my employees' conversation.

Counting the part-time workers, there were fewer than twenty of us. We were a friendly workplace, and I was a friendly president!

"If a tavern can't be enjoyed by nondrinkers, what kind of a tavern is it? Drinkers like places they can drink, sure, and water is wet. There's no new worth there! It's corporate's job to find it! That is why Halkara Pharmaceuticals must create new value! What I mean to say is—I don't really have anything to say! I don't know where I was going with that! The food is so good!"

"Oh, Prez, you're already drunk."

"Sometimes it does seem like you're always drunk, but you are actually drunk this time~"

"Please don't throw up today, Prez."

I'd just started drinking, so I was sober, by the way.

They were making fun of me, but amiably so—it was important to stay close to the employees.

"Ha-ha-ha! I'm not going to get drunk today! I am still the president of this company, after all! I can't make a blunder like that!"

"I've had to take you home from two drinking parties in a row already, Miss President."

"If you throw up today, that'll be a hat trick."

"No one's taking you home today."

"Ha-ha-ha-ha! I don't remember anything like that! You're all mistaken! I'm fiiiine!"

"Oh no, she's so drunk that she's forgetting things…"

"I don't think you should be drinking alcohol, Miss President."

"We should have the next party at her house so we don't have to send her home…"

My company was one without walls, so they could have conversations like this where even the president could hear.

It was a wonderful place where we could say anything we like!

"Well, if any of you don't drink, then please order as much food as you like! This place is so good, even nondrinkers want to frequent it!"

"Okay!"

"I'll eat till I'm stuffed!"

The food was exquisite even during lunchtime~

Their grilled-leek-and-fried-chicken set (six hundred gold) was particularly wonderful.

Burning your mouth on the sizzling-hot grilled leek, along with a generous drizzle of fermented-bean seasoning elvin on the also sizzling-hot fried chicken—it's all just part of the fun!

"Now, let's have our second round! Owner, can you mix the ale with Nutri-Spirits?"

I brought out some Nutri-Spirits, Halkara Pharmaceuticals's hit product. I could pull this little trick because I rented out the whole place.

Nutri-Spirits as a mixer is wonderful, too! I mean it! People who have never tried it before are missing out! It's nice with a bit of ice so it gets all chilly! Don't worry if it makes your stomach feel cold.

The owner grabbed the Nutri-Spirits and brought out the ale-Nutri-Spirits mixer. The ale was called the Breath of Ah Un. It apparently came from an ancient civilization with two gods called Ah and Un.

"Thank you for always choosing us, Miss President." The young elf-owner, wearing an apron, came straight to greet me. Most of the working elves looked young.

"Oh, this was an obvious choice. I come because your food is delicious, that's all."

"Ah, you're so good at your compliments. What should I say?!"

"I do best with positive reinforcement, so I am very conscious of what compliments I pay~ ♪ My family is full of its own problems, so I've lived looking for the bright side to things~"

My mother never scolded my brother, my sister, or me.

I personally thought she could stand to be a little harsher on my brother...

My mother has always been a little scatterbrained anyway. About twice a year, she mixes up sugar and salt and puts it in her tea... I'm not making that up. By the way, we would always drink it together, so we'd all get sick at once.

Stories about throwing up never bring anything good, so I won't say any more.

The point is, it's thanks to my mother that I grew up so well.

Right now, there were no people in the area who did not know of Halkara Pharmaceuticals. I planned on building an even bigger house with the profits from Nutri-Spirits and our other products. I already felt like I was giving back much to my family, but this was to make doubly sure.

I was a bit of a celebrity in the marquessate. At least, the restaurant owner here knew who I was. I came here up to three times a week, after all.

"I mean it; when I see you, Miss President, I feel like I can work extra hard."

"Oh? Do you mean to say I'm a connoisseur?"

"You have such a sexy body, Miss President~ I can't help but get excited when I look at your chest~"

"That is sexual harassment!"

My other female employees often said that to me; still, a girl saying it to another girl was most certainly harassment...

"Miss President, since you're going with the all-you-can-eat course, feel free to order things you don't usually get. We will work hard to make something delicious."

The owner was generous—a necessary quality for a trader.

"I do plan on ordering a wide variety, yes~"

I made a show of looking down at the menu, then clapped it shut.

"Then I hope you don't mind me asking for some secret-menu items," I said, putting on a cool front.

I didn't actually know if there were any secret items, though. First-time visitors might embarrass themselves saying that, but we were on good terms here.

"Even if you don't have a secret menu, I'm all right with the regular menu. But, well, perhaps I'll have your specialty, or something like it. I just wanted to order something from a 'secret menu' at least once at a restaurant."

A Nutri-Spirits mixer was already a secret-menu item—well, more like my own original menu item, though.

"The secret menu? I can't say we don't have one."

There was a bewitching glint in the owner's eyes.

What?! There is?! It was worth asking!

I expected no less from Mellow Revelations. Their flexibility was what made it so appealing.

"This is a little dangerous, so we don't often serve it."

"Dangerous? In the spicy sense?" I couldn't handle spicy foods very well.

"No, not that."

"Then no need to worry! I will take responsibility for whatever happens, so bring it out!"

The alcohol was making me bold.

"All right! Just sit tight!" And the owner enthusiastically returned to the kitchen. Ten minutes later, she came back with a plate. "Here we go, our secret dish: elvin-dipped cockatrice!"

I was presented with rare slices of meat.

The outside was cooked, but the inside was still pink, while the dark elvin coated the bottom of the plate.

On the edge of the plate was a ground-up mound of wasabee. The combination of elvin and wasabee was a good one for elves, but—

"This is…"

"It's cockatrice. A valuable bird with the power of petrification. An incredibly dangerous thing to come across in the mountains unprepared."

Yes, I knew that much. Cockatrices were birds with snakelike tails, and they had a venom that could petrify its prey with a bite.

They couldn't eat their prey once it was stone, so they often starved to death, which made their numbers few and valuable. It was still a mystery how such a stupid creature came to be... It must be an evolutionary mistake...

But enough about the cockatrice—

"This is practically...raw, isn't it?"

We elves did not have the custom of eating meat that wasn't fully cooked. Some of us would eat raw egg because they believed it worked well against a cold, though.

"Yes, intentionally so. Cockatrice is the most delicious when it's served rare! Grilled cockatrice is good, too, but to be honest, once it's fully cooked, it doesn't taste much different from regular grilled chicken." The owner grinned.

"Are you allowed to offer rare meat in Hrant...?"

I ran a company that sold drinks, so I was somewhat knowledgeable when it came to food regulations.

"*That's* why it's on our secret menu." The owner smiled again.

I wondered if the owner had a long history of mischief.

"We don't get shipments of cockatrice in every day, though. We just happened to receive some recently, so we're serving it."

Is that so?

That meant this was an illegal dish!

All of a sudden, I felt so shady!

"You've ordered the all-you-can-eat course today. If you're already full, of course, don't force yourself to eat it all. Eat as much or as little as you like. You asked for a secret dish, so we simply brought out something we thought you might enjoy."

I see! It was illegal to sell raw meat in a restaurant, but if you caught a cockatrice and decided to eat it raw yourself, the responsibility only fell on you!

"This cockatrice is *free*, of course. You've already paid for the all-you-can-eat course, so there's no need for any extra fees."

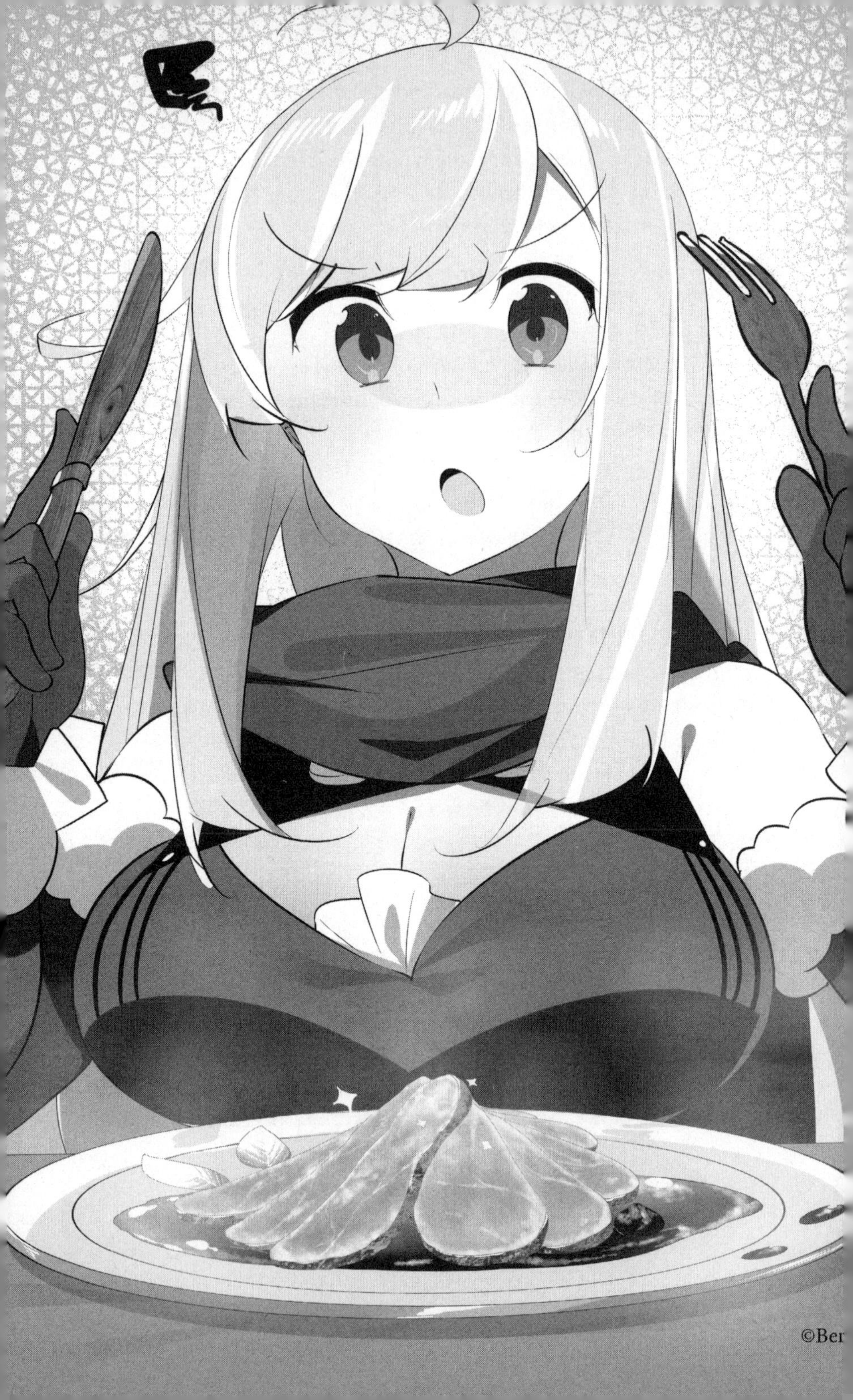

The owner was such an interesting person.

"Very well. Then I will have a bit."

I stabbed my wooden fork into the rare cockatrice meat...

...dipped it in the elvin...

...and put it in my mouth.

Oh! The cockatrice's natural sweetness spread throughout my mouth with every bite! And the salty elvin brought out that sweetness and umami even more!

"It seems you've discovered the true flavor of cockatrice, Miss President."

The owner smiled like a sage.

Ah, it felt like I'd opened the door to truth, too.

"Ever since we founded this restaurant, I've been determined to eat all sorts of birds and prepare cockatrice in a variety of ways. But it was only three years ago that I discovered that this primitive way of eating cockatrice was best. Every bird is best enjoyed in a different way... I am still developing these tastes."

You're very long-winded, owner. And quite annoying, to be honest.

I ate another slice, and another, putting them in my mouth one after the other. In between, I took sips of alcohol.

Oh yes, it went perfectly with the drink.

The taste of crime was truly exquisite. I suppose it would be nice to try something so tantalizing every once in a while.

*At Halkara Pharmaceuticals, we properly file and pay all our taxes, and we are not involved in any collusion.

"What, is that raw?"

"Whoa, cockatrice!"

"Isn't this supposed to be good raw?"

Oh, everyone else seemed fascinated by it.

"It's delicious! It's a special dish, only for today!"

Everyone had a taste of the rare-cooked poultry.

"It's so good!"

"I didn't know you could eat it like this!"

A delicious side dish with a delicious drink—that's the life!

The meal lasted for several hours, and the tavern was filled with laughter the whole time.

"Did you all have fun? I'm afraid we'll have to wrap it up soon here!"

At the end, I came to stand in front of everyone and spoke.

"Omigosh! You're not drunk, Prez!"

"It's a miracle!"

"I never thought I'd see the day!"

Please respect your company president at least a little bit.

Anyway, our drinking party was a great success! I didn't black out and throw up!

I didn't make a single blunder!

Three days after the party...

"Uuugh... I feel so heavy, like I'm carrying bronze swords all over my body..."

Feeling feverish, I came home a little after lunch.

My mother measured the temperature on my forehead. She typically had a high body temperature, so she was a good benchmark.

"Hmm, you are warm~ You're right in thinking you have a fever."

"I knew it... But it's the wrong time of year for a cold. And our family should be fine, too..."

"Sometimes your body just can't handle it anymore. Stay in bed today and rest."

"Okaaay."

It was times like these that staying with my family was a relief. I was thankful there was someone here to look after me.

I went to my room, immediately changed into my pajamas, and crawled into bed. "I suppose this means I need to get proper rest sometimes. Yes, I'll think of it that way."

*　*　*

Sleeping must have helped, because my fever went down in the evening.

I had my mother check the temperature on my forehead again.

"It's lower than mine. You don't seem to have a fever anymore."

"It went away in less than half a day. Our family sure fights off sickness well."

It was almost unusual that it would be gone so quickly.

"But keep resting, just in case. Why don't you take tomorrow off, too?"

"Oh, this is nothing, though. I'm totally fi— *Urp!*"

"What? What's wrong~?"

I could hear my instincts screaming at me to go to the bathroom.

"I need the toilet!"

But cruelly, the plate on the bathroom door said OCCUPIED.

Someone was in there!

"Please come out as soon as possible! Let me in!"

"Oh, Halkara. Can you wait a sec?"

My brother was inside.

"I'll give you a hundred gold, so please come out right now! Please, I beg you!"

"Fine… Can't afford to take any chances, so I'll make the best of it!"

Not funny—you need to take this seriously! He let me in, and I dashed into the bathroom.

—
——
———
————

I emptied the entire contents of my gut. And I mean everything.

I had a fever earlier, so I suppose I had a cold. To think it would be such an easy tell… I needed to drink some water before I got dehydrated…

My mother had a glass of water ready for me the moment I entered the kitchen. A mother's love was necessary at a time like this.

"Oh dear, Halkara, it doesn't seem like you're all better yet. Be sure to hydrate and rest well."

"Yes… My body is telling me not to push myself…" I stumbled back to my bed.

Ten minutes later…

"Waaaaaaah! Bathroom, bathroom, bathroom!"

It was really sudden! It was like a rock suddenly falling from above! And yet again, the plate on the bathroom door said OCCUPIED!

I knocked furiously on the door like a demon! *Knock, knock, knock, knock, knock!*

"Come out! Actually, you don't have to, but please just let me in!"

"You're scaring me, Sis!"

Now my sister was in there!

"Hmm, wait just three minutes~"

"I can't wait that long! It'll be a catastrophe out here! Do you want to know how much I can ruin the house in another sixty seconds?!"

"What…? You're making such a big deal about this… Hold on, hold on…"

"It's not my spirit that will decide if I can wait! It's my body!"

The body regulates the spirit—oh yes, I've learned about this theory in school!

Grrrrrrumble, grrrrrrumble…

That wasn't thunder. That was my stomach.

Grrrrrrumble, grrrrrrumble…

Was my stomach creating its own universe in there…?

"Sis, was that thunder? I don't like thunder…"

"Honestly, it's worse than that! Come out this instant! Unlock it, at least! Let's share! Let's share the toilet!"

"No, why would I do that?! You've finally snapped!"

"My body is indeed about to snap! Rather, it *is* snap*ing*! Too fast to stop!"

"I'm getting scared, but I can't leave! Just hold on…"

Hold on?

I never thought the day would come that I would so viscerally feel the meaning of a poem about waiting for a lover to return from battle... One second felt like an entire year!

If someone out there is going to yell at me for defiling true love, this is what I would say back:

You know what, I am in a much more dangerous situation than someone waiting for someone else to return from battle! This is a battlefield! A battle on the inside!

The door opened, and the second my sister exited, I leaped inside!

....

"...I'm so tired."

My face had gone gaunt. I doubted soldiers on the front line, who would never receive their rations after the supply routes were cut off, would ever look as haggard as me. And walking itself was turning out to be a task...

I decided to grab some water in the kitchen again.

"Are you all right, Halkara? Your symptoms are quite serious, aren't they?" My mother worriedly offered me a cup of water.

"No, I'm okay... Everyone has had tummy problems befo— I'm going to the bathroom!" I ran down the hall.

Come to me, toilet!

This time, my father was about to enter the bathroom.

Why do they keep using it at the same time as me?! Is it because we're family?!

"Stop right there!" I yelled.

My father froze in place.

I took my chance to slip into the bathroom.

"Hey, Halkara, it's not fair to jump ahead of someone else. Aren't you past your rebellious phase? I know you make more money than I do, but you should respect your parents a little more... Now, if you told me you would give me a million gold if I stood down, I would obey."

"Dad, your daughter is unwell... Please be a little more considerate of her needs..."

....

Even my easygoing self finally realized something.

Something was off.

I wasn't just a bit under the weather. This wasn't just some random coldlike illness.

What was going on...?

Maybe I should go to the doctor, just in case. Most places were closed because it was nighttime, but I had a feeling I should visit an emergency outpatient clinic...

I realized immediately that would be pointless, though.

"My stomach would never last the time it takes to reach the hospital..."

A second wave would most certainly come along the way. No, the second and third wave had already come and gone, I suppose. I was losing count.

Considering I was so unwell I couldn't walk fast, I decided I couldn't head out; I was not confident enough that I could be safe for thirty minutes. I could barely sit still for five or ten minutes, so I couldn't do anything at the moment.

I staggered down the hall to the kitchen.

"Halkara, you shouldn't go to work tomorrow."

"Okay... I don't think I'd be able to get to work, so I can't even physically go..."

"Should we call a doctor right now?"

I suppose having one come over was our last resort. I didn't want to do that, but I didn't think I had any other choice...

"Yes, please... Sorry for the trouble..."

Afterward, my brother and sister went out looking for a doctor, while my father left to buy some easily digestible and healthy foods.

I lay in bed with my mother looking after me.

"Here, have some water."

"Thank you..."

I had a glass of water at regular intervals. That was about all I could do to protect myself.

My family was indispensable…

They mercilessly sponged money from me for eating out, but they were reliable when it came to times like this…

"You've been going to the bathroom less frequently now. Though it's still about once every fifteen minutes."

"It is so much better for me mentally to think of the fifteen minutes of peace I have… Positive thinking, positive thinking…"

"You're recovering. Hang in there."

"Yes… At this rate, I may be able to set a new record for the number of times someone's gone to the bathroom in one day…"

An hour and a half later, my brother brought home a doctor.

I told him about my symptoms. I mean, it wasn't like I had very many symptoms to begin with, so it was a very short talk.

"—Which leads me to believe you just have a cold, but…"

The doctor wore a puzzled expression.

Oh no, please don't tell me I have a life-threatening disease…! Please just answer casually, *Oh yes, you just have a cold*!

"Ah, Miss Halkara… Have you, by any chance, eaten any raw meat in the past couple of days?"

That was a very specific question.

"Ha-ha-ha, why would I ever get the chance to—? Oh gosh, I ate so much!"

Just a few days ago, I ate rare cockatrice meat at Mellow Revelations… Was that it…? That would be it, wouldn't it…?

I suppose there was a reason why it was on the secret menu…

How brutal… What a price to pay for flavor… But if the most delicious meat in the world was going to give me diarrhea like this, then no thank you!

"It seems you have. When you get food poisoning from poultry especially, it causes the stomach to react like this. But it will get better in a few days, so you'll be fine if you drink plenty of water and rest. It won't infect anyone else, so there's no need to worry."

"All right, I understa— I need the bathroom."

The worst part about this food poisoning was that the moment I knew I needed to go to the bathroom, I couldn't delay going any further...

Normally, the body exhibits a response when it's about time to go. This sickness offered me no preliminary announcement...

I could hear the doctor laughing behind me, saying, "Take care~"

The bathroom was practically my room now, and as I sat there, I suddenly realized something.

"Other people beside me ate that secret dish..."

As I thought back, I believed I saw everyone at least take a bite.

"If everyone gets ill and ends up down for the count, then work at the factory would come to a halt... Wouldn't that cause huge losses...?"

My stomach started hurting for reasons other than food poisoning...

Afterward, I stopped the doctor as he was on his way out.

"Excuse me! I have a question about my employees!"

The doctor was rather shocked when I ran at him with terror on my face.

As it turns out, it was totally fine.

When I arrived at the company for the first time in three days, everyone was working normally. Although I did know they'd been doing their work properly because I had my mother come in and check the day after my food poisoning symptoms flared up.

"Oh, Prez! Morning!"

"Good morning!"

Judging from the loud, hearty calls, I could tell they hadn't been cooped up in bed.

"Good morning. Has anyone fallen ill in these past few days?"

"Nope."

"Not that I've heard, no."

"...Then don't worry about it. It's nothing!"

I asked the doctor, and he said there was a clear divide between people who were okay with eating rare meat and people who weren't, even if they ate the same things. It seemed I was the only one who took a hit.

In a way, I was the chosen one.

"Oh, that's right; while you were out, we got an offer from someone in the west who wants to make an order. It's a tool-shop chain with a lot of branches out there."

Ooh! So much luck had come my way for all that I'd suffered! The rainbow after the storm!

"Very well! I will check in on the details and get to work!"

"Oh yeah, Miss President, you look really healthy for recovering from a cold," one of my employees said with a puzzled expression.

"Oh~ That's because I've been able to do a lot of detoxing these past few days."

There wasn't a single scrap of waste left in my body!

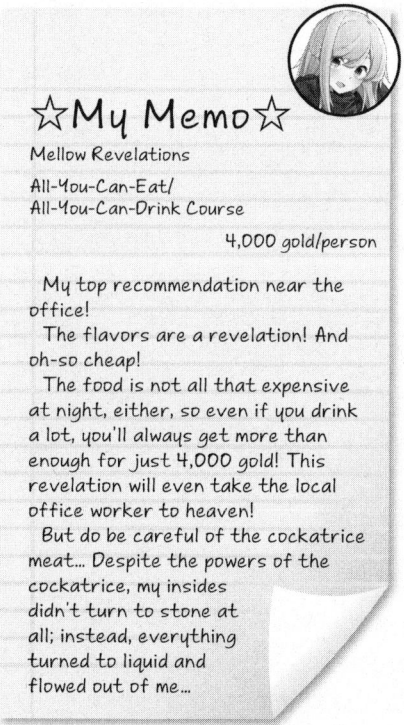

☆My Memo☆

Mellow Revelations
All-You-Can-Eat/
All-You-Can-Drink Course
                4,000 gold/person

My top recommendation near the office!
  The flavors are a revelation! And oh-so cheap!
  The food is not all that expensive at night, either, so even if you drink a lot, you'll always get more than enough for just 4,000 gold! This revelation will even take the local office worker to heaven!
  But do be careful of the cockatrice meat... Despite the powers of the cockatrice, my insides didn't turn to stone at all; instead, everything turned to liquid and flowed out of me...

IS IT TRUE THAT **INGREDIENTS YOU GET YOURSELF** ARE TASTIER THAN INGREDIENTS YOU BUY?

SHE LOVES EATING!

Hello, I am Halkara, president of Halkara Pharmaceuticals.

It's gotten rather cold recently, hasn't it? The province of Hrant, including the Wellbranch Marquessate, is not really an area that sees much snowfall, but we do get a healthy foot or so every once in a while.

And when you want to warm up on cold days like this, there's nothing better than Halkara Pharmaceuticals's Warming Herbal Bath—is what I would like to say, but there is something even more effective out there.

That is…hot pot.

That day when I got home, the whole family was going ahead and getting the hot pot ready.

"Oh, you're home."

My brother looked very hungry already. Just the other day, he successfully got hired for the fourth time this year, so we were celebrating with him at the seat of honor.

That just meant he'd been fired or quit himself that many times, but…it was our family rule not to ask too much about that. That was because of my mother's gentle style of authority.

And pressuring him about his situation after all this time wouldn't actually help… Though elves were long-lived, if someone didn't have their act together by the age of a hundred twenty, then they probably never would.

"Halkara, go wash your hands. We'll get started when you sit down." My father was sitting in the hot pot administrative seat.

It was customary for Wellbranch elves to have someone act as the hot pot administrator when it came time for hot pot. This person was in charge of putting in the meat at the right time and saying when it was time to eat. It was a mealtime standard with a long-standing tradition.

"All right. I'll go wash my hands."

When I was finished, I immediately took my seat.

That was when I saw what kind of hot pot we were having today.

"Oh, mushrooms."

There were all sorts of fungal delights sitting in front of me.

Mushroom hot pot was very popular with elves. With so many trees and forested areas in elven lands, there was no shortage. Elves have always been very careful about cutting trees down, but we don't feel guilty about picking mushrooms.

Our values went like this:

Elves = Trees > Flowers, Ferns > Mushrooms

And so mushrooms have always had a secure place as an ingredient. That concludes our minilecture.

"There were all sorts of mushrooms for sale at the neighborhood market. See, there's iron mask mushrooms, azaleashrooms, and grinning man mushrooms, too. Aren't they incredible?"

My mother seemed to be having a grand time. Also, the name *grinning man mushroom* came from when you cut it vertically through the middle; the cross section looked like a grinning old man. It didn't cause laughing fits when you ate it or anything.

"Ooh! These are incredibly rare. I'm surprised you found them."

"It's the season for them now, so there were tons out for sale. The moment I saw them, I knew we just had to have hot pot~"

"Hey, let's hurry up and eat. The pot's boiling already!" My sister thumped her wooden fork against the table impatiently.

"Sure. Then first, I'll go ahead and start with ones that need a thorough—"

"Dad, wait!" Just as my father was about to put in the mushroom, I stopped him.

"What is it, Halkara? I'm the hot pot administrator today. If you want to do it, then go for candidacy next time."

This hot-pot-administrator system sure was a pain…

…but I still had to stop him.

"Mister Administrator, I request you carry out a poisonous mushroom check! Please allow me to confirm these are indeed edible!"

"Whoa, hey—poisonous mushrooms? Hey, honey, were these poisonous?"

"They're not poisonous, but they do make you suddenly sleepy, so no driving carriages after eating them~"

That could indeed be called poisonous. That wasn't an acceptable effect for food.

"And these ones might cause nausea, dizziness, or chills."

"Those are definitely not safe! Please be careful when you go shopping! They have this risk because the mushrooms at the market haven't gone through proper sellers!"

Mushrooms were wonderful because they were rich in nutrients and came in a variety of textures, but it was very difficult to tell on sight which ones were poisonous and which ones weren't. But our elven predecessors often made the mistake of eating a lot of poisonous mushrooms, so we had more of a tolerance for it compared with humans.

I safely removed the poisonous mushrooms, and we finally started our mushroom hot pot.

Mushroom hot pot was reliably delicious. And despite the name, we put in meat and, later, flour dumplings as well, so the texture was perfect, too.

But—

"This hot pot feels like it's lacking that special something."

—my sister didn't seem satisfied, swirling around her fork with her hand. She was dexterous with the thing, but she sometimes stabbed and hurt herself.

"You've eaten quite a lot of that 'lacking' hot pot. The rule is that if you have any complaints for the hot pot administrator, you're supposed to lodge those before we get the pot ready."

This administrator system sure was a pain...

"But, like, I'm an elf, too, right? So I've studied wild grasses and mushrooms at school and stuff. But we only have a few of them in this pot, though."

Elves learned about plants in detail, so even my sister, who currently worked at a nail salon, knew a considerable amount.

"'Cause this is mushroom hot pot, but we don't even have any archbishop mushrooms, chivalric stools, or kingshrooms in here."

All the mushrooms my sister named were extremely expensive ones—a single stem could cost thousands and thousands of gold.

Kingshrooms, most notably, were called the kings of the mushroom world. Good thing, too; *cabinet ministers of the mushroom world* didn't have the same ring to it.

"A customer who came into the nail salon before said she'd eaten a kingshroom. She said it was so delicious, she's never looked at mushrooms the same way again."

"What...?" my father said. "You can't just get those anywhere...and it's not like you can just pay someone to get your hands on it immediately... It rarely ever shows up in the shops..." He made some sound arguments.

Not only did it have an absurdly high cost, but just finding it was extremely difficult.

"You're right~ I guess elves are the ones picking the mushrooms for sale in the mountains, so most of us will eat any rarities we find ourselves. I might've had a kingshroom once in my life already~"

"So you *have* had it before, Mom! Aww man, I want one! I wanna eat a kingshroom!" My sister started spinning her fork even faster. She was so selfish.

But I could kinda see her point.

I wasn't here to brag, but I did start my own company, and I was making quite a bit of money. I wasn't here to brag, but I did occasionally dine with clients in restaurants where it cost twenty thousand gold per person. I wasn't here to brag. I wasn't bragging.

But those were things one could obtain by paying money.

So long as you brought twenty thousand gold to a restaurant and weren't dirty enough to be kicked out for violating the dress code, then you could eat.

But if you wanted to try the elusive types of mushrooms that my sister brought up, you had to find them yourself, or you were out of luck.

In that sense, one could say they were ultrarare mushrooms.

I had eaten plenty of different foods in many restaurants thus far—

—but rare ingredients did have a different appeal to them.

"All right! Leave it to me!" I stood up with grand purpose. "Next time I have off, let's go to the mountains! Then let's gather up all the rarest mushrooms to eat and have a mushroom hot pot fit for a king! Let's eat so many kingshrooms that we get sick of them!"

It was times like these that I needed to show off as an older sister! How do you like that?! Are you swooning yet?!

"Whaaat? That's such a pain. You can go on your own, Sis."

That's when I knew my parents had failed us.

"No, you are coming with me! Ingredients you collect with your own hands and your own blood, sweat, and tears are much more delicious!"

"Whaaat? Mushrooms that other people pay for are way tastier~"

Our opinions were truly opposed!

"No! Come with me! You are coming with me so long as you don't have any other prior engagements!"

For some reason, I had to end up forcing her to tag along, but either way, we were going mushroom hunting.

The next day I had off, my sister and I went to a mountain that was well-known for mushrooms.

It was called Mount Shroom, after all. If there weren't many mushrooms here, then I was going to file a lawsuit.

We carried backpacks filled with some food and towels, and we had also brought along a basket for collecting mushrooms.

Grass didn't grow during the winter, so it was the perfect season to find mushrooms on the lower mountains that didn't have snow.

"Well then! Let us collect all the rare mushrooms we can find! Let's do this! We will have the best mushroom hot pot ever tonight!"

"...Yeah, okay. I wish I never said I wanted to eat any rare mushrooms." My sister started out markedly unmotivated, but I was sure her mood would get better as we found more good mushrooms. "Just don't get lost, okay, Sis?"

"It's okay. I have a map, you know!" I patted the map. "I may have a reputation for carelessness, but I am not foolish enough to forget bringing a map to a mountain. We will be okay this time!"

"Yeah, I want to believe you, but we'll have to leave the path when we go mushroom hunting..."

The mushrooms that grew right by the road would already be picked. That meant we would have to enter the mountain through a side path.

"That won't be a problem. When we leave the path, I will be sure we only proceed straight ahead! Then we will certainly come across a marked path!"

One hour later...

"Hmm...? This is strange... The paths don't meet up in the spots they're supposed to... And where are we walking anyway? We should be coming across a real path soon; otherwise, something is off here..."

When we saw a spot that might have some mushrooms, we left the path and pressed forward into the wilderness.

The strategy had gone well up until a point.

While we didn't find any rare mushrooms, we got quite a lot of mushrooms that weren't for sale in the shops. Our basket was starting to feel a little heavier.

But…we weren't finding any paths at all…

"I knew you'd get lost, Sis!"

I heard a complaint come from beside me. *I wish she would let me concentrate on the map right now.*

"How strange… Even if we are just a bit off our travel route, then I would simply make a small detour. I planned this very carefully, you know!"

"Ugh, just let me see the map. Gimme!"

My sister snatched the map from me. I had a feeling she was going to take control of the whole mission.

Three seconds after she took the map, she said:

"Hey, this is a map for a different mountain, isn't it?"

That theory would mean the premise for everything we were doing was wrong!

"Of course not. Even I can read the words *Mount Shroom*."

"Look, there's a bit in the corner here that says *Quick Advice*. Read it."

My sister gave the map back to me.

I didn't think anything weird had been written there…

There are several places across the province of Hrant called Mount Shroom. This map is for Mount Shroom in Notter County.

Make sure you don't end up in the wrong Mount Shroom.

"This map is for a different mountain!! I messed up!!!"

"There's no point if you bring a map for the wrong place! What are we supposed to do, Sis?!"

"These place names are confusing, so let's make a suggestion to the government that they change the names so that this confusion can be avoided."

"That's not the kind of solution I'm asking about. I mean, what are we going to do now that we're lost without a map?"

My sister's stare felt chilly. Perhaps because it was winter.

"...Hmmmm... Hmm."

"After the Quick Advice section, it says, *Smaller Mount Shrooms come with a great risk of getting lost, especially since mushroom picking means leaving the marked paths. Please go with an expert.*"

Pat.

I put my hands on my sister's shoulders.

"...You are the big sister now."

"You can't just flip-flop who's older depending on the situation!"

"...Then you are the leader. I charge you with all the power."

"What...? It's not like I know the geography of this place well, either... I'm not even good at hiking... I'm a beginner..."

"This mistake has left my mind blank. It would be even worse if I led the way in this situation."

"Sis, here's a double-digit problem. What's 55 plus 75?"

"5,575."

"I guess I *have* to lead... Let's turn back for now, then... That way, we can get back to where we started..."

And so with my sister in the lead, we started our trek back down the mountain.

One hour later...

Before us was a tall waterfall, one we didn't see on our way up.

"We are seriously lost, Sis, and it's getting worse..."

"It's times like these that we should keep a positive attitude. Look, this waterfall is gorgeous, isn't it? And we are lucky that we can fill up on water."

We would break if we didn't force ourselves to cheer up. Drinking clear water could calm us down; we wouldn't get any good ideas if we panicked.

I went to the water's edge, scooped some up with my hands, and drank it.

The tasteless, odorless liquid purified my body! I never thought water could be so sweet!

Perhaps water was the greatest ingestible thing in the world?! No animal or plant could live without it.

For a long time now, I had encountered many failures when it came to food, so maybe it was time I concentrated on water instead. I didn't care about culinary oddities or delicacies anymore.

I suppose one could say I'd had an epiphany.

And thanks to that, an idea that might take us out from the mountain came to me.

"I know! It's simple!"

"What? Did you make a breakthrough?!"

"There's a waterfall, so if we follow the river downstream, we will eventually exit the mountain!"

"Sis, read this part under *Quick Advice*."

My sister immediately showed me the map with a cold look.

If you are a beginner, be sure NOT to follow rivers downstream to proceed down the mountain, as it will frequently take you to steep waterfalls and slopes. Without the proper precautions, this will put you on a path toward impassable cliffs. However, if you find yourself unable to climb up the steep slopes you went down to get there, you won't even be able to turn back. You will be stuck.

That was me!

"An amateur's ideas don't bring the best results, do they?! I'm sorry! We will start from scratch! But we can't even start from scratch!" I fell to my knees in disappointment. "Or perhaps, this is the end… I have no regrets in life…"

"No, c'mon! You're not hurt or anything, and the sun's still out—you're giving up way too early! Seriously, let's think of how we can get out of here!"

"But it's so cold at night in the winter. We're done for..."

"There isn't even any snow here. We can do this!" my sister urged me, and we started walking.

Standing still wouldn't make anything better— Hmm?

"If we stay put, our family will realize we haven't come home and then send a search party for us, wouldn't they?"

"...Sis, they think we've gone up a different Mount Shroom."

Well, I suppose we have no choice to walk with our own two feet!

Another hour later...

"*Gasp*, I found it!"

As I walked through the forest, I found something.

"What? Did we make it back to the path, Sis?!"

I pointed to a spot at the base of a tree.

"The ever-elusive mushroom, a kingshroom! We finally, finally found it! Our hardships have been rewarded!"

"...We're in a crisis right now, Sis. I can't honestly be excited about this..."

My sister wore a little frown, but she did harvest the mushroom properly. We were not going to be knocked down for nothing—despite how lost we had been so far, we still got what we came for.

But right at that moment, a terrible tragedy befell my body.

Oh yes. I was hungry.

"**Grrrrrrrrwwwwllll~**"

"Your stomach is insanely loud, Sis."

"Oh, we haven't had lunch yet. And I'm hungrier than usual because we've been walking around the mountain."

"Oh, you're right. We haven't had anything to eat."

We sat right there on the spot, unshouldered our backpacks, and took out our lunch.

We'd brought several slices of bread with different kinds of jam generously slathered on one side. Then we put another piece of bread on top to make a jam sandwich.

The choice was deliberate—sweet things were effective in recovering the energy spent climbing the mountain.

"We might be eating a little late now, but let's have our sandwich and get a fresh start."

"Yeah. If we can get home like this, then we'll be heroes for getting the kingshroom."

My sister also smiled for the first time in a little while.

And so I first took a bite of my strawberry-jam sandwich.

"Oh~ How wonderful! I feel the sweetness spreading throughout my mouth and healing me!"

My sister nodded as well. "You're right. I never thought a jam sandwich would taste so good!"

As a meal, there was nothing special about it.

I doubted there was anyone who would look at a jam sandwich and feel it was unique.

But to us in this moment, it would be apt to say there was nothing tastier.

I could tell my body was overjoyed to have something so sweet.

"Next is the apple-jam sandwich. This one is so refreshing and mellow!"

"Oh yeah. We're in the middle of a mountain, but it feels like we're in a café in town."

And suddenly, I wanted to keep trying.

A roused spirit wasn't such a remarkable thing, but I was motivated to keep going and reach my goal.

"Next is the blueberry jam. Oh yes! What a wonderful acidity it has!"

"Sis, you've got jam on your mouth!" My sister laughed at me.

Enough energy had returned to us that we could afford to laugh.

"Oh gosh~ I could eat all of them at this rate."

"But, Sis, we don't know when we'll make it down, so shouldn't we save a little for later…?"

My little sister was relatively more of a pessimist than I was.

"I understand what you're trying to say. But if it is going to provide energy for us anyway, then isn't it the same to eat it all right now? And we will have less to carry if we finish everything. And that means we'll be spending less energy!"

"Now that you mention it, that sounds right to me, too... But you just want to eat it all, don't you?"

Oh, my sister was so smart. She understood me so well.

"Oh well, I'm sure it'll work out~ Let's not be so stingy and polish it off right now~"

"Sometimes being worried is a good thing, you know! That's not going to fix our situation!"

Then, at that moment, I felt someone watching me.

I whirled around, and a boar was approaching.

Oh, it must have been attracted to the smell of the jam sandwiches...

"Let's get out of here! I doubt boars will go so far as to attack elves, though..."

"Sis, they're coming from the other direction, too..."

Several boars were coming from behind my sister! And there were several cockatrices behind them!

We were surrounded!!

Our nice little lunch had ended in peril!

"What should we do, Leader...?"

"Stop trying to push responsibility on your little sister!"

"I hate to brag, but I have no ideas."

"Good thing you're not bragging!"

"I will shove all the remaining jam sandwiches in my mouth!"

"Yeah, if they're after the jam sandwiches, then they might come back."

"Eating one in front of them will be like taunting them—what a thrill!"

"Now is not the time to be getting a kick out of a superiority complex!"

As I sat there without an answer, the boars slowly drew nearer.

I doubted boars ate elves, but we would be in truly deep trouble if we ended up lost and injured in this empty mountain. And we would be dead if we were petrified from a cockatrice bite.

"H-here, we should threaten the boars first! Intimidate them!"

"But, Sis, I don't know how to intimidate a boar!"

I had no choice. I was the older sister, so I must risk my life…

I stood to protect my little sister, then turned to the boars and yelled:

"You will all die right now! You will die! Get out of here, or you will die! And the cockatrices will die, too! Fly away!"

"What on earth are you talking about?!"

"I am threatening them! My strategy is to frighten them with prophecies of doom and destruction!"

"They don't understand words! Just scream at them or something!"

The boars and cockatrices were getting closer.

I was out of ideas… Not that I really had ideas to begin with…

"I have no regrets in life…"

"Don't give up! Keep fighting!"

But then—

—something flew right past me.

In the next moment, an arrow plunged right into the head of the boar in front of me—

—and with a dull *thud*, it fell to the ground.

It was probably dead.

More arrows embedded themselves in the other boars, and they slowly fell, one after the other.

The other creatures must have sensed the danger, so they scurried off.

"…The prophecy of the boars' death has been realized… I didn't know I had such hidden power…"

"That's because you don't!"

A male elf, equipped with a bow and some arrows, poked his head out from among the trees.

"Y'all decided to have a picnic on the mountain without anything to protect yourself against the critters? That's dangerous."

"Are you a hunter…?"

"I am. I hunt in this area. You're mushroom pickers, I see. Well, good luck. I better take care of those boars before they get too gamey." My sister and I exchanged glances.

We were sisters, so that was all we needed to understand each other. We knew right away that we had to say something.

""Excuse us, please tell us the way out!""

◇

The elf hunter guided us safely off the mountain.

"My, what an adventure~"

"It wouldn't have been an adventure if you hadn't brought the wrong map, Sis…," my sister complained, but our mission was successful.

"Oh, all's well that ends well. We got the kingshroom and other rare mushrooms!"

"I guess…I can't not acknowledge that…"

The family unanimously agreed we would have mushroom hot pot that night.

I was curious about the kingshroom. What sort of flavor would it have in the end?

Other mushrooms that I'd known about but had never tasted filled our basket.

"Then I will be the hot pot administrator this time." I respectfully lowered the kingshroom into the pot. I was drooling before I even got to eat it.

"All right! It's cooked. Everyone, please eat! Enjoy the taste of the king of the mushroom world!"

My sister and I popped a bit of the kingshroom into our mouths at the same time.

As for our opinions—

"…It is delicious, yes, but not enough to bring me to tears."

"If anything, those strawberry-jam and apple-jam sandwiches were way tastier."

It didn't taste bad, but the flavor was a little...lacking. After all the trouble we went through, this was it?

"A rarer ingredient means it's become a higher-quality ingredient, and then someone decided the rarity means it must taste good~ I suppose it's a problem of perception~"

My mother made a good point. She was right. There was no rule anywhere that said rarer foods meant tastier foods...

The next day, I had a spaghetti lunch at a restaurant. One serving was eight hundred gold.

A thought came to me as I gobbled down the food.

How divine was it that one could have such reliable goodness for just eight hundred gold...?

As a company president, I was reminded of the importance of supply chains—and I matured a little in my job that day.

The End

☆My Memo☆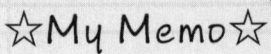

Homemade Mushroom Hot Pot

Maybe we should've gotten some boar meat from the hunter.

Even elves get lost in the woods. (I just made up that proverb.)

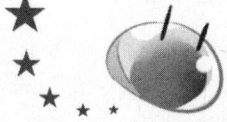

Afterword

This is Kisetsu Morita. Long time no see!

We have finally reached Volume 9 of *I've Been Killing Slimes*.

A lot of the earlier novels came out in such short intervals, so it doesn't feel as though a lot of time has passed, but I had no idea I would be able to get this far. This is all thanks to your support. Thank you so much!

Now, I have all sorts of announcements today.

First: The *I've Been Killing Slimes* series has surpassed one million units sold!

Wow… This is truly unbelievable. There's another digit on the number. It's so important to just keep at it. At this point, my only thought is *I really have had amazing luck*, but I'm still happy!

Next: The ninth volume's limited-edition version comes with the third drama CD, which features Falfa and Shalsha in all their glory as they play detective!

I never thought there'd be so many drama CDs… When we did the first one, I didn't think we'd make this many, so the story was pretty similar to the type you'd find in the original novel with all the same characters. However, now that there's a second and third CD, we've been able to tell stories that have a different POV.

I hope to show you the story of *Slimes* in all sorts of new ways!

Third: The comic adaptation of *I Was a Bottom-Tier Bureaucrat for 1,500 Years, and the Demon King Made Me a Minister*, starring Beelzebub and drawn by Meishi Murakami, has begun serialization in *Gan-Gan GA*!

I never imagined my spin-off work would get a manga, too!

I just keep coming back to the thought of how good my luck is... Maybe this is the result of having visited every shrine and temple in the country. I should make an effort to do another round in the future, too.

This is a total tangent, but as I was saying this and that about shrines and temples, work came in for a book on Buddhist statues. This is indeed Buddha's providence!

Well, all that aside, this spin-off manga will include stories that are not in the original novels and new characters in the future (I mean, there were only six stories in the original books anyhow).

Actually, when it was decided there would be a comic version of the spin-off, we agreed that I would add a whole bunch of short stories that would count as additional episodes, and then Meishi Murakami would draw chapters based on those stories. It's essentially the first time that one of my stories will be presented as a manga first instead of as prose. I hope you're looking forward to that!

Next topic: Volume 4 of Yusuke Shiba's comic adaptation will be going on sale in April!

Please check out the newest volume of the manga—there are more characters, and the level of cuteness goes way up!

By the way, the first volume of the comic adaptation of *A Mysterious Job Called Oda Nobunaga*, all three volumes of which are on sale through GA Bunko, will go on sale in April as well! Riku Nishi's art for the manga is so elegant and sleek. I hope you check this out, too!

* * *

    I still have more: When this volume, Volume 9, goes on sale, Movic will be releasing two types of plastic file-folders that'll use the novel's cover art! We've had them made through campaigns before and whatnot, but this is the first time we're getting official merch on sale! Yay!
    Everyone, please use these folders for your studies or in your business. Advertising for this series has been very effective, so I'm terribly grateful. Those who are worried about it getting all banged up through use, I would be even more grateful if you bought one extra for safekeeping (direct marketing!).
    Once they realize *Slime* merch sells well, they'll make even more stuff, and I'll be terribly happy, so please and thank you!

    This is the last topic. The wall-scroll sweepstakes we did last time in celebration of the simultaneous release of Volume 8 of the novel and Volume 3 of the comic successfully came to an end! Congratulations to those who won a wall scroll! I'm sure some of you don't know what to do with it because it's much bigger than anticipated (I certainly don't), but I would be happy if you put it up anyway.

    Wow… So many things to talk about. It's essentially just an announcement page in the guise of an afterword now, but I am truly thankful to have so many things to announce.
    The series will be reaching its landmark tenth volume next time. I never even thought we'd get this far, not at all. I would be happy if I could keep going, little by little, forever.
    In this volume, we introduced a new daughter (?) named Wynona. Benio has drawn so many wonderful illustrations again, including ones of the new characters. Thank you so much!
    I didn't even think we'd get to see Halkara's little sister (still no name yet) in a full-color illustration!
    It's thanks to all of you who are supporting the series that we've managed to cross the line of one million copies sold. That is most

certainly not something I alone could accomplish, so I honestly believe it is the result of good luck. I am so, so thankful.

The world of *I've Been Killing Slimes* will continue to expand! I plan on introducing even more characters! I hope you will stick with me!

Kisetsu Morita